I0721869

TIR-LANAN

SILVERSWORD PASS

SNOWPEAK MOUNTAINS

THE TOWER

THE WINDING RIVER HAVEN

TALES FROM LYTHINALL

A Collection of Stories From Around Lythinall

MICHAEL D. NADEAU

TALES FROM LYTHINALL

Copyright © 2021 Michael D. Nadeau

All rights reserved

"Skullgate Media" and associated logos copyright © 2021 Skullgate Media LLC

www.skullgatemedia.com

ISBN 978-1-956042-99-3

Ebook ISBN 978-1-956042-98-6

First Edition: 2021, Michael D. Nadeau

Cover art by David Eskridge, licensed through Shutterstock

Cover design and internal layout by Chris Vandyke

ACKNOWLEDGEMENTS

This is dedicated to my wonderful wife, Sheila, for putting up with Karsis the bard all these years. Without her support and love, these stories would never be possible. Shout out to my friends for always having faith in me and supporting my many stories I wrote them as gifts. Our many adventures play out in my head as I write these exciting stories. Alan P. for the great advice and edits, and Sam & B.K. for believing in me in the first place.

MAP OF LYTHINALL
And Surrounding Regions
S'REN-SELLERE
NORTHERN BELT
TIR IANAN
SILVERSWORD PASS
THE WATCHING WOODS
SNOWPEAK MOUNTAINS
LYTHINALL
THE TORN HILLS
WYNDRAL
THE BELTFLOW RIVER
DAELYN
NORHIL HOLD
THE WINDNG RIVER
HAVENAR
THE HIDDEN VALE
NORTHERN RUN ROAD
SEILD MOUNTAINS
THE MISTY WOODS
END OF THE WORLD
KERAGAN HOLD
EVERKNIGHT
RIVER VALE
CAERLYN HOLD
ALRIN
FOREST OF THE LOST
WHITELEAF LAKE
TERAFAR
SOUTHERN RUN ROAD
THE SERPENT RIVER
BARRIER MOUNTAINS

TALES FROM LYTHINALL

A Collection of stories
from around Lythinall

CONTENTS

TALES FROM LYTHINALL

WELCOME TO LYTHINALL
A BEGINNER'S TOUR

"Long and long ago, even to the memories of the oldest of the elves, the gods of this world argued and fought. The source of their fighting is something that we mortals will never understand, but their conflict lasted for centuries. This divine war devastated this entire world, which we call Seren'Dir, sending mountains crumbling and breaking the very lands asunder. Seeing the destruction they had wrought, at last the gods stopped and pondered for eons on how they had almost destroyed what they loved. They eventually came up with a solution, one that of course involved us. Each god would choose a mortal champion and invest a tiny bit of themselves within them, working through these beings instead of clashing directly with each other. These powerful beings, called incarnations, would work towards their god's aims and goals, living the decades away without growing old as other mortals do. Although powerful and ageless, the incarnations were not, in fact, moral, as they could be slain.

During these early years, great forests covered most of Lythinall, from the Barrier Mountains to the Northern Belt.

Elves, faeries, and other sylvan folk freely roamed through these woods as they battled dragons for dominion. Even though dragons are resistant to the forces of nature and most magic, the elves' mastery of the elements pulled the great beasts out of the skies, entangled them in roots torn from the earth, and punctured their hardened scales with ice. The elves also had to be constantly on guard against the excursions of the warlike oran and the larger ogrann that would come from the Shield Mountains to raid from time to time, and worked to stem the tide of these evil beings. Then the humans came.

Humans migrated from the far southern lands, moving into the lower end of the great forest of Mist'rien. They treated with the elves and offered assistance against the dragons and oran, who had started streaming out of their mountain homes in force. The two races worked together for many decades without incident, eventually forging a truce with the great dragons, with many of the great beasts going into slumber. For a time, all the people of Seren'Dir live in harmony. However, nothing that good can last forever.

It was shortly after this that things started happening rather quickly, in the grand scheme of things. Dar'Krist, incarnation of death and corruption, was sealed away by the other four incarnations for heinous crimes against the people of Tir-Novran to the west of Lythinall. With the help of the elves, he was locked away in the southern Sea of Irace in a great tomb of ice and the remaining incarnations helped survivors of the ruined city relocate to a secret island to rebuild.

Back in Lythinall, the elves had their own misfortune that would start the great decline of their race. The humans and elves went to war, and the effects were devastating to everyone involved. No one knows what started it, or who was responsible, but what followed was the turning point for both races. Thousands of human warriors fell to the blades of elven blademasters and elven magic. Humans couldn't cast magic so they were forced to develop other ways to contest the mighty elven archmages. So vicious was the fighting that the faeries refused to participate at all, stepping sideways into the moon and disappearing from Seren'Dir. In the end, the elves were victorious, and the remnants of the humans were taken into slavery. For centuries they the elves ruled over humans, yet were not unkind masters. The elves taught the humans the ways of nature and of the forests, taught their young in schools, and trained those that they felt they could trust as warriors. This lasted for over two hundred years, but then fate intervened once more: the incarnation of death was released from his prison deep in the sea of Irace and set off after his hated enemies, the elves, seeking revenge for their part in his imprisonment.

The elven lords threw their human slaves at him in waves; the resulting death-tolls were appalling. Hundreds, if not thousands died, many rotting away at the slightest touch of the powerful being's hands. Once the human slaves were shown to be useless against the incarnation, elven archmages hurled spells from on high and great knights led their forces against him. Eventually, the elves' magic encased him deep within a coffin of earth. The battle destroyed the western part of the Mist'rien and it was renamed The Valley of Khaerl, after a brave elven blademaster who sacrificed himself to bring Dar'Krist down. They took the coffin of earth to the north, and buried him down deep, weaving a mighty spell of Sealing over the earth that locked him away. Alas, the war against the incarnation was but another catalyst, bringing to light something even darker than his deeds.

During that war, some elves admired certain humans for their for their bravery, and thus, the first pairings began. Even though such couplings was frowned upon heavily, more than a few elves took humans as lovers, and a couple years later the first of the half-elves were born. The elves continued to keep the humans as slaves, but a few now roamed the elven cities as consorts and spouses and were given certain privileges. In this era, fate reached out its cold hand and intervened once more, starting what would be known as the bloodiest war known to all of Lythinall.

You see, one of the pairings was with the greatest archmage of that time, Ill'lyth G'harr. In her arrogance, Ill'lyth thought to teach her lover the art of magic. This was an abomination, as only those with elven blood could cast magic; when her transgression was discovered, the elven council, by a forty-one to one vote, banished Ill'lyth and her human consort to the Southwestern part of Lythinall, but that was not enough to stop the corruption that the archmage had begin. Many others went with the couple, feeling their banishment to be unjust. They had fallen for the honeyed words of Ill'lyth and broken free from their ideals and morals. These renegades started their own community and taught yet more humans the art of magic--but in the end, it backfired horribly.

Elves, by their very nature, are connected to the elements around them, and to the very fabric of the world. They learn to cast their magic by asking the elements to help them, with an understanding that the elf will keep nature's balance. Air, fire, earth, water, and ether. It's all about the question posed by the caster, and the elements answer the best they can. To master such an art takes decades of study and meditation... but the short-lived humans didn't have that kind of time. The humans, and many of the half elves who lived along side them, were warriors and conquerors. They saw every challenge as something to overcome instead of a lesson from which to learn. Whenever they were taught something, they rarely continued their studies afterward, unless it was to gain more power from the study. For these humans, magic was not a question—it was a demand, and the elements were to obey. The archmage either didn't see this, refused to see it, or embraced it. None will ever know now.

In any case, what resulted was the destruction of the very nature around them. Some elves in this new community were horrified once they saw that the humans were destroying nature instead of keeping balance with it. They called out to the elves of the north for help to stop them, but it was too late. The renegades of G'harr--the name they choose for their new community--slew most of these elves and declared war upon their brethren in the north.

The human sorcerers, a title they bestowed upon themselves, fought with their newfound power, tearing up great trees and hurling them like spears against the elven cities. Whole swaths of the great forest were destroyed in titanic battles, and the destruction that followed tore apart rivers, lakes, and woods alike. The great forest became a battlefield, and even a weapon against the elves; worse, their human slaves rebelled at the same time. The elves were fighting a war on two fronts and they were losing fast. For over ten years, the elves struggled against the G'harran elves and human sorcerers, but in the end, it was an unlooked for ally that saved the day.

A large group of human slaves, led by a warrior named Drennel, stopped fighting against the elves and joined instead joined them against the sorcerers. They remembered the teachings of the elves and saw how the sorcerers were destroying nature. Although none of these warriors knew magic, they were instrumental in turning the war around by sheer force of will, and they pushed the sorcerers back to their new lands and out of the elves' territory. Thanks to Drennel and his forces the elves triumphed, but even so the destruction was great.

The victors did not celebrate, nor did they rejoice. The great forest of Mist'rien was no more. Now it was only three small fragments. In the south of Lythinall lay the Forest of the Lost. Near the End of the World lay the Misty Woods. Lastly, in the high north, below the Northern Belt was The Watching Woods. The elves turned their backs on their allies and disappeared into the Snow Peak mountains and never ventured around Lythinall again, except for the odd elf here and there. The humans, led by the great warrior Drennel, settled in a large area nestled between three rivers. They named this Everknight, a name that Drennel took as a surname to match. He became King and under his knowledge, the land of Lythinall prospered once again. One decade turned into another, and the memory of the elves vanished from most of the human's minds. They became myth and legend, as did the stories of their kind. Only the bards and the kings' own line knew the truth.

It was in these new times that the men and women of Lythinall worked hard to tame the land around them, carving out an existence from the remnants of the war. After a few years a brave company of adventurers formed and rode across the land, cleansing it of monsters so that humanity could spread out to frontier villages and grow in safety. The Companions of Everknight were mighty heroes, delving into elven ruins and fighting off awakening dragons. They were led by the prince of Everknight and included the legendary bard Karsis. These famed slayers of evil ran for many years, eventually settling down across Lythinall as they aged and the land prospered under their protection. It is in this age, the age of new heroes, that you find yourselves thrust into, reading about the various heroes and villains in and around Lythinall. The stories you find herein are often footnotes, little things that make up grander stories that you may have already read, or will hunger to read after knowing what lies within these pages. So--delve in, if you dare to learn of the missing parts of the Land of Lythinall, but be warned: it won't always be pleasant and oftentimes you may be drawn in too deep. Never fear though, you can always climb back out. The question is: will you want to?"

— KARSIS THE BARD

FOREST OF MIST'RIAN
KANTHALIANAR

❦ 2 ❦

DRAGON'S FALL
THE HIGH KING AND THE DRAGONS

Harav'in strode across the courtyard as elves rushed to get out of his way. He was in a hurry and had no time for anyone on this day of all days. Harav'in Alansil was a wizard, as well as the general in command of the elven forces for the northern region of Lythin'all. Today he was meeting with the high king and the other generals to discuss the war against the dragons. He was tall for an elf, cresting a little over six feet, with his long white hair falling to his waist marking his station in elven society. Hair length was a sign of prestige among the elves, and wizards were close to the top of the societal hierarchy.

"Sir, why are we running down the common folk again?" the elf struggling to keep up with him asked meekly. Mas'ril Moonriver, Prince of Lythin'all, was in his fiftieth year—a babe really—and was learning from the general first-hand. Mas'ril was nearing five feet and still growing, his own long white hair bound in three braids that fell almost to his waist. He had piercing blue eyes and a sarcastic wit fit for a human.

"Because, *squire*, we need to get to the council meeting ahead of the others," Harav'in said through gritted teeth. If he could arrive before the other generals, he would be able to spread word of his new plans among the other councilors without interruption. He looked at the prince and closed his eyes briefly. He had come to loathe the young royal and cursed the day that High King Zen'ril told him to take the boy as an apprentice. *Teach the boy the ways of the field, Harav'in. Give him some backbone, Harav'in.*

The city of Tir-Vaniar was situated on the banks of the Belt-flow River—as the humans called it—as it flowed from the Northern Belt Mountains. The city was the shining beacon of the northern region. From here, battalions of knights and wizards, along with human archers, tracked down the dragons and tore them from the sky. For the last two centuries, the elven kingdom had battled the massive creatures for dominion of the land, receiving aid from the newly migrated humans a couple decades ago. Their timing couldn't be better, as the oran had been exceedingly active these last twenty years as well. The ugly creatures had increased the frequency of their raids, attacking settlements in search of food and slaves. The pairing of human and elven forces had been successful, even if the humans were barbaric in their weaponry, tactics, and vocabulary. Their lack of magic didn't help either.

"If you say so, general," Mas'ril muttered as he struggled to keep up.

"I do." Harav'in forced open the massive crystal doors with a gust of magical wind and gestured for the prince to enter first.

"I see you caused quite the commotion on the way in, general. Is there any reason you're in such a hurry?" High King Zen'ril Moonriver asked politely as they entered. The high king's robes cascaded about him and silver thread was woven through his hair like a crown. Without waiting for a response, the king tapped a small gavel to signal the assembled elves to take their seats.

The other two generals came shortly after Harav'in and

started their discussions on the dragons. Harav'in, of course, advocated for extinction. To him, nothing short of full annihilation would suffice. "We must hunt them down to the last flyer and exterminate the threat to our society. I plan for a full sweep across the forest with new traps and ambush tactics," he proposed to the council of his peers. *They had to see his reasoning,* he thought. *At least enough to pass the vote.*

"The resources needed to hunt down every dragon would empty the chests of every noble in the kingdom, never mind the north," Lys'lyll Ash'ashlyn harped at the dour-faced general. She was sitting in her chair rather than standing to address the council, as was customary, cradling her swollen stomach and rubbing her hands around the child that was expected any day now. Lys'lyll was the general of the southern region and opposed Harav'in on anything he brought up as a matter of principle.

"Always money with you Lys!" Harav'in countered, rising, his fists clenched at his sides.

"Calm thyselves, councilors," Zen'ril warned. The high king turned to eye the other councilors, who had remained silent in this confrontation, then sighed heavily. "Show of hands in favor of Harav'in's proposal?" he asked the assembly; twenty-six hands went up. "All right Harav'in, you shall have your annihilation. *However,*" he said. "That stands only if there is no way to parlay with them. If you can find me a dragon to talk to about a treaty or some resolution, then by all means *pursue that opportunity.*"

The council meeting was over and Harav'in basked in his victory, anticipating the war he had envisioned. He walked out of the palace and through the courtyard just as quickly as when he arrived, calling after the prince who lagged behind. He had to get to his men and begin constructing plans. They needed to prepare traps and magical ambushes, and he had to send word to the outposts. Those beasts would pay for their constant attacks, and the elves would rule supreme!

He came out of his reverie as he noticed an odd look upon Mas'ril's face. "What is it boy?"

MAS'RIL TRIED to catch his breath. They had walked for over an hour and for all that time he had tried to get the general's attention. They were heading towards the river bank and it didn't seem the man would stop before he walked clean off the edge. The young prince finally resorted to magic, asking the earth to hold the man's feet. "Ash'anti dir, hadar dosan kith," he whispered, pointing at the general. Harav'in stopped short, feet held in stone, and turned to look at the prince as if he hadn't heard him at all. *How insane is this man to not realize his feet were rooted by magic, or even where he was heading?* Mas'ril thought, staring at him. "Nothing sir, I just used magic to stop you from walking over the river bank." This was going to be a very long war if he had to be near this lunatic the whole time.

DRAGON'S STAND OFF

The dragon banked through the forest with an ease that shouldn't have been possible. He was far too large to be so agile and didn't even break the branches of the trees as he threaded his way through the canopy. His green scales blended in with the beautiful forest as he dove once more into the woods, scattering a group of sprites and relishing in the freedom of flight. Kanthalianar was five hundred and fifty years old, and glistening green scales covered his large frame. Dragon scales changed color with age and the green of his hide showed that

Kanthalianar was in his prime. In another two hundred years the scales would darken to brown, indicating he was approaching elder status.

He soared once more above the tree line and looked out over what the elves called Lythin'all in their language. He smiled when he thought of how the humans pronounced it. *Lythinall.* Those crass beings had no flair for the pompous elves' vocabulary. He had dealt with both races off and on over the last fifty years since the humans migrated into the great forest of Mist'rien.

Kanthalianar, or "Kanth," as he liked to be called, banked sharply as another dragon flew dangerously close to him. "Garentifranor! Easy lad!" Kanth bellowed, turning on his wing and pulling up quickly, beating his large wings slowly as he hovered above the trees.

"Oh, you're fine, Kanth. Rest easy—I wasn't anywhere near you," Garen said with a sharp laugh. He was young, only into his blue scales at the age of two hundred and sixty years. He was much smaller, but quicker, and had a mischievous streak eight miles long.

"What brings you barging into my alone-time, bluewing?" Kanth asked.

"Have you seen Florenvarial? She was coming to meet me in the open glade this morning, but never showed. With the ongoing attacks, I'm actually worried," Garen confessed, all mirth fading from his voice. The two dragons had an on-again, off-again romance that had blossomed early in their white scales.

Kanth grew serious, knowing that the young one had a right to be worried. Dragons did not give their word lightly; when they did, they always kept it. He sighed, thinking of the two centuries of fighting against the elves, and knew that prospects weren't good for Floren. He wondered—not for the first time—why they were fighting at all.

The elves and dragons had been at peace for the first half millennia of life after the War of the Gods, only coming to serious blows after the elves had begun to colonize every aspect of the great forest with their over-glorified cities. They had driven out dragons from their lairs; slaying some and forcing others to flee for their lives. Eventually, the elder dragons had called a conclave and decided to fight back.

They thought it would be an easy thing, but the elves' magic proved troublesome. Even though dragons were resistant to the forces of nature—and most elven magic—the elves' mastery of the art pulled the great beasts out of the skies nonetheless, entangling them in great roots from the earth, and even freezing them in ice. Neither side had profited from the fighting and the rumor was that the council was going to call for the total destruction of the elven cities during the next conclave two days from now.

"All right Garen, let's fly to the glade and see if we can find traces of her. Slowly, though. No reckless charge like you usually do," Kanth ordered, knowing the youth all too well.

Garen nodded his acceptance and flew behind the elder dragon.

They soared through the forest, weaving and banking around the huge trees and avoiding the elven cities. The faeries hid at their passing and he smiled at the fear they put into the lesser races. They flew down one of the well-traveled ways to the glade, slowing and landing to creep up without being seen. It was a marvel of the great beasts that something so large and colorful could remain so inconspicuous. Within minutes, they heard elves speaking about some 'trophy,' and Kanth's stomach tightened in worry for Floren.

"Wait for my signal," he said as the older dragon crept forward.

❧

HARAV'IN STRODE towards the captured dragon and frowned. The great beast had flown right into their trap, a great network of spidersilk ropes strung through the trees and reinforced by magic to hold even the powerful monsters they were hunting. Once tangled, the beast would fall and be assailed by spears and swords until it perished. He frowned because the dragon was still alive. "You there, captain. Why in heaven's bright sky is that beast still breathing!?" He was livid that they disobeyed a direct order, and wanted to know why they wished to be punished so severely.

"General, we—" He was cut off by a female voice coming from the bushes near the clearing.

"*I* ordered them not to, General," Lys'lyll said with a harsh tone to her voice.

"How *dare* you?" Harav'in spat as his hand drifted to his sword. "You have no right to—"

"I have *every* right, *General*. The order from the high king himself was that if there was any way to speak to the beasts we shall make the attempt. I think if we have a hostage, then that may open up a line of communication." Lys'lyll slowly drew her own slim sword.

Harav'in walked over, disdain fighting with rage across his elegant features, and stepped right in front of her. "*I* am in command here, Lys'lyll, and I order you to stand aside so we can finish off this creature," he shouted.

Then his day got even worse.

UNLIKELY ALLIES

"I'm afraid that may be a bit of a problem for me, *elf*." A great green dragon stepped into the clearing as it spoke.

Mas'ril noticed the beast's chest was puffed out, no doubt ready to unleash flame, yet it hadn't just yet. The first sign of magic, however, and the prince assumed they were as good as dead.

"Fan out! Take arms and prepare to battle!" Harav'in shouted commands to the soldiers in the clearing, finally drawing his own sword and casting a glimmering shield of magic before himself. The elven warriors fanned out, drawing their weapons and raising their shields as they circled the captured dragon and Lys'lyll. "Mas'ril, to me!"

Mas'ril knew that he shouldn't be staring, but he had never seen a live dragon before. The one they captured hadn't seemed so big and scary, but then the large green-scaled one came through the trees. This one was much larger than the captured blue, and much more intimidating without bonds holding it against the ground. When he heard his name, he snapped out of his reverie and hastened to the general's side. "I'm here, General."

"Good. I want you to tighten the spidersilk around the dragon's neck to the point that it starts to cut the scales." The green's head snapped around towards the general. "Yes, dragon. Another step and your friend here dies."

KANTH WAS AT AN IMPASSE. If he attacked, Floren might die. He saw that they had used spidersilk, probably reinforced with magic if he knew elves at all... and he did. He doubted the child there was strong enough to carry out his master's orders, yet he couldn't take that chance. "You do realize you won't save any of your men if you kill her?" Kanth said loudly, watching the elves flinch as the bass of his voice reverberated through the forest.

Floren's head came up then, tears streaming down her scaled face as she struggled against the formidable bonds. "Leave me, Kanthalianar, and flee. I can see the young one's power. Even *you* are in danger!"

Kanth knew that Floren was unique amongst dragonkind, being able to see magic in others, like unicorns sometimes could. He hesitated, unsure now whether he could save the young blue. Thank the Gods above he had told Garen to stay back until he gave the signal. He knew the young blue would've acted rashly in this situation; hells below even *he* wasn't sure what to do.

MAS'RIL WAS ready to step up and take the leap into becoming a true warrior by proving himself in battle. Then he saw the tears of the great beast and all his resolve flew out of him like so many petals upon a strong wind. For the first time he knew that all the fighting they had been doing was *wrong*. That *they* were wrong. He heard his father's voice telling them to find a way to talk to the dragons and knew he had to forge his own path in this. "Ash'anti ethir, brek dosit draco!" he called, invoking the ether to free the creature. The spidersilk ropes went slack and fell away.

Harav'in turned–his face a mask of pure rage–and struck with lightning speed. He plunged his sword into Mas'ril's chest, the blade thrusting from the young elf's back in a spray of blood. Barely had the prince cried out before Harav'in charged towards Lys'lyll with murder in his darkened eyes. Mas'ril saw the general meet her with confidence that lasted exactly three seconds. The seasoned general was suddenly on the defensive, fighting for his life.

She's so fast! Mas'ril thought as he grew weaker. He saw Harav'in feign a slash at her stomach, anticipating her quick thinking. When he swung high instead, he asked the wind to slam her backwards. The gust lifted her from her feet and sent her rolling across the field.

KANTH WAS APPALLED that the elf would turn on the young one so violently. He had seen the courage in the young elf's face and was moved by the act of bravery in the presence of his superiors. The young elf surely knew he would be held accountable, but had not foreseen the violence to come. Then the man attacked the one with child and Kanth could no longer stand idle. He rarely became involved with other races' politics, but *this* went too far. He stepped forward, his massive bulk forcing the nearest elves to retreat or become squashed against the trees. Some of the blades cut into him, but most glanced harmlessly off his scales. Kanth let out a roar into the face of the elf who held the bloody sword, tossing him away with the force of his voice alone. He then cradled the female elf in his claws and turned to Floren. "Grab the boy!"

The massive green dragon turned towards the edge of the clearing and saw Garen crashing through the trees, his eyes narrowed in anger and fear. He had heard the signal that all was not well and had come charging in as planned. *Good, for once that might help,* Kanth thought as he turned and beat his mighty wings, taking off into the trees at speed. The backwash from his wings threw most of the elves off their feet.

Floren grabbed the boy as swords slashed into her underbelly, and took off. "Hold on young one," she said as she glided behind Kanth.

Garen charged into the clearing with a mighty roar, spinning and lashing out with his tail, sending four elves that had just regained their feet flying across the clearing. He took off after the two other dragons as another elf regained his feet. "We're taking hostages now?" Garen asked as they flew off into the deep woods.

Kanth was about to answer when the elf with that bloody sword threw a huge spear at Floren, taking her in the wing and sending her plummeting to the ground. She cried out and dropped the boy as she spiraled down to crash into the forest floor.

"Florenvaril!" Garen roared, racing to her aid. He grabbed her and lifted her through the forest, beating his wings frantically to get her away from the battle. Within minutes they were clear.

HARAV'IN SIGHED AND stalked towards what was left of his men. "Get up and let's get the wounded back to the city. Collect the dead and transport them as well," he said, not seeing their faces. When no one moved he turned and noticed that all of them held their weapons at the ready, eyes threatening. "Oh, you're all against me then?" he asked as he drew his dagger and readied his sword.

"For the murder of the crown prince, Harav'in, I place you —" The elf never finished. He dropped his sword and grasped his throat as Harav'in's dagger jutted from it, cutting off his voice and his life.

They all came at him then, with spells and blades, but the elder general was also an accomplished wizard. He had never fully banished the darkness within himself, something every wizard had to accomplish lest the magic turn their heart to evil.

Now he could feel it tighten and consume him, the final step taken. Harav'in was more than a match for them, even in numbers. Within minutes he was alone: wounded, but triumphant. He burned the bodies, calling upon the element of fire to make it look like a dragon attack, then used the ether to transport home.

THE PRINCE AND THE UNICORN

Avaryn walked cautiously towards the body and sniffed. He had seen the dragon drop it and wondered if it was food or waste. It smelled like an elf, so maybe not food. Dragons were thought to eat people, but in reality, they rarely did. Oh, they killed them, that's true, but they didn't like eating them, from what he had seen. Avaryn shook his head and tossed his shimmering silver mane. The sun glinted from the single horn upon his brow like firelight shining from crushed pearls. He stomped a hoof as he neared the elf and saw the body twitch in response; he was shocked that the frail thing was still alive. Avaryn gently rolled the body over with his muzzle to see what had happened to it. The elf was very young, maybe only fifty years if a day. *Hold on young one*, he sent telepathically to the young elf. He lowered his horn to the chest of the boy and let his healing powers flow into the dirty wound. Connected like this he could feel the ebb and flow of the heart, which was very weak, and he concentrated harder to keep the elf alive.

Mas'ril came around slowly, his eyes fluttering open weakly. He saw the vague outline of a horse and knew that someone had come to save him from the mad general, Harav'in. Then the full memory of the events flooded back and he shot upright. The young prince regretted this immediately as his pulse pounded in his head, his stomach turned in knots, and his heart began to beat so fast he thought it might escape from his chest and flee of its own accord. "Oh, that wasn't smart," he said as he rubbed his head and tried to focus.

I'm glad you're alive, young one, he heard a voice in his mind say.

"Did someone just speak in my head?" Mas'ril asked the treetops. He stood slowly, using the horse's shoulder and horn to help him with his balance. Then he realized that there *was* a horn and let go, stumbling backwards and almost falling once more. "Sweet Goddess! You're a unicorn!"

I am. Thank you for noticing, the unicorn's thoughts boomed in his mind. *We must go, young one. Those dragons may be back for you.*

"I rather think the dragons are the ones I need to find," Mas'ril said slowly, not believing his own words. Something was wrong though. Where was everyone? "Why am I in the middle of the forest? I was with other elves in a clearing," he asked. He couldn't believe he was talking to a unicorn. Mas'ril hadn't ever seen one in person, though he always wanted to. From what he understood there weren't many left.

The dragon that was carrying you dropped you when it fell out of the air. I waited until it was gone then came out to see what it had dropped. If you're going to go looking for dragons, you might want to rest more first. You've been through a lot and I wasn't even sure I could heal you enough to keep you here on this plane.

"You're afraid of dragons?" Mas'ril was shocked—he had always thought that unicorns got along with other mystical beasts.

No. I'm not afraid of dragons. I have a healthy respect for them, yes, but not fear, the unicorn answered as he led the elf towards the thick bushes. *I'm more worried about what the dragons may do to you.*

Mas'ril followed the unicorn and realized he didn't know what to call him. "By the way, my name is Prince Mas'ril Moonriver. What do they call you?" he asked quietly, not wanting to alert any elves still around of his survival. He still couldn't believe that Harav'in had tried to kill him.

A prince? You are far from the palace, my lord. I am called Avaryn and it is good to meet you. The unicorn stopped and turned its head towards Mas'ril and bowed slightly, then walked on. *There is something about you that speaks of destiny. I can sense some greater thread of fate attached to you, young lord.*

"Yes, well, the general of the northern regions tried to kill me because I helped a dragon escape. He wants to eradicate all dragons and actually thinks he can do it, but the war has gone on long enough; we have to find a way to coexist." Mas'ril ignored the whole 'greater destiny' speech and ran right into the back of Avaryn as they continued to walk. "What is it?" he asked, looking to the canopy above for signs of trouble.

You want to end the war with the dragons? Your people have been fighting them for decades and suddenly you think it should end? Avaryn shook his head back and forth. *You speak like a true king of your people. Oh, what a wonder you will make on the throne one day, if you live that long.* He turned to the prince and pawed the ground with his hoof. *Most of your people wouldn't even think to treat with the dragons.*

"Actually, my father insisted that if a way to do so presented itself one should take it," Mas'ril said.

Avaryn stopped and moved aside some brush with his horn, revealing a small den. It was nestled in a bush and had boughs overhead to shield one from the rain. *Here is where you may rest. It is a deer's den that has long been empty. After that I will point you in the right direction.* Mas'ril nodded and sat cross-legged, closing his eyes and breathing deep to enter the meditative state that for the elves was as close to sleep as they would ever come. *Stay here and rest. I'll go see if I can find your dragon.*

AVARYN WALKED AWAY and began to search for a dryad tree. He wondered, not for the first time this day, why he was interfering. Dragons and Unicorns usually stayed well away from each other out of mutual respect, yet the destiny around this powerful young wizard was impressive. It took little time before he found what he was looking for. *Hello, dear dryad, can you help me?* he asked.

A green mop of hair popped out from a hole in the tree. Leaves fluttered from it and fell to the forest floor as the dryad shook her verdant locks. The woman had light green skin and brown freckles, wearing only a shift of interwoven leaves. "Dear unicorn, what do you want with one such as I?" she asked in a rich voice.

I'm looking for a wounded dragon, with a companion or two. Blue scales, maybe? he asked, bowing his head in respect to the dryad.

"Oh, them! Yes! They are in the far glade past the lazy stream, an hour's walk from here." she answered giddily, clapping her hands together.

I thank you great lady--may your leaves fall only when you wish them to. He backed away and went to find the prince once more. Avaryn wouldn't go with him, but now he knew where to send the young elf. When he returned, the young prince was already up and stretching his legs. His blood-soaked shirt fluttered in the breeze, revealing a raw and pink patch of flesh where before there had been an open wound. *I've found your dragons, young lord. I will show you the way, but will not travel with you. Dealing with dragons is not a unicorn's affair, but I will see you upon the path before I leave you.*

"I understand, brave Avaryn. You have done quite enough for me already, not least of all saving my life. I owe you much and I hope that we meet one day again," Mas'ril said.

I very much think that I will see you again prince, if not today then another. Now come, the way to peril lies this way. He bobbed his head at the young elf and trotted away. Mas'ril followed with a sense of purpose and not a little trepidation. The unicorn's predictions of his fate weighed heavily upon him and he tried to shrug it off for a later day. He had bigger things to worry about right now.

THE PRICE WE PAY

Kanth paced around the large clearing—the site of a magical battle last year with a contingent of elves—and scowled. "Is she going to be all right Garen?" he asked, worried that Floren wouldn't be able to fly for a while. With the elves this close, it wouldn't do to stay in one place for long. He looked at the elven woman he had saved lying unconscious on the pile of leaves and closed his eyes in contemplation. He had taken her to protect her, but couldn't say why. *Instinct? Because she is with child?* he thought.

"Floren will be fine," Garen said. "She needs to rest until the tendons reattach. She'll have to walk for a while. That spear was designed for *us*, Kanth." Garen held the broken haft in his massive claws and showed the elder dragon. The head was wickedly barbed and twice the size of a typical elven spear.

Kanth sighed. "I'll have to carry her, then. Those elves will be coming for us, do not doubt that. The one leading them was single-minded and will not stop until we are all dead." He looked at the female elf again as she stirred, contemplating his brash decision to save her.

His thoughts were broken when his keen hearing detected footfalls in the surrounding forest. Kanth shifted forward, imposing his bulk between the others and the side of the clearing from which the sound was coming. Then Kanth received the second surprise of his very long life.

It was the young prince, walking quietly and sliding from tree to tree effortlessly. Nary a twig broke nor leaf shuffled at his passing, yet the dragon could still hear him. When he came into the clearing he swallowed deeply and muttered to himself. "Well, when the dark one runs..." The young prince stood straighter and faced the dragons. "I mean you no harm," Mas'ril said,

Garen snorted. "Harm? What could he possibly do alone?"

Kanth sat back on his haunches and smiled. *This was the brave one!* He thought. *And he wasn't dead, after all.* "Welcome, young elf. We wish you no harm, either, while you are at peace with us."

"Maybe *you* don't," Garen growled from over the green's shoulder.

"Easy, Garen. This one saved your love. He was repaid for his chivalry with deception and violence. Let us hear him out." Kanth wasn't usually the voice of reason, but circumstances demanded it.

"Very well, Kanth." Garen eased back to Floren's side, stroking the sleeping dragon's back with his long tail.

Mas'ril took two steps forward, his hands shaking and his face beaded with sweat. "I am Mas'ril Moonriver, prince of the elves. I was told that if there was some way to end this war without shedding more blood, that I was to take it. Offer me a solution that I can take to my father and I promise on my life that I will try and bring us all peace," he said, his voice never wavering despite the fear writ plain across his face.

"Wise words, my prince. But alas, you are too young to trust in this." Kanth said, "Elves will make their rules and pass their laws regardless of your intentions. Mistake me not, your acts of bravery and compassion will stay with me for a *very* long time, but I just can't put my race's faith in one so young."

"Then put that trust in me, dragon," the female elf said weakly from behind him. "I know not how you live, Mas'ril. But we have another problem besides the war."

"What is it, general?" the elven prince asked, concern tightening his features.

"The baby," she said flatly. She hung her head and tears started to fall. "I tried every spell of healing I know, but I need a wizard. I have to get to the city fast, or I shall lose my child."

"Well," Kanth started slowly, trying not to sound crass, "Why don't you just magic yourself back there like you people always do?" He saw the young prince flinch and realized he must have crossed some line.

"Because, majestic one, the ether we travel with will harm the child. No. I must travel by conventional means."

"Garentifranor, help me up," Floren said, suddenly awake. Garen lent her a wing, and she turned herself to face the elves and lowered her head. "I haven't ever seen courage like yours in an elf. I owe you a debt of life, and to a dragon that is a mighty thing indeed. This means that you and your family are always safe from me and I will always try and help when I can." She closed her eyes and sighed, "Garen, you once said you would do anything for me. Does that still hold true, my love?"

Garen's scales bristled with anger, then the rage left him as he looked at the blue scales of his soulmate, and bowed his head. "Yes, Florenvarial. I said that, and I mean it still."

Floren smiled, her rows of wicked teeth gleaming. "Then

will you help me fulfill my debt? Will you carry these two to the city of the elves in the north?"

Garen nodded.

"I will help as well," Kanth said, moved by the compassion of the two bluewings. Besides, Garen would most likely open his mouth and get himself killed if he went alone. "You can send a message to your people with your magic, can you not? To warn them that we are coming?" he asked the elves.

"Yes, the winds shall carry our words before us. We will tell our people to stand down, and to summon our best healer, Adrilian, for the general," Mas'ril said, suddenly assuming an air of command that belied his young age.

Kanth nodded approval and took the young prince upon his back while Garen took the general. They launched into the air and soared above the trees. Into the clouds they went, slowly so they wouldn't harm their passengers in the gusting winds. Little did they realize just how far reaching their decisions would impact their peoples in the centuries to come.

CONSEQUENCES

Emerging from the clouds above the city of Tir-Vaniar, Mas'ril hastily threw up a shield of compacted air to block the hundreds of arrows flying at them from below. "Hold!" he called as both he and Lys'lyll worked feverishly to counter spells being hurled at them. They landed hard in the courtyard, scattering dozens of elves. Kanth's roar sent them tumbling back in fear, scrambling for cover as Garen spread his wings out defensively. Once the gathered elves saw Lys'lyll, they stood down. The elves stared in confusion, then pointed to the palace steps. Mas'ril's heart sank as he slid down from the dragon and saw his father held in mid-air by some invisible force.

"Isn't it a good thing I received your message?" Harav'in

asked as he stepped out from behind the king. "I have your father here in a spell web; threads of magic stand ready to cut him apart if anything happens to me."

"What do you want, Harav'in?" Lys'lyll said, fighting the pain in her stomach.

"What I *want* is for Mas'ril here to prove his loyalty and slay these two dragons. Only then will his father be released." The wizard grinned as he gestured sharply, and the king screamed in pain as his body jerked about within the magical bonds.

"Stop!" Mas'ril called. His eyes met his father's and he saw both pride and sorrow at the same time. The prince knew they couldn't slay the dragons and hope to end the war in peace. He knew what had to be done and it fell to him to be the one that did it. The unicorn's words of destiny came back to him then and he closed his eyes. *I'll kill you slowly for this Harav'in,* he thought as he gathered his will and shouted the words that would haunt his heart forever. "Ash'anti fra, wan, fros dosit kith's shir!" he called to both the air and water, asking them to freeze his father's heart, ending the stalemate and letting his father die quickly. Mas'ril knew his father was as good as dead, but this way his will would be done. The last act of his father was to smile with pride at his son.

Lys'lyll's eyes watered as she drew her sword and called it out, "The High King is dead! Long live the High King!"

"What have you done?!" Harav'in screamed as he spun towards the palace. He met a staff to the chest as a red-robed elf came out of nowhere.

"And that is the end of you, general." The elf said as he walked by the prone general to Lys'lyll's side. Adrilian Everence was one of the most accomplished wizards in the north, if not the entirety of Lythin'all. The venerable elf's crimson robes and long hair flowed about him as he ran his hands over the general's stomach, whispering quietly.

Mas'ril walked towards a now restrained Harav'in, his tears falling from his eyes like water from an overfilled cup. He said nothing as he stopped in front of the man and slowly drew his sword. The fear in the disgraced general's eyes was clear. Mas'ril sighed, knowing that he couldn't go through with his thoughts of killing the wizard. He turned his sword to point to Kanth and Garen and smiled, knowing what he would do. "This man is yours, Kanth. Take him, now named Dragonslayer, in good faith, and let your elders know that the elven king wishes to discuss terms of peace between our peoples."

Kanth bowed and took his offered gift, the general screaming as they flew off into the azure sky.

EPILOGUE: THE TRUCE

It took three days to hear back from the dragons. The day they returned, the courtyard was emptied for their arrival. Garen and Floren weren't there, but Kanthalianar arrived with two other dragons. One had light brown scales and the other was deep crimson. They discussed the elven cities and what the dragons wished to change, and within a tenday they had a workable truce. The elves would halt their territorial expansion and the dragons would leave the cities that were already established alone. Some of the dragons even went so far as to go to slumber, letting the elves have the forest to themselves for the time being. It was so easy that Mas'ril couldn't understand why they had fought in the first place, then he remembered Harav'in and knew what had caused the war. It had been selfishness and hate.

ONLY A DAY later and Kanth was bored. All this formal talk was for dragons older than he. He had only come to see the young high king. He had never seen so much bravery in an elf before and he wanted to thank him for all he had done. Their reunion was short, as duty calls to those in power, yet it filled his heart to see the young king smile. Soon Kanth was back to soaring upon the wind through the forest. He banked and flexed his wings, gliding through the trees and up into the canopy once more, breaking through the foliage in a shower of shimmering leaves and spiraling towards the clouds.

ISLE OF NOVRANTIR
WOODS OF CALM
AMONG HIGHGRASS
HILLS OF F'NAR
PLINTH RIVER
BRIDGE OF YAIL
LAKE OF SORROW
INSIDE TREES
HORN MOUNTAINS
FOREST OF TRANQUILITY
BENEATH SKY

❧ 3 ❧

THE TIME BEFORE DARKNESS
DAR'KRIST IN NOVRANTIR

In the Beginning...

The man jogged lightly, knowing that they were right behind him and that no amount of speed would outdistance the magic the elves were using. He so despised elves, and he couldn't believe that the other incarnations had banded together to take him down. As the living, breathing, embodiment of their respective gods, the incarnations were usually at odds with one another on principle only. It seemed that things had changed when he destroyed that elven city. *They had it coming,* he thought, smiling at the memory of destruction and death. Death! That was his name, as stupid as it sounded. All five incarnations had met over a century ago, under a flag of truce, and decided to change their names to avoid being worshiped by the humans that had come up from the southern plains. The humans had migrated to all parts of the north, mingling with both the elves in Nov'ranen and in Lythin'all. So now they all had names dealing with what they saw in themselves. Rubbish, all of it. He should know, he was one of those humans, although he was far older than any of them now. He was tall, seven feet if he was an inch, with a long mane of black hair. The man called Death wore black clothes and a cloak that seemed to flutter, even without wind.

He followed the ocean, keeping the crashing waves on his right as the elves came running behind him, propelled by their magic. He should've known as soon as the great city of Tir-Novran fell that he would have trouble, but he honestly didn't think they would *all* come for him. He sent his *sight* out ahead of him, seeing the distant cliffs like they were right in front of him, and located a path down to the edge of the water. Following the sound of the crashing waves, he stopped at a landing to stand his ground. He would meet them here, on a field that would favor a martial fighter rather than have to deal with their ranged attacks as well. Let them come, he would show them the meaning of death.

War ran easily with the wind assisting him, his long white hair flowing out behind him like a glorious standard of battle. He was tall for an elf, cresting over six feet, and had piercing blue eyes. *By all the gods above, Death will pay for what he has done,* he thought as the grim scene replayed in his mind. He would never forget what he had seen in the ruins of Tir-Novran. Never. He gripped the blade in his hands a little tighter and ran on, knowing that the incarnation of death had nowhere to go. War was wielding one of the three great treasures of the elven people, an artifact that could actually hurt a being as powerful as himself. The sword Chal'ice was glorious, etched in elven runes and edged with silver. "Can you see him, Time?" he called out over the rushing wind. Gods, they were almost flying!

"Yes, he went down the cliffs towards the ocean," Time said, keeping his response curt. He had control of the magic on all of them... while running.

Thank the goddess he's an incarnation, War thought, as he looked ahead at the cliffs, *or he would've passed out long ago.* Time was the incarnation of magic and was only about five feet standing on his tiptoes—on top of a rock. He had long white hair tied up in a single braid, laced with purple flowers: flowers that weren't doing so well going this fast. He had lost most of them and that made his frown even deeper; he worked hard for his appearance. Time also wielded one of the three treasures, the Vanen'il. It was an orb, with a golden glow and an inner warmth. It was a wondrous creation, able to protect whomever held it from any sort of power or affect—like the field of death given off by the very man they were chasing— or even their own weaknesses to the elements. They each had one weakness, not known to one another, and that one element would damn near cripple them when exposed to enough of it. War's was water, and he hated the rain with a passion. Just looking at those waves below was making him sick.

"Well—I, for one, will be glad when this is all over and we can go our separate ways again. You all make me nervous." The shaky voice was from a very slight elf with a malicious smile. He didn't seem that dangerous, except when he drew his twin daggers, then all bets were off. Shadow was the incarnation of, well, shadows. His god, Norar, was the patron of the less than honorable thieves and cut throats of the world, and the others rarely even talked to him. He had shoulder length white hair, sticking out of his hood and that very same hood concealed his eyes from everyone. He looked over at Fate with that mischievous smirk he always wore when he was thinking about trouble

"Shadow, you *would* say that. Look, we all agreed to put him away, if we had agreed sooner, that city wouldn't be choked with the bodies of the dead," Fate said, scowling at the sneaky elf running next to her. She had long white hair that reached down to her waist, and eyes so green that they almost glowed. She had been the personification of beauty long before she was made an incarnation. She held the third elven treasure: Saten'Kind, a staff of pure, polished, white wood, unknown to any tree in nature. It would harm any evil it touched and if used defensively it would charm anyone the wielder wanted to. It had brought the humans and elves together these last fifty years, and they had made great strides in living together. Not so over in Lythin'all, or so the stories told.

War heard Time ask the wind to slow their rapid approach as they neared the winding path. *Gods above, that man is good with magic,* War thought as he slowed to a brisk walk, leading the way down to the landing. As they approached the dangerous incarnation, War saw Death whip off his cloak and throw it at Shadow as they neared; the little elf actually yelped out loud when the cloak attacked him.

"Shadow, meet my cloak. It fed back at Tir-Novran, but it always likes a snack," Death quipped, but then they were on him.

War went on the offensive. He knew Death had been an incarnation for a great many years, more than anyone here, and he was by far the better fighter. One on one like this, it would be tough, especially with his sword in this cramped space, but he had trained for centuries as well. Death spun, kicking at War's midsection. War caught his foot in his off hand, but Death kicked up with his other foot and slammed it into War's head. Death put his hand down to catch his fall, and rolled to the cliff wall as the others flanked him. War stood, rubbing his head. If it weren't for the Vanen'il, he would be severely weakened by that hit, powered by an incarnation.

"Death, you have gone too far! It is time you were dealt with." War swung his blade around and regretted it instantly. He took a kick to the chest and stumbled back, cursing the cramped space. "Ash'anti dir hadar ea pera balen," he whispered, asking the earth to ground his footing as he went back in for more. He wasn't as adept at magic as Time, but he was still a wizard. He saw Fate swing her staff and instead of blocking the wood that would hurt him, Death just ducked and pulled Time into the swing, rolling around to put them all in front of him once more. *Hells below, this man is good,* he thought, as they closed in on him as one.

"You can't win Death. You are outnumbered," Fate growled, clearly irritated. She wasn't suited for battle of any kind.

"Oh, I'm sorry, was I supposed to *let* you kill me?" Death said, kicking out and landing a solid blow to Time's lower back as the wizard stood once more.

War came in with his sword, hitting Death in the shoulder. He opened him up good, but the incarnation ignored the hit and focused on the others still. Where was Shadow? He looked up as Death's cloak came fluttering by, thrown by the lithe incarnation.

Death snatched his cloak out of the air and dodged the first dagger coming right behind it. The second one, however, slammed into his ribs. He threw his cloak at Time and spun around War, lashing out with a powerful kick towards the incarnation of shadows. The solid hit sent the little elf flying out well beyond the cliff, spiraling down to the water below. It had to be over two hundred feet to the crashing waves and the gods above knew he wouldn't survive *that* impact. "One down three to—"

"Murderer!" Fate screamed as she went at Death with all she had. "Why do you despise all life?"

"I don't despise *all* life, just all *elves*," Death said quietly, more for War's hearing than anyone else's. He pulled power from the very earth under him, something he had been practicing ever since his god, Krist, had told him how. Everything had vibrations and gave off power, so as long as you could perceive it the right way, you could draw on it. His already strong frame was increased threefold, and he grabbed the arm of War, twisting it and used it to impale Fate with War's own sword as she came at him. It wouldn't kill her—incarnations healed much faster than normal mortals—but it would take her out for a bit. She hit the blade and dropped her staff, crying out in shock and pain, clutching at the powerful sword in her belly.

"Fate, no!" War cried, trying to turn and face Death. "How?" He let go of the sword in shock, and stumbled back.

Time whispered a quick spell while wrestling with the cloak, then threw it at Death as he cast yet another. "Ash'anti fir leven oa fra, wan hary fros!" Time yelled, urging the elements to action.

Death shivered, feeling the heat leave the air around him. If he was going, he would take one of them with him. He took two strong hits from Wars' fists on his back, gritted his teeth, and pushed through the pain. He grabbed the impaled incarnation with one hand and the sword with the other. He pulled the sword sideways, nearly cutting Fate in half, then threw the blade at War. "Farewell brother," he called, already feeling his limbs icing up. He hugged the body of Fate tightly as the ice fully engulfed them. She was dead before they were frozen solid.

LONG MOMENTS of silence went by before War picked up his blade and walked solemnly over to gather up the fallen staff. It felt warm to the touch and his tears fell on the wood like spring rain. He had never told her he had loved her, his own fault to be sure. Sadly, it wasn't the only mistake he would live with. "Well done, Time. Now what do we *do* with him?" he asked, a quiet melancholy to his usual edgy voice.

"The spell I worked up calls for him to be held in a vault of rock, deep under the waves. The waters this far north will be cold year-round, especially that far down," Time said, wiping his tears away and straightening his back, "At least that is the theory."

"What's stopping him from getting out?" War asked solemnly. "You saw how strong he can be. Can't he break out?" The incarnation looked out at the sea of Irace and watched the sun dip low on the horizon. He shivered involuntarily at the thought of being kept under those waves. It certainly didn't feel like victory.

"I'm going to use the three artifacts to power the spell. As long as they are intact, and are not used to undo it, it will keep him in there forever." Time closed his eyes and called forth a vault of stone around the body of Death and Fate. He used the air to lift it out over the ocean and plunged it down deep, then asked the water to hold it there. He tied all of that to the three items with the element of ether, for stability, then swayed on his feet.

War shook his head; that was a lot, even for an incarnation. In fact, he didn't think anyone else could've done it alone.

Sometime later, as they travelled north once more, they ran into a line of refugees. They were a mixed company of elves and humans and looked to the powerful beings for guidance. War and Time conferred and came up with an idea, one that would benefit all involved. They would relocate the survivors to the hidden island that they had trained on and help them begin anew. They would teach them to guard the three treasures and to be ever diligent against the evil that lay under the waves. They renamed the island Novrantir, or secret city, in remembrance of the city that was destroyed by Death. They had to make up some of the story, to avoid leading the curious to the site, but in the end the elders knew that they were to be obeyed. The sword Chalice, the Orb of Light, and the Staff of Kindred—as they were to be called by the humans and elves alike in the years to come—were interred in three separate cities. Incarnations can be very persuasive when they want to be so things went well for over three hundred years, but all good things eventually come to an end.

DESTINY CALLS

The people ignored her as she walked down the beautiful cobblestone path, kicking the fallen leaves as she tried her best to not feel lonely. Yoril Everbright was an outcast, in every sense of the word, and no one would even tell her. She was just over five feet tall, dressed in her white training leathers that contrasted with her vibrant violet eyes. She had short white hair that fell in her face as she bobbed her head at the people that passed by. *I don't know why I bother to be polite, they all hate me anyway,* she thought as she crossed the streets of the city. Yoril was an anomaly: born of an elf and a human, she was never supposed to exist. The elven priests had said she was not possible, that the two races were incompatible, yet here she was. One would think that she would be hailed as a miracle, but no. Everyone looked at her like she was an abomination.

The elves hated her because she wasn't pure and the humans disdained her because she was part fae. Worse than all of that was the fact that the two races lived in harmony despite their differences; the only thing they hated was her. She stopped and stared up at the open sky through the sparse white trees and had to smile despite her mood. The elven city of Beneath Sky was one of the most beautiful places on the isle of Novrantir, yet she would give anything to leave it. Irony seemed to love her. Most of the public buildings had no roofs—all the better to see the open sky above—and the rain and other elements were kept out with magic. She walked on, hurrying now as she realized she was late, once again, for cadet training. Yoril arrived at the Sacred Chamber and was met by the Mistress-at-Arms lightly tapping her foot.

"Late again, miss Everbright?" sighed Mistress Urien Ashbow as she walked past. Urien was the trainer for the Home Guard, the most dangerous post one could find on the Isle of Novrantir. The Home Guard was responsible for guarding the sacred treasures that kept the magical seal of Jera functioning, imprisoning the dark god's beast. Their lives were the only thing that stood between the safety of the world and a hideous evil that would destroy them in a heartbeat. Urien turned and walked behind Yoril as they both entered the chamber that held the sacred Staff of Kindred, one of the three artifacts that powered the seal.

"All right, settle down," she called out in her stern voice to the other cadets. Mistress Urien was very tall for an elf, a little over six feet tall, and her long white hair hung down in three braids that bounced off her black leathers that signaled her as a master. "Today's lesson is something that you've only heard in whispers or at bedtime from your parents. Today we will go over what you need to know about the gramayre." She smiled at the chorus of gasps from the cadets. "As always with what you learn here, this is for your ears only. Nothing heard here is to be told to anyone. Not to your families, friends, or even nobles." She scowled as a young elf raised his hand. "Yes, Myst?"

Mystanshir Nightstar was liked by the others as much as boils on your eyes or vomiting up sharp rocks. It's not that he was repulsive—far from it—but his family had been disavowed of noble rank and there wasn't much that was worse in elven society than a disgraced noble... except, perhaps, being a half-elf. The scandal that threw House Nightstar into obscurity was the worst kind: infidelity. Elves joined with a life partner and it meant just that. *Life.* Elves lived for a very long time, so when one of them swore their love to someone, they meant it. To throw that away was almost as bad as murder; Alana'vyn Nightstar should've known better. Her family was stripped of noble rank and shunned by most other elves, which coincidentally led to Myst's budding friendship with Yoril. They were both looked at like misfits.

"Mistress Urien, do the Gramayre really exist?" He sat back in his chair and smoothed his long white hair back out of his face. At a very young eighty-five years old, he was handsome by any standard and he knew it. He was a little over five feet tall and cut a dashing figure in his white training leathers, with his pale skin and deep silver eyes.

"That is the point of this lesson plan, young cadet," Urien said casually, looking around the inner chamber with narrowed eyes.

Yoril followed the trainer's gaze and her sharp mind registered what Urien must have noticed. The regular guards were absent, leaving them all by themselves. *They probably just left to give us some privacy, to lessen the intimidation effect,* she thought, dismissing her growing worry.

"Sorry," Myst said, lowering his eyes. He always talked about the stories of the Gramayre as if they were real and not just to scare children into going to bed on time; although few of his age shared his belief, Myst thought the ancient blood mages were truly real.

"To answer your question though, yes. The Gramayre were humans who tired of only the elves being able to cast magic.

They petitioned powers from the deep Hells for the ability to cast magic, yet did not get what they expected. They had to sacrifice elves and use their blood to fuel this foul magic. They started around two hundred years ago, but they were thrown down by the Council of Magi. No trace of them has been seen since those dark days." She paused as most cadets took out parchment to take notes, settling her gaze on Yoril. The half-elf had yet to write anything down over the last year of class; she didn't need to. Yoril had an excellent memory and could always remember anything said to her, as long as she was paying attention.

"Because of this, their magic can pierce our magical shields, and cut through most defenses, but thankfully they are just as vulnerable to swords as any person of flesh and blood."

"The powers they contacted, were they demons? They don't really exist, too—do they?" Malis Talian asked with a note of smug defiance to her voice. The girl always thought she was right, though she almost never was.

"Oh yes, they were—and they *are*—very much real. Demons are crafty and not at all like the stories make them out to be. Most people hear of demons being horned creatures with tails and wings that were covered in flames. The stories say they were summoned with magic into chalk outlines that supposedly kept them bound and restrained. That's not even close to the true horror," Urien said, pacing now as she continued. "Demons are beings with immense power that dwell in-between the worlds and can only reach out to this world through magic, like the rituals the Gramayre used. They come in varied shapes and sizes, mostly formless things, and they only want one thing: souls. Once they get inside your mind, they attack your soul and devour it, then leave you an empty husk as they flee back to the space between worlds." Urien shivered and Yoril knew it had nothing to do with the chill in the fall air. "However, we've gotten off topic. Today's lesson is supposed to be about the Gramayre. You all have to be ready, as part of the Home Guard, to defend the treasures in each of the three cities where they are kept."

Yoril's hand went up, but she spoke before Urien could call on her. "Why can't we just keep all the artifacts in one spot? Surely, they won't attack the cities head on, will they?" She had always wondered why they kept them apart. Actually, she wondered about a whole lot. "And how did we even come by these treasures if they are so powerful?"

Urien arched her eyebrows at her questions and smiled. "We'll start with the three treasures; the Staff of Kindred, the blade Chalice, and the Orb of Light." She looked at the cadets seriously, her smile fading. "These powerful items were brought to the survivors of a great tragedy on the mainland over three centuries ago by incarnations of Davalar and Syll. They led the survivors here to this island and helped set up the Home Guard, along with the three cities." She saw the faces of the cadets at the mention of incarnations and continued before anyone asked any more questions. "The incarnations told us they had sealed a great beast away and that these items would keep it there, deep in the Sea of Irace. The survivors were told to keep them in separate places, because of how powerful they were—they couldn't fall into the wrong hands." She paused as the cadets murmured their disbelief. "When powerful beings tell you to do something, you do it."

"So, we guard the Staff here?" Myst asked, sitting up and paying attention now. The only thing he loved more than stories of the Gramayre were ones of the incarnations.

"Yes, but like I said, the Gramayre haven't been active for centuries." Urien tensed as something in the room changed.

.   .   .

Yoril cringed as a deep voice boomed from behind them all. She had been paying attention and still hadn't sensed anyone enter.

"That changes now," a man said. He drew a dagger which dripped blood as he casually whispered something to himself. A red pulse raced towards the Mistress-at-Arms over the young group, smelling like sulphur and death; a bolt straight from the deep Hells.

"Down cadets! This is not--" Urien's scream was cut off as the red pulse severed her right arm and carried on to scar the wall with a blackish red soot. She fell to both knees as a black rot spread quickly up her arm. Despite asking the ether to heal her, she was dead in less than ten heartbeats.

Yoril saw some of the cadets laugh and ignore the Mistress-at-arms as she fell and tried to warn them. Whispers of 'It's only a drill,' and 'Good effects,' flew around the group. She knew better; there was never any blood in any of their drills. Yoril drew her sword and backed towards the Staff of Kindred, somehow knowing that this wasn't going to end well. She saw Myst draw his own thin blade, rolling to the side and crouching behind a pillar just as another red pulse cut down three cadets who were still laughing. That's when the room exploded into chaos.

Cadets screamed and drew their weapons, some fleeing for the chamber doors, some rushing headlong at the intruder. Yoril looked at the man and shuddered. If anything matched her imaginings of what a Gramayre looked like, it was standing right in front of her.

The man was tall, well over six feet, and dressed in a long black robe. He had a black beard and deep black eyes that said he was not only here to kill everyone and but was eager to do it. He cut down cadets with blasts of both red and black bolts now, smiling whilst he did so. Worse, he wasn't even asking the elements to do it like elven wizards did. Instead, he was using that dripping knife. *That must be elven blood on that blade*, she thought, as she saw the man cut down the young cadets one after another, none of them even coming close to proving dangerous. He was ancient and powerful and none of the cadets stood a chance against him. The Gramayre walked to where the Staff of Kindred rested and laughed when he saw Yoril guarding it. Her shaking hands held her slim sword firmly, yet she knew this fight wasn't going to be won with direct force—if it was going to be won at all

"I've slain all of your friends and yet you still think that you're going to defend that staff?" he asked, sounding intrigued by her defiance.

"You didn't though." Yoril said as she tried to steady her voice. She finally understood what all of her instructors always said about fear. You either let it win, or you used it to win. She saw Myst crouching behind the man and knew that she had to draw attention to herself. She took a deep breath and stilled her nerves. She was probably going to die horribly, but she would be damned if she was going to do it shaking like a frightened animal.

"I didn't what now?" the man stopped and looked at her, tilting his head and scrutinizing her with a careful gaze.

"You said that you killed all of my friends. You didn't." He came closer but still hadn't blasted the life from her yet. A few more feet and they might have a shot. She shifted her feet like Mistress Urien always told them to do before they engaged the enemy and moved her balance from the back foot to the front for a quick lunge, then smiled nervously at the Gramayre as he studied her. This was going to hurt.

"Oh? Did I miss one?" He looked around with an exaggerated sweep of his arm, still holding the dagger as it dripped blood.

"No. It's just that they weren't my friends." Yoril said, as a matter of fact, and lunged quickly at his chest with her thrusting blade. It struck the cloth of the robe like she had hit a stone wall and the shock of it threw the blade out of her hands. She felt a numbness shoot up her arm as he stepped up and grabbed her by the throat, laughing a cold deep laugh as her blade clattered to the floor in the eerie quiet.

"Silly girl—you should've known I would ward myself for a frontal attack, or didn't the instructor go over that with you? Oh, that's right. I killed her before she could get into that. I mean, what elf doesn't know that anyway?" the Gramayre asked, his confidence showing in his arrogant smile.

"She's not an elf; she's a half-elf, and apparently smarter than you," Myst said as he slammed his sword through the back of the man and out his chest. Yoril gasped as she watched the stuff of nightmares fall to its knees. Myst withdrew his blade slowly with trembling hands. It was stained with black blood. The Home Guard rushed in then, battering the doors open and shouting orders. Once they saw the carnage, they started calling for the healers. Myst just stared at her, like he could only see Yoril.

"What are you staring at?" Yoril asked, breathless now that the threat was gone. Myst had that ridiculous smile on his face and she found herself smiling back despite the horrific ordeal.

"Oh nothing. Just the hero of Beneath Sky." He winked at her and started answering questions as the Home Guard flooded the inner chamber and pulled them away from the body of the Gramayre. They were, of course, ignoring her altogether. He answered their questions curtly, drawing them away from her so she could sit and breathe. The Gramayre were back and after the sacred treasures, but now their plan was laid bare and measures could be taken. She knew then, that destiny had picked both of them, unlikely heroes, to save the realm. Gods above, was the council of nobles going to hate that.

DESPERATE PLANS

Yoril stood in the rear of the council hall and thought about running right back out the front door. She was so far out of her depth that she couldn't even see their shoes from where she was. These meetings were for the important people: wizards, nobles, and merchant guild masters. Every single person better than she was. "Hey!" she yelped as something prodded her in the back.

"Let's go, hero—they want both of us," Myst said, smiling at her as he stuck her in the back with his foot, gently pushing her forward. At his proclamation every head turned to stare at them and the whispering started in.

"Not me, you," she retorted, knowing that she would likely be ignored on general principle.

Myst stopped and faced her, in the middle of the entire room. They were halfway into the room and in full view of the council table and everyone could hear them. She knew that he was counting on that. "Listen right now, Yoril. The *only* reason we are here right now is *your* bravery in baiting that maniac. I couldn't have gotten that close without you keeping his atten-tion. I thought you were dead but I had to go slow, praying that he wouldn't attack until I was in range. That was the single bravest thing I have ever seen."

Yoril almost cried. No one had ever said anything like that to her in her life, including her own mother. She knew that on some level it was for show, but she could see in his eyes that he meant it. She mouthed the words 'Thank You' and walked with him more confidently. She looked up at the elevated dais and the table of seven nobles, and her confidence started to waver. She stopped at the little table set up for the two of them and pulled out a seat, waiting to sit until the room quieted down. Myst had no such compunction.

Myst walked behind Yoril and whispered in her ear. "I'm in absolutely no mood for these people." He sat and put his feet up on the table, smiling defiantly at the seven and crossed his arms, feigning boredom. One of them scoffed loudly and Myst smiled even wider.

A throat cleared and quieted the room. "Let me start by saying how glad we are that you two made it out of this alive." Lariel DeLanril wasn't the oldest person on the council, but she certainly looked it. Being human, she showed age easier than the elves that lived for centuries rather than decades. At forty-five winters she was by no means 'old', but compared to the fair skinned elves, she might as well have been. The female councilor had blond hair and blue eyes that complimented the yellow silks that she favored. She stood and inclined her head to the young ones before her. "However, a few of us are unconvinced that the story you tell is the truth."

Myst was on his feet in a heartbeat. He was shaking with anger and it didn't so much as creep into his voice rather than leap there. "How can you sit there and say that!? The Gramayre killed Mistress Urien and you say we made it up?"

Ereval Ashstaff rose swiftly to her feet as Lariel sat. "We aren't saying you made it up, young Nightstar; we just don't believe that he was Gramayre." She made a calming gesture to them both before she went on. "What we have here is tragic, there is no doubt of that, and we all mourn the deaths of those cadets and Urien." She walked off of the dais, down to their level with grace and style. She was three times the age of Lariel, yet looked only twenty or so winters. Her long white hair was tied up in a bun and her green eyes matched her floor length dress. "However, the notion that the Gramayre were behind this horrible attack is pure nonsense."

"They saw it for themselves Ereval!" Thandyr Tetheren rose to his feet, shaking his fist. "Are we going to just ignore first-hand accounts?" He was in his thirties, with short brown hair and a thick beard that hung down to his broad chest. At over six feet he was a giant among the smaller elves and his long white dress coat fluttered as he walked down to confront Ereval. He looked back at the representatives from House Silvertree, House Degreth, and House Goldenleaf and frowned. The three houses hadn't said a word, partly because this wasn't their city. They were from the other two cities and were on the council as representatives of nobility.

"Please, councilors—control yourselves. We will take their official statements and *then* plan on what to do." Alan'ya Starfire was the oldest elf on the council of nobles, but you would never know it. She was vibrant and beautiful and as a priestess of Ollian, goddess of beauty and love, she was the perfect mediator for a situation with heated emotions. Her long white hair was the same length all the way around and pulled back in a knot. Instead of a messy appearance, however, it added to her innate sexuality in a come-hither sense that most men couldn't resist. Her red silk robes hung on her slight five-foot frame showing her many curves and her smile was just pleasant enough to keep everyone happy with her. "Now why don't we sit and hear from the young... woman."

The pause was just enough to be polite but Yoril knew that it was a veiled insult. Not an elf or a human. As the other council members took their seats and calmed down, they signaled to Yoril to stand and give her statement. Yoril looked at Myst and nodded, standing and clearing her throat. "When the pulse of red light hit the Mistress-at-arms, I turned and saw the Gram...I mean, man. He was chanting and channeling what, I can only assume, was blood." She waited for the council to nod and she took her seat once more.

"So, you never actually heard this man ask the elements to attack Urien?" Ereval asked nonchalantly. "You only observed him after?"

"To a point, Lady. I also witnessed him cast again and again against the rest of the cadets, as well as cut them down with his blade," she said, remembering the horror and carnage. She shook her head as if to wipe away the images. If only she knew that they would never go away.

"So, point of fact, you were in the middle of a heated combat with a class full of cadets dying around you?" Ereval continued, driving her point home, as Yoril nodded woodenly. "So, one could say that the only thing you 'know' is that he killed the cadets with the weapon dripping blood, not actually flinging it at them with magic."

Yoril went cold and nodded to keep from throwing up. She hadn't mentioned that his *weapon* was dripping blood. She hadn't even said it to the guards that questioned them, however briefly; only that he used blood to cast. She felt Myst's hand on her leg as he squeezed it in warning as he stood.

"Lady Ashstaff," Myst began, his tone one of surrender, "we've given our statements to the guards and respectfully inform this council that the man was indeed Gramayre. If this esteemed council feels that we are lying, or are unable to remember the events properly, then we will take our leave."

They still think we're outcasts, less than worthy of their time, Yoril thought, as she walked towards the exit behind Myst. She assumed that some of the councilors were in on it, but had no idea how bad it was until Myst spoke in hushed tones.

"They will more than likely try to silence us within the hour. We have to get out of the city before that."

Yoril followed numbly behind Myst, unable to comprehend what he was saying. Surely, they wouldn't kill them? She could hear the council arguing and knew that they had failed to convince the majority of them. She knew as well that the chances of the staff being safe were slim. "Myst, we have to get the staff," she said quietly as they walked out and down the open cobblestone street.

Myst put his arm around hers and pulled her close. "I know, but first we have to get some stuff. They won't let us live, Yoril. We have to go." He walked arm in arm with her, to avoid suspicion. They could talk easier this way, being seen as young lovers to the casual passerby. "My mother will help us, but I have no idea where to go once we leave Beneath Sky."

Yoril shrugged as they hurried down the many streets, taking turn after turn to dissuade any pursuit from people that would want them dead.

NIGHTSTAR VILLA, BENEATH SKY

They arrived at Nightstar Villa and went in the back, just as they heard a woman's voice come from the front of the house. Myst looked around the corner in time to see the end of the exchange.

"No sir, I haven't seen my son since I heard of the incident. Isn't he at the council meeting?" Alana'vyn batted her eyes at the young human guard and smiled charmingly. He shook his head and turned around, walking away but keeping his eyes on the perimeter of the grounds.

Myst let out a breath he wasn't aware he was holding. "Thanks mother, but he will be back," he said as they came into the living room. "We have to get out of the city and soon." Things had gone so wrong, so fast, that his head was spinning. Luckily he had always been kind of an outcast and had learned to live on the fringes of a society that had shunned him. Not as bad as Yoril though.

"No. We have to get the Staff first," Yoril pleaded. "If we let the Gramayre get it then they will release the evil beast." She seemed to grow angrier as she spoke. "Once we have it, we can run to the cities of Inside Trees and Among Highgrass and take the other sacred treasures as well." She stopped as a knock on the back door startled them all. They held their breath... and then let it out as a familiar voice called out to them.

"You guys alive in there?" Xaniver Sirr called out to his childhood friends. Xaniver was six feet tall and well muscled, with sandy blond hair that always seemed tousled, and dark grey eyes. He favored white silks and plain breeches when he wasn't in his guard armor. The Sirr family house wasn't noble, but as one of the oldest human families in Beneath Sky, they might as well be. His father was Captain of the City Guard, and had taught him everything he knew. Xaniver had been training as a warrior all of his life and was one of the best swordsmen in the city for his young age.

"Well come, good *Sir*," Myst mispronounced his best friends name as Ser rather than Sear. It was a bone of contention that they went through more often than not and proved to be just the tension breaker that this tense meeting needed.

"Yeah, yeah. I'm just glad you two are all right," Xaniver said, looking at Yoril more than Myst. He had always been fond of the young half elf, ever since they met years ago. She didn't know he was alive though, and seemed oblivious to his awkward attempts at flirting, if you wanted to call it that. His flirting was more akin to jumping off of a seaside cliff and missing the water.

"Look, Xaniver, we have to leave. Can you look after my mother while we're gone?" Myst asked as he threw some things in a sling bag.

"Where are you going?"

"We have to steal the Staff of Kindred and get out of the city, Xaniver. The Gramayre are back," Yoril blurted out, then covered her mouth as an afterthought. Too late. Myst's mother ran off frantically packing for her son while Xaniver tried to work his mouth to no avail.

"I'm going with you," Xaniver finally said, and turned without waiting for an argument. Going to his horse, he pulled out his sword and his pack that he kept in case he was called to arms and walked back in, slapping the horse and sending it on its way back home. "We have twenty minutes before my father sees the horse without a rider. He will know something is wrong, and since I was warned not to come here, he will check here first," Xaniver said as he strapped his weapon on.

Myst wasn't going to argue. He knew that once his friend set his mind to something it was done. "Glad to have you."

SACRED CHAMBER, BENEATH SKY

Within the hour they were across from the Sacred Chamber once more and Myst wasn't thrilled about going back in there. Entering that place would bring all of the gruesome memories flooding back, but it had to be done. There were only two of the Home Guard stationed outside as the three tried to come up with a plan crouching among the trees. In the end Yoril decided to try magic. She wasn't strong, but she did know a few tricks that might help, and Myst wasn't very good at all except with air.

"Ash'anti ethir, cra'del lae kith doz," Yoril whispered quietly, asking the ether to help them sleep. Of the five elements she was best at Ether. Ironically, it was the most diverse of them all. They slipped by the two snoring guards and entered the chamber, stopping short when they saw that it had already been cleaned. Not that their memories would ever be wiped of what had happened here. "Quickly, over here," she said as they made their way to the staff.

"What have we here?" a deep voice said as they approached

the staff. Two more of the Home Guard stepped out smiling, but quickly dropped the grins as Xaniver swung his sword at them with purpose. They had never even seen him draw the blade.

"Get the staff—I'll take care of these two," the young fighter said confidently. Elves were very skilled at combat, as they had centuries to practice. However, a lot of them were lazy mainly because they *had* so long to train. Thankfully this was the case with these two. By the time that Myst and Yoril had the Staff of Kindred, the two guards were on the floor with minor injuries. "So much for the elite guard of the sacred treasures," Xaniver quipped, sheathing his weapon. Then he saw Yoril's face drop and swallowed. "Sorry, Yoril, I..."

"I know. They never took it seriously because the Gramayre were all gone. I wouldn't have though."

"I know."

"Can we go now? Or do you two want to continue to be awkward?" Myst asked lightheartedly, clapping his friends on the shoulder and sprinting out.

A little under an hour later the three of them were walking through the Forest of Tranquility on the way to the city of Inside Trees. They knew that there would be pursuit but felt confident that they would never expect them to flee towards another city. The pursuit would head towards the docks to the south and find nothing, giving them a good two days head start. Now they just had to figure out how to get the other sacred treasures before the Gramayre struck again. They clearly weren't thinking of how badly things could go wrong when fate played with mortals.

UNLIKELY ALLIES

Yoril was exhausted already. They had been walking for hours but at least there was still no sign of pursuit. The city of Inside Trees was roughly fifty miles north of Beneath Sky through the Forest of Tranquility. It was so named mainly because the patrols had eliminated anything remotely hostile, and because of the sweet Singsong lilies that would trill with a good wind. Stories told of a time, centuries ago, when it was populated by faeries, but those were just old tales. Myst had taken up singing after the first half an hour of no pursuit. Yoril mainly ignored him, but she caught the last part of the song he was singing and stopped dead in her tracks.

We go, we walk this road called life
We live, we dream, we die!
They call him the black death,
Forever walking on.

With every breath we sigh.
We hope, we pray, we die!
The fall of Tir-Novran
The everlasting fight...

Myst trailed off as he noticed Yoril looking at him. "What? Have I grown another head, possibly a third arm?"

"That song. That's the song about the destruction of Tir-Novran isn't it?" She had always been fascinated with anything about that city and its mysterious destruction. All anyone knew was that the survivors fled a terrible cataclysm and were led here by their saviors. It was all very vague.

"Yeah, it was the piece I had to learn during my bardic test."

"You never told me you were a bard!"

"I'm not. I didn't have the spark needed to be a bard. I took to the shadows after I failed the test and learned other ways to pass the time," he said smirking at her sideways.

"So, I hate to be the downer of the group," Xaniver started, "but what exactly are we going to do when we get to Inside Trees? It's not like we can just walk in and take their sacred treasure."

"Well, my initial plan was to get in with disguises, then scout out the chamber. But now that I've had time to think about it... I have no idea." Yoril's mind was running in circles with the past events. Walking through the forest was comforting, but when Xaniver brought up what to do--well, her mind went racing again.

Myst chuckled. "Don't worry, I'll sneak in, check it out, then tell you guys what their defenses are. Do we know what the sacred treasure is?" He opened his mouth to say more, but something seemed to catch his attention. He circled around Yoril, looking at her cloak, "Yoril, what did you do to your cloak?" he asked loudly, then leaned in and whispered to her. "Don't panic, but we have company."

Yoril looked around and saw them—two men hiding by the trees on the path ahead, and a third behind a tree to her left.

"What, did it rip?" Xaniver turned to look at Yoril; he must've seen the men as well. He pulled his sword and rushed the tree to Yoril's left, yelling a battle cry as he did.

Myst drew his sword and rolled his eyes. He turned as two men with bloody swords went at Xaniver. He threw two daggers, then rolled as a red blast arced towards him, narrowly missing and taking out a tree. "Gramayre!" he called as he pulled his slim sword and crouched behind a tree. "Ash'anti fra, sran dosan kithin!" He asked the air to shield him then stalked out to cover Yoril.

Yoril saw the men and froze. This couldn't be happening.

When she looked at the attackers, all she could see were the dead bodies of her fellow cadets. She gripped the Staff of Kindred and closed her eyes, wishing it would all just go away. Then a strong hand pulled her and she went down to her knees. She looked up as Myst blocked a sword that was covered in dripping blood, then kicked the man in the chest. Myst whispered to the air again and a third Gramayre went backwards into a tree, hard. Yoril saw Xaniver battling a man who kept blasting him with magic. He was taking the deep red blasts on his sword, which was starting to crack with the pressure. Yoril jumped as Myst took a blast to the shoulder, right through his wards, and fell to one knee.

No! I will not let them down! she thought, trying to figure out what to do. Then it came to her. The Staff! If this staff was one of the three sacred treasures, then it must have some use against evil. *Now I just have to figure out how to invoke whatever it is and pray to all of the Gods above that it helps,* she thought, gripping the staff tightly. Yoril stood and held it out at arm's length, facing one of the black robed Gramayre. "Hold this evil!" she commanded, then closed her eyes, focusing her will into the staff. An eerie silence greeted her as she cracked one eye open; the attackers were as still as statues, frozen by her will and the staff's power.

"Good timing, Yoril," Xaniver said. His cloak was covered in blood and one of his arms hung limply at his side.

"Xaniver, what happened?" She rushed over and looked at his arm, searching for the black veins that had afflicted Mistress Urien. Her heart raced with dread.

"It's fine, Yoril—just numb from the beating my poor sword took."

"I'm not sure what you did, Yoril, but thank Syll you did it." Myst walked around the three men, searching them for anything that could help identify who was behind the attack.

He retrieved his daggers and spun as an elf appeared out of thin air, walking towards them slowly, her hands out and empty. They all relaxed when they recognized her as Tan'lin Golden-leaf, one of the nobles on the council that hadn't spoken during their interview.

Her long white hair fell over her tan shoulders and her keen grey eyes seemed to appraise them all within seconds. "Hold, younglings. I mean no harm." Tan'lin lowered her arms and smoothed out her long golden dress as she walked barefoot towards them. She was beautiful beyond any elf or human, and she knew it. "I am Tan'lin Goldenleaf, and I agree with your rash decision to take the Staff of Kindred and flee."

"How did you find us?" Yoril asked, staring at the place where the portal appeared.

"I used my *sight* to find you, then I asked the ether to bring me to you."

"Want to go over that one more time?" Yoril said, a quizzical look on her face.

Tan'lin looked at Yoril and smiled. "Asking the ether to bring you somewhere, in this case, to you, needs the *sight* to work in conjunction. It uses the image you *see* in your mind when you ask, and if you don't keep a level head and calm mind, you could end up torn apart by conflicting images."

"All right, now why?" Always to the point, Xaniver was still holding his cracked sword at the ready. His arm was still limp, but he only needed the other arm to swing it.

"Don't worry—I am an ally. Besides, with the enemies you just made, you really need all of the help you can get. On top of that, I think that my city is next. I want to help you get the blade, Chalice, from Inside Trees."

"Why would you do that?" Xaniver asked, inching closer to Yoril.

"Ever since I heard Ereval at the council meeting, I knew in my gut that the Gramayre were back. I remember those dark times well and if I keep them from occurring again, I have to try something—even if it means treason."

Myst walked around the three men as Tan'lin talked and used his daggers to end their lives; their bodies fell to the ground as soon as they died.

Yoril gasped in horror at the merciless deed. She clutched the staff for support as all eyes went to Myst.

"It had to be done, Yoril. They're Gramayre," Myst said, as if that was all the explanation needed.

"But they were helpless!" Yoril said, looking away from the bodies.

"I wasn't sure how long they were going to remain frozen and I didn't want them coming out of it when we weren't ready."

"Yoril..." Xaniver started, placing a hand on her shoulder. He didn't get anything else out as she shoved his hand off and stormed away from them all.

"I know. It had to be done. It's just sad that we are killing so that we can stop killing."

"Yoril, where are you going?" Xaniver made to follow, but Myst held him back gently, shaking his head. "She has to work through this on her own."

Yoril stomped off but heard someone following and stopped, her heart racing. "What?"

Tan'lin sighed as she walked up, her bare feet making almost no sound on the forest floor. "You have good ears, Yoril." she started. "Look, I know that you don't like some of this. The gods above know that I don't either. Right now, though, we have to hurry before more people like Urien fall to the evil that has come to the island," she said, a tear falling down her cheek.

"You knew her."

"Yes. I was in the Home Guard with her over two hundred years ago. We grew up in Inside Trees together."

"All right. I think I understand why killing them was necessary, but that's only true because they were Gramayre," she turned to her companions, making sure they could see her face as she talked. "If any elves attack us, we try not to kill them. Is that understood?"

"I get it, Yoril. I'll try my best," Xaniver said, finally flexing his arm once more.

"Yoril, I'm—" Myst looked at her and stopped, his face a mask of pain.

"Myst, I need to hear that you understand." Yoril wasn't going into a city where he might kill just to protect her.

"I understand."

"Good. Now we can get you three to the city." Tan'lin smiled and started walking. "We just have to find a small pool of water. I hear the river up ahead so let's start there."

"Why water?" Yoril asked, a little confused. "Couldn't we just get there like you got here?" She had taken magic classes like any other elven child, yet this seemed way beyond the scope of what she had been taught.

"No. That only works for the caster. If I want to bring others with me, I have to use a scrying pool." Tan'lin stopped and looked at them, seeming frustrated. "This is why I gave up teaching—I just don't have the patience for it." She rubbed her temples and continued. "A scrying pool is a reflective surface in which you can view far off places, using ether. Once the location is fixed in the pool, you can ask the ether to open a portal and others can walk right through."

"We should get a drink once we get there." Myst said, eyeing Tan'lin, in that way he always did.

Tan'lin giggled and stared at him. "Not right now, young one. But maybe someday." They walked to the river and followed it northeast for a little while until Tan'lin found a small pool with circling eddies. "Perfect." She gathered them close and brought up a view of Inside Trees front gate. "Ash'anti ethir, yaw ce por ta car'cen." Tan'lin asked for the ether to open a portal and they all stepped through. The world seemed to bend slightly, then they were on the other side.

ENTRANCE OF INSIDE TREES

The sight that greeted Yoril took her breath away. Beneath Sky was beautiful, but this... this was something beyond that. The city of Inside Trees was literally the forest around them. Oh sure—there was a front gate, basically for appearances, but the trees beyond all held the houses of the elves and humans that dared live among their branches. Clearly a work of high magic, the trees had windows and doors in them, as well as walkways that spanned between them. These walkways connected over fifty trees together in a web of nature and the lights of the houses made it seem like sunset through the canopy. On the forest floor were the shops and smiths, all on raised mounds of roots and earth; Yoril had never seen anything like it.

"It's a lot to take in the first time. Follow me." Tan'lin walked in smiling at the guards and leading them towards the sacred chamber. "Once you have the sword, I will get you to Among Highgrass. Firiath Silvertree will be waiting for you there and lead you to the Orb of Light. He 's also on our side, yet time is precious." She waved the Home Guard away from the chamber doors and went right in, ignoring their looks of confusion. She was a noble and on the council; what the council said was basically law among the cities, so whether they understood or not, the Guard would obey her without question.

Xaniver bowed to the confused Home Guard and walked in behind everyone else. Once inside the tree chamber, they climbed a spiral staircase that wound around the inside of the massive tree. About twenty feet up it turned into another room with a single sword on a pillar. Yoril could see Xaniver staring at it, his eyes transfixed on the blade's beauty.

The sword was exquisite and surrounded by a halo of light that came from above. Even Myst stopped and stared, open mouthed, at the sword as it rested there. Yoril had to admit that it was amazing on a deeper level than just a weapon.

"Go on man, take it," Tan'lin said to Xaniver, clearly impatient. "If any other nobles come in, it could be trouble."

Xaniver stepped up and grasped the hilt, taking it down from the pillar with a slow reverence. He gave it a few passes in the air before switching it out in his sheath. He placed his old sword on the pedestal and stared at it longingly for a moment, then turned to them. "I'm ready, let's get out of here before I have to use this."

They left the chamber, but instead of going down they continued upward, Tan'lin leading them into another room with a huge mirror. "All right, Yoril, first lesson. Repeat after me." She grabbed Yoril by the shoulders gently and turned her to the mirror, whispering in her ear. "Ash'anti ethir, reva ea Among Highgrass."

"Ash'anti ethir, reva ea Among Highgrass," Yoril repeated, verbatim. Her flawless memory was coming in handy for once.

"Now—see that city? Focus on it, memorize it. Do *not* let anything else cloud your vision." Tan'lin sounded worried and shook slightly as she held her. "Now say this: Ash'anti ethir, yaw ce por ta car'cen."

"Ash'anti ethir, yaw ce por ta car'cen," Yoril said, keeping the city in her mind. A portal opened before her, the swirling glass revealing the main gates of a fabulous city. Yoril couldn't believe the drain on her mind and resolve it took to cast the spell. How did those archmages do this all the time?

"Hurry children—get the Orb and flee to the mainland," Tan'lin said as she all but pushed them through. "Hide them away or bring them to Lythinall. Anywhere the Gramayre can't find them." Tan'lin turned as the Home Guard began pounding upon the chamber door. "Go!" Then they were through the portal and gone.

FINDING THE WAY

Rav'ar Hawklin smiled as they gathered outside of the city. The walls were only ten feet high and made of woven grass... grass! He couldn't believe it when Ereval had told him about the city. He was sure she was leading them into a trap, but at seeing the feeble walls, he felt his confidence soar. Oh sure, she had told him the walls were sturdy and flame resistant, but they were Gramayre. All told, he had assembled ten of his brethren from the main cult and they were the first to strike the cities and try for the sacred treasures. He had heard that a lone Gramayre had tried for the Staff and alerted the elves of Beneath Sky, but their traitor had deflected the alarmists rather well. He straightened his long black robes and brushed the black hair out of his eyes. It was shoulder length almost all the way around, and shielded his blue eyes from sight on occasion.

"My Lord, shall we start the assault?" a youth asked. It was his first time on a mission with the order.

Rav'ar looked at the boy and nodded his acceptance. *Let's see what these walls can take,* he thought as they started to channel their powers together. The blood they had brought would only be enough to get in—after that they would need to slay some elves to stock up and make a push for the sacred chamber. He saw his brothers all cast at the wall by the gate and, though the wall did hold up rather well for grass, it melted quickly under the weight of their magic. He tensed as the elven and human guards came streaming out to stop them and waded in with his own magic, cutting them down without mercy. He was going to save most of his power for the Home Guard, but as he strode in and looked around, he was stunned to find that the Home Guard was nowhere to be seen. Were they waiting for them at the chamber? He waved three of his brethren to go to the sacred chamber while he prepared to take out any resistance here at the gate. *At least I have power to spare,* he thought. Then one of his men called out to him.

"Lord! Behind you!"

The call came too late. Rav'ar turned as a portal opened and a warrior stepped through. He raised his dagger, ready to blast the fool, when the man pulled his sword and swung for his head. Rav'ar barely spun out of the way, only taking a light cut on the shoulder, and threw a bolt of bloodfire at the man. The warrior took it on the blade and stepped forward, lunging straight at him. Rav'ar felt something sharp slide into his chest and cried out, more from the surprise of being hit than the actual pain. He dropped to his knees and saw of all the blood that was pooling on the ground. *What a waste,* he thought, as his vision went black.

SACRED CHAMBER, AMONG HIGHGRASS

Firiath Silvertree walked into the chamber and greeted the guards on duty with a quick smile and a deep bow. They returned the gesture, and as they did Firiath quietly whispered to the air in the room to leave their bodies. Gasping, they dropped silently and writhed on the ground. He waited until their eyes fluttered, then released the air so they would breathe. They would have a headache from the deep hells tomorrow, but they would live. He stepped up and grabbed the Orb of Light and turned to get to the city gate. If Tan'lin did her job, she would be sending the young ones to him soon and he wanted to be ready. He agreed with her plan to hide the treasures; he just hoped he could get it to them in time. That's when he saw Breven, the Captain of the Home Guard.

"Something I can help you with, Lord?" Breven asked, his dour expression speaking volumes in the quiet chamber.

"Breven, I wish you weren't here." Firiath shook his head, truly saddened by the thought that the captain would go down fighting. The man was strong with some of the elements, but not a full wizard. Still, he knew enough to not fall for the fast tricks that would get him out of this alive; that was a shame. "I tell you, in all honesty, that I'm taking this to keep it out of the hands of our enemies and I truly hope you believe me."

"Enemies? You mean my nephew?" he asked, pointing his sword at the bodies on the floor. Breven slowly circled, keeping his stance ready. "Ash'anti fra sran..." he couldn't get the rest out as he started gasping for air. Then he heard the shuffling behind them and spun towards the doorway.

Firiath saw Breven gasp and knew they had been infiltrated. The sounds of steel on steel rang out the minute the doors bashed open and two black robed Gramayre came at them with death in their eyes. They used their magic to take out the captain, not knowing that Firiath was more dangerous. "Ash'anti sonn, yanel ubel undra lae!" Firiath called to the stone floor. That floor rose in a perfect circle, a pillar of stone crushing them against the ceiling.

Firiath stashed the orb in his cloak and ran for the door. Syll forgive him—he wanted to save the captain, but the orb was more important. Out the doors he went, flying by the surprised Home Guard as they awaited their captain's orders. "Get in there, your captain is down!" he called as he ran on, down the smooth stone streets surrounded by edges of high grass. It was then that he saw the fighting at the gate straight ahead. Yet his spirits lifted as he saw the two that must've started this all; two young heroes that destiny had chosen to save them all.

MAIN STREETS, AMONG HIGHGRASS

Yoril was trying to stay behind Myst as they made their way to the sacred chamber. They had come out of the portal and stumbled upon Gramayre attacking the Home Guard. They had to fight their way down the street against at least ten of the wicked sorcerers. Between Chalice and the Staff of Kindred, they were making good progress. Yoril tried to stay focused, but this was another beautiful city that she marveled at. The edges of the avenues were lined with three-foot-tall grass, sporting flowers and small creatures that harmlessly skittered around. Even the walls seemed made out of woven grass and nature was all encompassing in every building and structure, just like Inside Trees.

"Down Yoril!" Myst called out as he spun, launching two daggers at a black robed Gramayre coming at them from the side. The daggers hit some sort of barrier, probably a magical shield of air, and clattered harmlessly to the ground. He slid Yoril behind him, putting her between Xaniver and himself, and drew his slim blade. The man raised his dripping dagger, yet screamed as his robe caught fire. The Gramayre dropped to the ground, trying to put out the flames. Myst lunged quickly, sliding his blade into the man's neck and spun back to Yoril.

Firiath came up to them in a rush. "There is no time," he started as they tried to talk all at once. "Take this and flee down the coast towards the river south of here. At the mouth of the river are the docks and a ship you can take." He handed Myst the orb and winked at Yoril.

Xaniver was covered in blood, none of it his. "Are you kidding me? I don't even know how we're alive at this point, never mind fleeing south with all three cities after us. Oh yeah and *these* guys trying to kill us!" Xaniver yelled, clearly out of his depth and losing it quickly. Physically he seemed fine, although killing this many people would do horrible things to a person when they stopped to think about it.

"That is the Orb of Light. With it you needn't fear *any* magic they throw at you. It protects you from any outside influence that you don't want to affect you, regardless of knowing what it actually is." Firiath ushered them to a side alley, out of the general gaze of the city guard as they still fought the remnants of the invaders. "They are mopping up the last of the Gramayre now, and soon they will realize the orb is gone. Now —out the front gate and go. I will stall them as best I can. May Syll guide your steps, young ones; the future depends on you." He pushed them towards the gate and spun, yelling orders to the city guard to go help the Home Guard at the chamber.

Yoril was in shock. It was all happening so fast that she really didn't have any time to process it all. One minute, she was just an eighteen-year-old cadet, hated by most everyone for her heritage, and now she was on the run for her life while trying to save them all from a horrible sect of blood mages. She stumbled, tears running down her face as they ran for the coast through the fields of high grass. Strong arms lifted her up and supported her and she turned to see Xaniver staring at her, tears of his own falling slowly down his cheeks. "I'm sorry..." was all she could get out.

Xaniver smiled through his tears. "I know how you feel. I'm away from home for the first time and I'm terrified I will never see my family again. Worse though, is the feelings I have held in about *you*. I've always been scared to let you know, for fear of being rejected, but this has shown me that I could lose you any moment. I love you Yoril. Please don't cry. I will always keep you safe, at the cost of my life if necessary... even if you don't return that love." He set her down and brushed her off, then started walking with her, guiding her along until she rested her head on his shoulder.

"I've always known Xan... I've just kept distant because I didn't want to bring shame to your family; loving a half-breed isn't the style these days."

"Awwww, I could cry too." Myst laughed as they both tried to kick him and missed, almost taking each other down to the ground. He laughed louder and ran on ahead of them, skipping through the grass.

Yoril was glad they finally got that out of their systems. Keeping things in like that could do horrible things to mages, and besides, it would be a shame to die holding that inside. It was a good long way to where the river met the sea, but at least they had a couple hours to get out of sight. She hoped.

ASHSTAFF VILLA, BENEATH SKY

Ereval turned away from her scrying pool in disgust. She couldn't believe that the councilors had helped those meddling younglings take the sacred treasures. She kicked a marble column and sent a vase tumbling to the floor in her anger and strode down the hallway, pushing her servants out of the way. She hadn't let the darkness within her take her heart just to lose out on being the one to release the dark beast. Ereval fumed again on her choice to use the Gramayre. They were a means to an end, but clearly they weren't working anymore. *Some days you just have to do the hard things yourself,* she thought, preparing to take a horse to her own private docks south of the city. She knew they would now head to the mainland and try for Lythinall. It's what she would've done, after all. Her boat was fast, and with her magic behind it she would make landfall earlier than they would. There she would take back what was rightfully hers and go on to glory. Death's beast would be released once more and she would be there with a smile on her face.

RELEASING EVIL

The boat ride was horrific. Myst had seen the ocean before, being near the southern coast of the island, but had never actually been on it before. Who knew that Yoril would get sick riding the gentle waves? She spent most of the trip over the side of the railing—Xaniver holding her hair and whispering assurances—while Myst kept checking their safety. The crew didn't know who they were, or what they were carrying, and it stayed that way. It took two days to get to the port of Anar, sailing around the Snowpeak Mountains, and by the time they got there Yoril was the first one limping off of the boat, followed by Myst checking the alleys as they passed.

Anar, located in the Old Lands, was one of the few cities still standing after the catastrophe all those centuries ago. Most of the cities, including Tir-Novran, were never rebuilt and fell into disuse. These days they were used by bandits, marauders, or monsters: dangerous places to be sure. More humans came up from the south, or migrated from Lythinall, but they never settled anywhere except around the city of Anar. They walked off of the ship and blended into the crowd seeking an inn to grab for the night. Myst took the lead, as the two love birds were still staring at each other off and on. "There's one—The Lashed Girl," Myst said, walking towards the dark walled tavern. It had a sign that hung on one hinge and consisted of a gagged woman with her hands tied behind her back.

"Um... no." Yoril stopped and stared at the sign, her face a mix of emotion.

"I have to agree Myst. This place just screams 'walk in with your weapon out', and it means trouble." Xaniver said, fingering his sword.

Myst stopped and turned to face them, an exasperated look on his face. "All right, I know it looks bad, but hear me out. We have never been off that island in our lives, right?" He waited for them to nod before he continued. "So, would it stand to reason that we would stay somewhere that we are used to?" He saw the realization dawn on their faces and smiled. Myst had talked to some of the sailors on the boat and found out what places were good to stay at and which ones weren't. He was fairly certain they wouldn't be looked for in a place like this. "Just keep your heads down and let me do the talking," he said, sauntering over to the bar. He stopped as he heard a shriek behind him and saw other patrons stand up drawing weapons in alarm. He spun, and saw Ereval holding Yoril by the throat with magic and using the threat of death to stay the blade of Xaniver.

"Nothing to see here, friends—go back to your filth and leave us be," Ereval said to the patrons, eyeing Myst as he walked back to his friends very slowly, hands in the air.

"How did you know we would be here?" he asked, sizing up the rest of the room to see if Ereval was alone or had help waiting. It seemed that she had some associates outside and he was angry that he didn't catch any of this sooner.

"I arrived hours before your ship and set up a place to stay before looking around the docks and waiting for your ship to come in. When I saw you all, I started tracking the magic of the Staff and waited until you stumbled in here." Ereval lifted Yoril a bit higher and the half-elf writhed in the grip of magic, struggling to breathe. "I had to wait until you were far enough away from them to strike—after all that orb is handy," she said, a purr in her voice as she smiled at him.

"Did you know she could do that?" Xaniver asked Myst, trying to keep the conversation going.

"No, I didn't. Guess I should've paid more attention in class." She had all but told Myst how to stop her. If he got close enough, the magic might fail because of the orb and Yoril would be free. *Now how to do that and keep her from killing Yoril?* he wondered. He inched closer, but he saw no way out of this situation.

"Stay back, Mystanshir, or she dies." Ereval placed her other hand behind her and waved her associates in. "Now give my associates the items you stole and we can end this charade." Four gramayre came in and went to the two heroes. They took both the sword and the orb when Myst and Xaniver handed them over. "Now back up and we will be on our way." She pried the staff out of Yoril's hands and backed away slowly, finally throwing the young half-elf at Xaniver and walking out the door laughing.

AN HOUR later Yoril was still taking slow, gasping breaths, forcing air into her strained lungs. It was the longest couple of minutes of her short life, and one experience she would never want to repeat. She should be dead, she knew that, but why she wasn't was anyone's guess. She could still feel the magic holding her throat and how a little bit of air was allowed in just to keep her conscious. Only an extremely powerful wizard could do that. "Myst, we have to go after her."

Myst patted her on the back softly. "I know Yoril, but let's get you on your feet and breathing first; you need to rest a bit."

"If only we knew where this supposed 'beast' is that she would be trying to free it would be a little easier." Xaniver said, clearly frustrated.

"Excuse me, but did you say the 'beast'?" a woman asked, as she stood up by the fireplace.

Yoril had noticed her staring at them the past hour and narrowed her eyes as she approached.

The woman walked over, looking at Myst in particular, and let her gaze drift up his legs to his face. She pulled the hood back from her curly blond hair and smiled with her ice blue eyes, stopping three feet away from them. Then she turned her gaze to Yoril.

"What if we did?" Myst asked, looking at Xaniver sideways with a scowl.

"I happen to know the story of such a beast, imprisoned centuries ago in the Sea of Irace… or so the tale goes."

"We've got to catch her, where would she be headed?" Yoril didn't have time for pleasantries; they needed to go soon or they would lose her. She didn't think that Ereval would use magic to get there, as no one really knew where to look, but she might be tracking this 'beast' the way she had followed them. They could still catch her if they hurried, even if she had an hour head start.

"The story mentions following the coast until the cliffs led down to the sea. That only happens near the cliffs west of the southern bridge. I'd say two hundred miles, give or take a mile." The woman walked back to her chair and grabbed her pack, slinging it over her shoulder as she went back to them. She was dressed in finely cut clothes, the kind Yoril had only seen on nobles in Beneath Sky.

"What do you think *you're* doing?" Myst asked, looking her up and down.

"Well, I figured I would fill you in on the rest as we travelled." She walked up to Yoril and held out her hand. "I'm Brylana Raredrom, bard and traveler."

Yoril took the hand skeptically, yet sensed the sincerity coming from the woman. "I'm Yoril, this is Xaniver, and that is Myst. *Now* can we go?" She smiled and led them out of the Lashed Girl without looking back, despite protests from the rest.

They got horses, for a good price, and rode south in haste. Yoril knew that they would have to push the horses to catch Ereval, but felt confident that they could get there in time, knowing where they were headed. They just had to.

SOUTHERN COAST, OLD LANDS

They rode for three days, pushing the horses as much as they could, and talked as they camped at night. They learned from Brylana that the 'beast' had been trapped in a place called *The Vault* by two very powerful elves, who then took the survivors of Tir-Novran across the sea to a secret land. Yoril had to laugh at the prospect of her home being a secret land, and Xaniver actually did laugh out loud. They traded stories and learned a lot about the Old Lands. They already knew it was a lawless place that was home to bandits and such, but what they didn't know was that some of those bandits and marauders set themselves up as Warlords. These ruthless tyrants controlled their territories with iron fists and pain.

On the third day they could see riders some distance ahead and as they came over the rise, the three young heroes heard Brylana sing a little phrase and saw a faint mist fall around them.

"What in the name of Syll was that?" Yoril asked, staring at Brylana with a critical eye. She had trusted her fully up until now, but with that show of magic, she had her doubts.

"I think the elves call it magic." Brylana answered sarcastically.

"What I think she meant was—how did you do it without elven blood?" Xaniver finished for Yoril, as he fingered the slim blade Myst had given him to use.

Brylana looked askance at Yoril and sighed. "It's bardic magic."

"We only have elven bards where we come from," Myst confessed. "We never thought anything of them casting magic."

"Well, it is slightly different from elven magic. For one, you have to be playing or singing, and second it never really hurts anyone. It can't be used in battle to wound, but it can prove handy otherwise." She waved her hands out wide as if to prove a point. "I clouded our presence from casual sight, so if they turn around, they won't see us," she said, laughing a little. "But if that bitch up there is a wizard, it will do absolutely nothing if she wants to *see* us."

"Well, thank you again Brylana, I am in your debt," Myst said, smiling that smile of his that he used on most women —*most* meaning every pretty one he saw.

"Oh, stop trying to seduce her. It hasn't worked so far, it isn't going to now," Yoril said, rolling her eyes. Myst had been trying to seduce the woman each time they stopped for the night, to no avail; this was something he was not used to. While elves mated for life once they found love, before that they tended to have fun where they could find it... and he was *really* good at finding it.

"I would complain, but I know we've been fawning over each other just as bad," Xaniver said to Yoril as she stuck her finger down her throat and made gagging noises.

They rode down the coast, following the dark figures in the distance and eventually saw them disappear over the cliff. They slowed as much as they dared and walked the rest of the way down the trail once they got to the cliffs. It hugged the cliff wall and was only about four feet wide, winding down to a small, circular landing. As they hurried quietly down the winding path, they heard chanting rising above the crashing waves. There on the circular landing stood Ereval Ashstaff, her arms raised high in the air as the water crashed and churned over two hundred feet below. Around her stood the Gramayre, holding the three sacred treasures and swaying silently.

Yoril watched Myst give them a quick hand signal to stay there as he crept closer. She looked on with tense shoulders as he crept slowly towards what she could only call certain doom. If they could get the Orb of Light, then they would have a chance against the magic of the Gramayre and the elven wizard. If Myst could grab it and toss it back, then she would breathe easier, or at least breathe. She was so engrossed in Myst's stealth that she failed to notice that the Gramayre only numbered three, instead of four as they had back at the Lashed Girl... until it was too late.

Out of nowhere, Brylana dropped down to her knees, holding her stomach and gasping in shock and pain.

As Yoril watched in horror, a blade slowly slid out from between her clutching hands. "*No!*" she screamed without thinking, seeing the Gramayre behind Brylana. The assailant pulled the sword out of the bard and kicked her over the cliff, then pointed the bloody sword at Yoril and summoned a red mist. Before the red mist fully formed, Xaniver was there. He pulled Yoril behind him and faced the Gramayre with his drawn sword. The mist gathered around him and held him, sticking to his arms and legs like tar, slowly burning into his armor.

Before Yoril could act, she felt her arms, feet, and torso pinned as the very ground beneath her spiraled up, engulfing her like an earthen tomb. She turned her head, the only part left free, and saw Ereval look at them with a frown on her face before turning back to her chanting.

Myst sprinted the last few feet to the Gramayre holding the Orb of Light and punched his dagger into the back of the foul blood mage. In that instant, Ereval finished chanting and a pulse went out to the sea, making waves down far below as it travelled.

"Do you think that orb will save you?" Ereval asked, as she

sauntered over towards Myst. She pulled her own thin blade using very steady hands. She switched her blade from left to right, then back again, showing her skill with the weapon and that she was inclined to use it.

Myst was going to say something sarcastic, but something, all the way down in the water, came rising up and towards them all. It came fast, creating quite a wake as it did, even giving the Gramayre pause as they backed up. Myst looked at Ereval, looked behind her, then back at her again. "I think that's for you," he said, backing up towards the wall. He had a dagger in one hand and the orb in the other, and kept the frightened Gramayre in the corner of his vision at all times.

"You really expect me to fall for that one?" Ereval asked, actually laughing. But when she saw the looks of her followers as well, she glanced out over the cliff towards the sea and drew in a sharp breath. There, coming up over the cliff and rising over two hundred feet from the sea was a huge block of stone, crumbling away to reveal a tomb of misshapen ice.

Myst made a break for Yoril, throwing his dagger at the Gramayre behind his friends up on the path and striking the man in the eye. The blood mage tumbled over the cliff as Myst felt something try to snare him, but it must've fallen apart when it got near the orb. Once he got within ten feet, he saw the magic start to unravel around Xaniver and Yoril, then they turned to the remaining Gramayre and got ready, keeping a wary eye on the scene by the cliff. What they saw would stay with them for the rest of their days.

FROM INSIDE THE rapidly melting block of ice, eyes that hadn't seen anything in centuries gazed at what appeared to be an elf... and narrowed in hate.

"What kind of beast is this?" the elven female asked,

backing away slowly. She appeared to be talking to herself. "Is it even going to be intelligent?" She walked forward once more, cautiously now as the ice broke apart and crumbled away, freeing his arms and hands.

The man called Death heard her chant and cast magic upon herself and had to laugh, or try to as his throat sputtered and he coughed violently as he took his first deep breaths of the clean air.

"Oh, powerful beast! I humbly take credit for unleashing you upon the world once more. Pray, do me this one favor I ask of you?"

"I don't think so." Death's cold voice finally cleared and he could once again feel his legs as the magic faded quickly. The last of the ice cracked and dumped a body on the dirt cliff ledge. He looked down and kicked it for good measure, sending it over to land by the black robed figures cringing by the cliff. He stepped out and stood tall and proud, his long black hair wet from his icy tomb. He shook his arms to get the feeling back in them and looked around, letting his gaze drift back to the female elf. He grinned, the smile never touching his eyes.

"What do you mean, you don't think so?" The female elf asked. "I am Ereval Ashstaff and I have freed you from your prison!" She stopped and itched her arm, then her other arm before narrowing her own eyes at him. "This is absurd. How is it that a mere human..." She started to speak again, but stopped as the very flesh on her body began to blacken and wither. She spit a mouth full of ash on the dirt and fell over, lifeless.

He hated that condescending tone. Death stood before them all and watched the robed figures wither away and was rather pleased with himself. He was about to leave when he heard a soft whimper up on the path. Death looked up and saw three younglings staring, so he smiled coldly at them. *I wonder what we're calling ourselves nowadays?* he thought. He went by

Death mainly because the other Incarnations had all chosen names to fit their new natures, but now he didn't know who they were or where they were. *I'll go back to what I was called before; Dar'Krist.*

DEATH COMES

Yoril trembled with fear. She used the ether to *see* if the man had magic like the Gramayre and almost went numb from what she saw. This man—if that was what he truly was—held such power that she could actually feel it coming off of him like the heat from a bonfire, yet it wasn't the magic she was used to at all. She had seen the Gramayre and Ereval wither away before her very eyes, and he didn't really *do* anything. Then Mistress Urien's lecture came back to her. Urien had said that the beings that delivered the treasures were incarnations. *They were Davalar and Syll's Incarnation, so this must be Krist's Incarnation. They didn't lock away a beast—they imprisoned one of their own!* she thought as the thing in black clothes turned towards them with a cold smile. Then she realized she was whimpering out loud.

"Well, I'm glad we're all here," Tan'lin said, appearing behind Yoril and Xaniver. "It seems my gambit has paid off," she continued as she bowed to the Incarnation.

"What? You're working for the gramayre?" Yoril asked, trying to keep her distance from that thing in black.

"No, Yoril, I am the Incarnation of Ollian, and I used you three to release my brother and my predecessor," she said, looking at the fallen body. She closed her eyes briefly, then looked back at her long-imprisoned brother. "My name is Tan'lin and I mean no ill will towards you," she said as she walked to the front of Yoril to face the Incarnation of Death.

"Well, I *am* a little surprised that an elf helped free me,"

Dar'Krist said, staring at Myst. He clicked his tongue. "Make those two elves." He waved his arms out in a grand gesture towards Tan'lin and shook his head. "Forgive me if I don't trust you, Tan'lin. I have been betrayed by my fellow Incarnations before. I think I will just kill you all and be on my way."

Myst swore and cast quickly. "Ash'anti fra gra ea lae itims hary," he called to the air as he crouched down low.

Dar'Krist braced himself, yet nothing happened. "You're weaker than I expected, elf," he spat venomously.

"Wasn't aiming at you," Myst said as the Staff of Kindred and the sword Chalice skittered across the ground towards his friends.

"Well played Myst," Tan'lin said, hopping over the relics as they went under her, landing on the balls of her feat.

Yoril grabbed the staff out of the air and backed up, ready as Xaniver picked up Chalice. Now they had something to defend themselves with at least. They were still dead, but they could try. Maybe with Tan'lin they even had a chance. Yoril still couldn't believe that the councilwoman was an Incarnation, too.

Dar'Krist smiled. "That was a good trick and one I didn't see coming, but it won't help you. I wasn't worried about those trinkets when Incarnations wielded them; what makes you think I'm in any danger now?" Dar'Krist rushed the Incarnation of Beauty as he finished, hitting her three times in rapid succession; she dropped her like a stone. He spun around the Myst, pushing him back towards the edge of the cliff and faced Xaniver with a balance and grace that none of them had ever seen.

Yoril saw Dar'Krist hit Xaniver low and then kick him in the head, the man she had loved falling back into her arms. She laid him down gently, and stood, watching the incarnation stalk after Myst. The ancient being was keeping them all in his vision as he lunged for Myst, kicking out and missing as the agile elf Myst rolled under him and towards Yoril. She would only have one chance.

Yoril swung with everything she had, silently calling to the staff to banish the evil it struck. The white wood hit a *very* surprised Dar'Krist squarely in the chest and time seemed to stop for a moment. Yoril felt the world explode in white brilliance, throwing her back to the ground near the Tan'lin's limp body. She looked up as her vision blurred and saw the edge of the cliff give way, dumping the man down into the sea over two hundred feet below, his powerful hands scrambling for purchase as he desperately clawed the crumbling earth. Yoril looked down at the staff in her numb hands and her eyes went wide. The white wood staff was blackened and charred from the impact with the Incarnation of Death.

"Are you all right?" Myst said, coming to her side, his voice quiet in the silence that followed the devastation.

"Yes, I think so. Check on Xaniver, he wasn't moving." She started crying, the stress of everything weighing heavily on her. She couldn't believe that they had been duped into releasing this evil into the world.

Myst went over and turned Xaniver over as the warrior tried to stand. "Easy there, man."

"Yoril... where is she?"

"Relax. She's over there, worried about you. You two go cuddle and I'll see about the beautiful woman over there," Myst said, winking at them and rushing to Tan'lin's side, gently shaking her. "Hey, it's over, we won."

"It's not over," Tan'lin said without opening her eyes. Her wounds had already healed, yet the bruises still showed.

"Tan'lin, he fell off the cliff. That's well over two hundred feet down."

"He's an Incarnation. We heal pretty quickly and can come back from a whole lot more than what you three can dish out.

Was he close to the edge?" She opened her eyes now and propped herself up on her elbows.

Yoril limped over with the charred staff. "Yeah, it broke under him and he went with it. Why?"

"Because if he was close to the edge then he can break his fall, hitting the water slow enough to only irritate him. We *have* to get out of here." She stood and asked the ether to heal her wounds fully, as well as Xaniver's; they grabbed the items, including the now blackened staff and went up the path to the plains above.

Dar'Krist felt like a mountain hit him in the back and did a little dance while it was there. His arms and neck felt like they were on fire and he was having a hard time convincing his eyes to open. He was under the water, trying to stay conscious, and holding his breath. Thank the Gods above that he could hold his breath a *very* long time. He broke the surface of the water, his arms protesting loudly at the exertion, and looked up at the far cliff. He had survived what Shadow had not, mainly because he could grab the wall of the cliff all the way down. His leg was still shattered, and he was pretty sure his ribs were kindling, but they would heal. It would take him a while to find his way up again, but when he did... they would pay dearly.

FOREST NORTHEAST OF THE VAULT

Myst walked into the woods and breathed a little easier. Tan'lin was blocking any magical *sight* that Dar'Krist might use to find them and the trees would block their view from normal sight. They had traveled almost sixty miles, in two days, and were still weary from their encounter.

"All right guys, let's stop for a minute and regroup," Tan'lin told them solemnly.

"You need to ambush us again?" Myst asked sarcastically. They hadn't talked much in the last two days, except to berate her about getting them into this in the first place. They blamed her for the Gramayre. Even though she swore that she hadn't actually brought him back, only showed them where the island was, her explanation didn't help any.

"I truly regret the deaths of the cadets and Urien, but I didn't think one would go lone wolf like that. I had convinced them to hit Among Highgrass first and not for another couple of days. Trust me when I say that will haunt me for the rest of my life, and, as an Incarnation, that could very well be forever."

"Should we make a fire?" Xaniver asked, changing the subject.

Tan'lin sighed, "Normally I would say no. However, it won't matter since he is an Incarnation. I've blocked his *sight*, but he can use it in other ways so he probably knows where we are, just can't pinpoint us. Yet." She gathered some sticks and whispered quietly to ignite them. The Incarnation of Beauty sat down and stretched her legs, staring at them with sad eyes.

"You have more bad news?" Myst asked, seeing the look on her face. He had a feeling deep in his gut that he wasn't going to enjoy this.

"Not bad news, just that I haven't told you everything. I not only wanted to set my brother free; I also wanted to start something." She paused for a minute then continued. "I wanted you three away from the island to start over here, on the mainland. Lead the people here, throw down the warlords and build it up again. It will take heroes to do this, and you won't be alone, there are others."

"Others?" Xaniver asked, curiosity written all over his face.

"You'll find them. They are everywhere, just waiting for

someone to follow. And you three can lead them." Tan'lin stood and looked up at the canopy above them, as if she could see something they couldn't. "Show them how to stand up and fight for what's right and build a nation that stands for good once more." She let out a breath and looked back down at them, a certain softness to her beautiful eyes.

"But what about the Incarnation of Death?" Myst knew that he would never stop coming for them, he had seen that look on others before, never mind an immortal being.

"That is a little easier than you might think. For centuries the elves of Lythinall have kept humans as slaves. They taught them the ways of nature and of the forests, trained their young in schools, and trained those that they felt they could trust as warriors. Dar'Krist will eventually find his way there, seeking vengeance for some past horror that the elves visited upon him, and it is my idea for someone to lead him there now."

"That's horrible!" Yoril said, rising to her feet. "How many will be slaughtered?"

"You misunderstand, Yoril. The elves of Lythinall have mastered magic in ways that few here have thought of. The best of us on Novrantir are but babes to their might. If any have a chance against him, it is them."

"I'll do it," Myst said, standing up and dusting off his clothes.

"But you haven't rested yet?" Yoril said, dread written all over her face.

"It's all right, Yoril. I'm feeling pretty good right now. Don't worry, I'll lead him on a chase that will take him right into Lythinall. But I want two things." He had an idea, something to help both his conscience and the people of that land.

"Name it," Tan'lin said, her eyes smiling at him mischievously.

Myst looked to Xaniver, then to Yoril, nodding at each in

turn. "I want the sword and staff. I'm going to place them in Lythinall for someone to find so that they will have weapons to fight the coming darkness."

"Not the Orb?" Tan'lin said, sounding skeptical.

"No. The Orb I want to keep hidden right here, In this forest." He saw the looks on both Tan'lin and his friends and laughed. "If it is here, then *we* will always know where it is and if he comes back, we will know where we can get the one weapon to stop him with. In theory, that is."

Tan'lin clapped her hands like a little elf at Kristmas. "I love it! Well thought out young one."

Xaniver rose and handed him Chalice and Yoril gave him the blackened staff.

Tan'lin walked over and laid a hand on Myst's shoulder. "The staff still holds a great power, but it's anyone's guess as to what that might be after what it has been through." She hugged him, whispering in his ear so that the others couldn't hear. "Find me in the Old Woods when you come back and we can have that drink."

Myst smiled at her as she stepped away, knowing that he would indeed make it back now. He hugged his friends tightly. "I wish you both the best and please watch each other until I return." Myst turned and fled before Yoril could get anything out. He would break down if he said anything else to his oldest friend. As he fled through the woods, he broke dead branches as he passed, making sure that he was leaving subtle traces of his passage.

Yoril watched her oldest friend go and tried not to start crying. She had to be strong now, for everyone. "Let's go, we have to get to Anar and start talking to some of the people that can help, and I think I know of just the inn to start in."

"You're kidding," Xaniver said, his mouth hanging open. "I know you're excited to be doing this Yoril, and gods above know I want to make my family proud, but we have to live through this to tell them."

"You wouldn't be talking about the Lashed Girl, would you?" Tan'lin interjected, a bright smile on her beautiful face.

Yoril nodded, wondering what the Incarnation knew of the place.

Tan'lin laughed and sat back down next to them. "All right then. In the morning we will use magic and travel there. That place is always full of fun," she said with a wink to Xaniver.

"Oh, gods above it's like Myst as a girl," he said, putting his head in his hands.

"Oh youngling, I haven't been a *girl* in many years."

Yoril laughed, unshed tears still hanging in her eyes. "You should quit while you're ahead Xaniver."

❦

IN THE MORNING, Tan'lin worked her magic, calling on the ether to bring them to just outside Anar. They started working on gathering heroes to their cause. They found people quickly, their call like flame to dry grass. The Incarnation of Beauty left them after three days, not wanting to be involved in this process herself. Her goddess just wanted her to start it, not be a part of it. As she walked out of the city and into the wastelands of the warlords, she reflected on her road here and finally let herself grieve over Urien.

Tan'lin knew there would be sacrifices—her goddess had told her that—yet she never thought it would be a friend. Letting Dar'Krist out of that prison wasn't her choice, but she obeyed her goddess when commanded; only fools pretend to know the will of gods. She traveled on to the Old Woods after letting go of the grief and sorrow, intending to wait for Myst, just in case he lived through his journey. It had been a while since she had enjoyed some company like his.

EPILOGUE: TIME MOVES ON

Dar'Krist walked with purpose. He worried when he noticed it was only the young elf he was following, but then again, he didn't have anything against the humans. No, he wanted the elf. He had been following him for more than three hundred miles so far and was getting irritated with the young one's schemes. One day he would veer left and head north, then another he would aim south, then turn and bolt for the east. The incarnation thought that the elf was fleeing, yet he didn't seem to be running on fear. *More like mischief,* he thought as he shook his head. They had passed by the Old Woods days ago and were deep into what used to be called Lythin'all, back when he was called Death, and he was shocked to see most of the forests vastly thinned out. *What could've happened here that the trees never grew back?* he wondered as he sent out his *sight* once more searching for where the elf was heading today. Dar'Krist *saw* him, far ahead and heading straight through the forest, yet he was slowing down. Then he saw why. The young one had found an elven city. Dar'Krist shrugged and picked up his pace, gaining slowly on the young one and his sworn enemies.

TIR-ANIEL, LYTHINALL

Myst walked on, exhausted. He hadn't dare rest for long periods of time with that thing behind him and he *knew* it was following him. He had tried to lose the ancient being by changing directions and leading him in various ways, but he always knew when he changed back. He had been in Lythinall for a couple days, looking for somewhere to hide the staff and sword, when he happened upon the outer patrol of an elven city. They brought him across a swift river and into their great city.

It was called Tir-Aniel and he was welcomed as a visitor quite freely. He wasted no time in sneaking down to their armory and stashing the sword in an old dirty sheath. *One down,* he thought, as he went back up the stairs to the inner courtyard. As Myst snuck out the back of the city, their horns blared. He knew what was coming. He ran south and came to the great river once more. He rested in an old hollowed out tree, almost forgetting the time it was so comfortable. He left the staff there and circled back to the west, not getting close enough to see what happened to Tir-Aniel. For reasons that he refused to admit to himself, Dar'Krist had stopped following him.

Myst made it to the Old Woods in time to meet Tan'lin, never looking back. He knew, deep down, it would only upset him to know what had happened. It would give him nightmares for the rest of his long life that he probably paid for with an entire elven city. He had his drink, and the pleasure of the Incarnation of Beauty, then set out to find his friends.

About a year later, word came to the three heroes from a traveling bard. After months of fighting, the elves had imprisoned the Incarnation, far in the north. Unfortunately, the elves of Lythinall now had another war on their hands, but it was one that didn't concern Yoril or her friends. For now they had their own fight.

They had cleared the ruins of Tir-Novran and thrown down one warlord, but now had two more coming for them. They renamed the city Sirr, after Xaniver's family name, with plans to call their new land the very same. Xaniver and Yoril married and had two beautiful children, who learned to fight like their parents and the crusade to free the people continued. None of them ever returned to Novrantir, as they were busy for most of their lives at that point, yet Xaniver's father did journey to see them from time to time. The rest is history and is a story for another day...

STREETS OF G'HARR

※   4   ※

SHATTERED IN DARKNESS
GRAF AND THE MAIDEN

Cirith Ellwood slammed the door to her villa open and stomped up the wrought iron stairs. She was beyond the normal confines of upset and was edging into the realm of angry. She was a noble in the court of G'harr and for the hundredth time that pretentious, self absorbed, bastard had treated her like a filthy commoner! Storming down the hallway she slapped a vase off of its marble stand and sent it crashing into the wall. The expensive art object disintegrated into tiny pieces and she didn't even bat an eye. Kicking open her bedroom doors she grabbed a silver statue and started to throw it into her full length, gold rimmed mirror, then froze. She could see herself in the reflection and didn't recognize the hate filled woman starting back at her.

Cirith was short, only reaching a touch over five feet tall, and weighed all of eight stone soaking wet. She sported long red hair the color of fresh strawberries and green eyes that seemed to take in everything around her. She was also one of the most competent sorcerers in G'harr, second only to the man that drove her to wreck anything in her sight this very evening: Sorcerer King Ran'cian Ashren. He had slain the former king two years ago and assumed the throne, and not one of them dared to do anything about it.

"I'm guessing he didn't take too kindly to your suggestions this evening?" The man strolled in as if nothing was out of the ordinary. Declan Reis was Cirith's lover and confidant. He was also her slave, but they had progressed beyond most of that over the years. He towered over her at an impressive six and a half feet, and filled out his frame weighing seventeen stone. His short brown hair was kept long, barely hanging into his deep brown eyes, and he had a winning smile that most other nobles dreamed of owning. He also had no magic in him whatsoever. Not one ounce of it.

Cirith spun, still holding the silver statue as if she was going to throw it straight at him, and almost did. She took a breath and lowered her arm, turning away. "He actually called me his mutt. *His mutt!*" Cirith dropped the statue and turned towards the closet, but a strong hand rested on her shoulder.

"I'm sorry," Declan said with a softness to his voice.

"Take. Your. Hand. Off. Me," Cirith demanded in a hushed tone. She whispered a command to the air to push Declan back against the wall and heard him grunt as he slammed into the wood, actually cracking it. She turned, her eyes smoldering. "I have told you time and time again. You are my *property* and you only touch me when I *allow* you to."

"I'm... sorry... mistress," he forced out, the air pushing against him still, holding him there like a painting that she could admire or burn at her leisure. He was at least six inches off of the floor, and his face showed the pain he must surely be feeling.

It wasn't the worst she ever gave him, but she could see it took him by surprise. She told the air to stop and turned her back on him. She really didn't mean to hurt him, but her mercurial temper sometimes got the best of her. "Now. I wish to be alone. If you have nothing of import to do I want you to clean the bath house."

Declan flexed his arms and hung his head, shuffling his feet like he had bad news. "Mistress," he said with the meekest voice she had ever heard.

"What, Declan?" This slave was trying her patience—and it was as thin as a whore's wardrobe right now.

"I have someone who wants to meet you, to discuss the recent problems you have been having," he said, closing his eyes.

Cirith didn't know whether she should embrace him or kill him outright. On the one hand, he cared for her enough to risk death conspiring with someone against the Sorcerer King. On the other, more reasonable hand, he had conspired with someone and probably included her name. "Who is it?" she asked through clenched teeth.

His face full of surprise—probably because he wasn't on the floor bleeding from any number of fatal wounds— he cautiously looked her in the eye and drew what might be his last breath. "It's Xalrin Blaine, Mistress."

"*What!?*"

"Hear me out."

"Are you out of your *mind?* That sorcerer is on the black list for a reason. No one likes him, least of all me!" She stormed up to him again, fury etched on her beautiful face, and grabbed his shirt with both hands. "He killed children, Declan. *Children!*"

Declan seemed taken aback. "I didn't know that... but look, he is the best choice to get that upstart Ran'cian out of power." He would've continued, but her stare cut him off.

"Declan, if we work with that man the people will never take me seriously in court." She wanted Ran'cian gone as much as the next woman; the twenty-year-old was powerful and causing quite a stir among the nobles with his new rules these last two years. But Xalrin...

"We don't have to openly work with him. Xalrin said that when he gets here, he will—" Declan's face turned sideways as she hit him, her hand striking so quick that he didn't even have time to flinch.

"When he *gets here?*" She hit him again as she screamed, slapping him so hard that his whole body turned with the impact. *He invited a child killer to my house? I think I'm going to be sick,* she thought as she watched him spin, then stormed off. "When is he going to be here?" she asked.

"Is now too soon Madam?" Xalrin asked casually from her front door, his smooth venomous voice pervading the quiet of the house. Xalrin Blaine was dressed in the typical black robes and cloak, cut in the southern style with the high collar. His short hair was perpetually messy and he had intense silver eyes that made everyone uncomfortable. His smile never seemed to touch his eyes.

"Get in here, you knave—quickly before you're seen." Cirith pulled him into the house and closed the door, pushing him into the spare room ahead of her.

❦

DECLAN TOOK HIS LEAVE, knowing that what they discussed was not for a slave's ears. He should be in there though; after all, it was his idea to contact the sorcerer for his mistress and overthrow the sorcerer king. He smiled as he left the house for a walk, never knowing that it would be his last.

CAT AND MOUSE

The sorcerer king of G'harr watched the man leave the villa and smiled coldly, signaling a guard to follow and end him quickly. Ran'cian Ashren was extremely intelligent for one so young and everything was going according to plan. He was barely into adulthood—twenty winters this very month—and had figured out what was going on immediately upon receiving the anonymous letter about threats to his rule and a conspiracy to take his life. He knew exactly who was behind such a devious plot.

He flipped his long black hair out of his deep blue eyes and motioned for the guard to advance, following them with measured steps in his high black boots. As they neared the entrance to Cirith's villa, he smoothed his white silk doublet and straightened the ornamental gold cape, announcing Cirith's doom in his deep, booming voice. "Arrest the noble, Cirith Ellwood, for acts of treason and conspiracy to commit regicide." He lowered his arm and the guard charged in, one man already flying back out the door as the female sorceress put up a valiant fight. Within minutes she was bound and gagged, dragged to his feet like the mutt she was. He had only lost five guards—not bad. Ran'cian smiled at the man walking behind the guards of his own volition and bowed ever so slightly at him.

Xalrin did a double take at the display of respect. "I trust you found my notice of conspiracy, my Lord?" Xalrin asked as he walked by and patted Cirith on the head. She shouted through the gag and struggled to get free.

"I did indeed, Master Xalrin. Now, what do I owe you for this little favor?" Ran'cian asked while slowly pulling a knife out of its sheath. He stared at the blade longingly, like it was an old lover.

"I have been blacklisted from the courts by that bastard you killed. I would just like to be able to come home and show my support for the new sorcerer king," the dark robed man said with a confidence that seemed shaky.

Ran'cian knew that the man needed access to the old archives to complete his latest work; he always did his homework on the dangerous people around him. "Ah, of course, that little bit with those kids. Nasty business, that." He walked over, hands behind his back and feigned boredom. This man was one of the *truly* dangerous ones, he knew that, but he was also someone that could get things done when needed. Someone Ran'cian was looking for, just recently, in fact.

"I suppose that could be remedied... if certain things were agreed upon." The sorcerer king let that hang there, baiting the man with hidden promises. This wasn't his usual tactic, but he had to tread carefully with the man known for skinning children. The king laughed as Xalrin nodded his head like an excited child, his enthusiasm written all over his face. Ran'cian's spies had informed him that the man's research had hit a dead end, probably because the things he needed to research were banned from the general public, and for good reason.

"Name it my Lord, and it shall be done."

"Formalities, formalities. We can get into that later. For now, though, you are in." Ran'cian turned away, pausing for dramatic effect. "Oh, and try not to anger me or draw too much notice though. I would hate for Cirith to have a cell-mate." He watched as Xalrin nodded again and hurried away to whatever black mischief he was going to do, then turned his attention to his captive. "You, my dear, are going to be my toy for a little while. Your attitude in court hasn't gone unnoticed and, as usual, I have to make an example of *someone* to make the others fall in line," he said as he patted her on the head like Xalrin did, mainly because he saw how much it had irritated her, and quietly commanded the air to lift her up. He grabbed her shirt and pulled her along like a pet, Cirith floating in the air behind him like some sort of perverse balloon. Ran'cian laughed as she thrashed helplessly in her bindings. "Don't worry, you will rot in a cell for a time. Then, when I've had enough time to spread word of your betrayal around court, I think we will have an execution." He walked away, ignoring the stares of other nobles coming out to see what was going on.

His back straight and his walk confident, Ran'cian guided her all the way back to the Golden Palace, making sure to take the most public way so that everyone could see. He had to make an example of the ones that got too brave. He had killed the former king of G'harr just two years ago and was still amazed at how easy the coup had been. No one liked the man, and when Ran'cian had made his bid they all backed him, mainly because they all thought he would fail. No one knew how powerful he was though, and in the end, his power was what had pulled him through. They all tried to pull his strings those first couple of months, but after three of them died, they stopped trying.

Magic usually was limited to elves and even half-elves, but even humans with a bloodline of elven ancestry could channel the forces of magic. In G'harr, sorcerers were prevalent, bending the natural order of magic and forcing the elements to do their bidding. Here even fully human sorcerers could wield the elements, but not as powerfully as the elves. It was the secret of G'harr and the reason they hadn't been wiped out centuries ago by the northern elven nation. Ran'cian himself was one of the most powerful sorcerers seen in over a century, his own little secret as well, and he had all but quelled the courts of G'harr with his ruthless magic and temper.

Yet now they were at it again, every year it seemed, and he needed a full-proof way to set the nobles and other sorcerers in their place. Xalrin was his ticket to having his very own lap dog on a leash. Yes, his plans were coming together nicely, and he couldn't see anything that could foil them.

THE MAN IN THE SHADOWS

The man let out more rope and pulled a small metal spike out of his inside pocket. The stone face of the building was old and placing the spike in the groove was easy. Hammering it in at this height, without alerting anyone to his presence, was the hard part. Placing the rope in his mouth and biting down to keep it in place, he reached in and took out his mini hammer. He softly pushed the spike in with three quick hits as carriages rambled below, timing his hits with the shouts of the drivers or elations of their passengers. His harness in place, Grafton pulled the rope and lowered himself down slowly to the fourth-floor window.

Grafton Jalmes was tall, whip lean, and fit, with black hair that hung down to his shoulders. The thin leathers he wore seemed to be in good condition despite being smeared in black charcoal. Once at the window, he hung there for a minute, holding the rope once more in his teeth, and quickly pulled out his tiny diamond sliver. The sliver was just that—a tiny piece of a smashed diamond that was stick-thin and rock hard. He traced a circle in the thin glass of the window and caught the piece with deft hands as it came free. Quickly reaching in whilst simultaneously holding the rope in his teeth and while holding the piece of round glass in his other hand— all the while eighty feet above the cobblestones—he opened the window and climbed inside, quiet as death. This would've seemed impossible for anyone else in the world, but Grafton wasn't anyone else. He was the Incarnation of Shadows.

The gods created the Incarnations because they wanted a way to solve their quarrels without wrecking the whole of the earth, so they chose mortal champions to do their dirty work for them. Incarnations did not age, and some have lived for so long that they were *very* good at a lot of things, especially things like fighting styles, weapons, tactics, and other activities necessary to remain a live for so long. Unfortunately, they also had a weakness. Each Incarnation had one element of nature that's anathema to them.

Grafton's was wind. Not even a strong wind mind you, but a breeze light enough to blow your hair around felt like knives dragging across his skin. Incarnations were also very resilient, healing very quickly from most damage and all sorts of poisons, but they could still be killed by mortals and immortals alike. They usually worked to promote their gods' will, as well as actively blocking the other incarnations' movements of their god. Grafton had only been doing this for about two years and he had taken his new powers to the extreme ever since. There was nothing that he couldn't do—well, from what he had tried at least. He was always good with his knives and could hide like the best of them, but now... Now that he could almost disappear at will, he had become so proficient as to be invisible.

I thought I told you to go to Alrin and stop that wandering bard...

The voice in his head was clearly displeased. It usually was. It was also *awfully* loud. "I know you said that, but this guy was rumored to have that tapestry of the unicorn in that glowing glade," Grafton whispered aloud. He knew who the voice belonged to—he just refused to talk to it in his mind. He smiled as the voice didn't reply. Instead, it gave up and left him to his own devices. The voice belonged to his god, Norar himself. Or so it claimed. It's not like he was struck by lightning or saw a burning bush to solidify its claim; the headaches were enough.

Grafton crept into the study on the fourth floor, disabling the lock with a quick thrust and twist of his diamond sliver—he refused to call it a pin—and let his gaze drift over the objects placed around the room. They were all kept on marble pillars, a small base of red silk under them, and each was unique in its own right: a vase etched with golden dust, an amethyst gem the size of his fist, a key made of silver set with a small ruby, and what he had come for in the first place—he tapestry. It wasn't on a marble pillar like the rest. Instead it hung behind one with the description sitting on the pillar for its viewers to read. Unfortunately, it was much bigger than he'd anticipated.

"Well, this ought to be fun," he whispered to himself as he looked around the room before going any further. If he owned these priceless objects, he would have a trap of some kind to stop people like him. It took him a moment but just when he thought he might have been mistaken, he saw it. The trip wire was placed in such a way that most thieves wouldn't see it, being at waist level instead of near the ground. At this height, any light they brought with them would make it hard to notice, especially if they were sweeping the floor. Grafton quickly followed the wire and took out the small wooden box he kept in his inside pocket, sliding it over the wire and attaching it to the wall where it went into the small hole. He was guessing poison darts, but he wasn't going to find out tonight. With the wire firmly held by the box, he cut the rest and proceeded to the tapestry, taking it down gently and rolling it up. He left the gem and the other items; he really didn't care about the money. Just like that he was back at the window, smiling like a kid with a new toy. No, money wasn't why he was here—it was purely for the thrill. That, and he'd always loved the old stories about faeries and unicorns; one could say he was obsessed.

Out the window he went, hooking up to the rope and sliding slowly down the tall building instead of up to the roof. He was almost at the bottom when the horns sounded, most assuredly signaling his presence. Cursing under his breath, he scanned the upper windows, looking for lights or people looking for him. He saw a head stick out right where his rope was.

Well, that is really inconvenient, he thought as he clicked his hook and slid down even faster. If it was him up there, he would cut the rope as soon as... then he was falling. It was only fifteen feet or so—still painful but nothing that would slow him down too much. He was more upset over the fact that they had found him. Stashing the huge, rolled up tapestry in a bush near the rear of the mansion, he made his way back to the front and waited behind the door. When it opened and the guards flooded out—looking for him, of course—he slipped right behind them and back into the house. He backed up to the wall and crouched, using the shadows to blend in with the furniture. Two more guards came by, heading outside of the main doors and left him alone in the house.

Now I can find out what happened, he thought as he snuck up the stairs. No one expected a thief to sneak back into the house they'd just robbed and, truth be told, he shouldn't be doing it. It just irked him they'd noticed his presence. He *never* got caught and this alarm thing was bugging him. *I couldn't have set it off, so what did?* he thought to himself as he climbed from the second floor to the third.

Grafton heard someone coming down the stairs from above, their heavy steps telling him that they were in a hurry. He shifted to the corner and stayed perfectly still, crawling into the shadow of a small desk on the landing. He watched as whoever it was went running by, a huge amethyst in his hand. *Son of a priest!* Grafton couldn't believe that there was a *second* burglar —and a bad one at that. He stuck out his foot at the last minute. The man tripped and went tumbling down the stairs rather loudly. Grafton watched as guards rushed back inside, tied the man up and called for help. Satisfied that he wasn't at fault— and glad to have the distraction—the Incarnation of Shadows slipped by the chaos and out into the bustling night streets of G'harr.

MAIDEN IN DISTRESS

Grafton walked the cobbled streets with his prize over his shoulder, sticking to the back roads as much as possible. He would stash the tapestry in his room at the Blackened Staff Inn until he left the city, which should be any day now; he just liked to visit places he had never been before.

The massive city of G'harr was the capital of the region with the same name—and if the legends were true, named after the elven archmage that led her subjects here—and was situated on the banks of the Shallow Lake. The city was dominated by its biggest monument, the Golden Palace. The palace was massive, having four huge domed buildings with a tall tower in the middle. There were other large structures in the city, but none compared to the Golden Palace. It was home to Sorcerer King Ran'cian and his noble court, as well as the schools of sorcery and military tactics. The city itself was clean, if dark, and the city guard was bolstered by ranks of lesser sorcerers to keep the peace. The air of fear and tyranny pervaded the empty streets once the sun went down, and anyone out at this time was surely up to no good; Grafton felt right at home.

After he'd had stashed his new tapestry, Grafton walked around the perimeter of the Golden Palace as it was one of the other sights he had wanted to see while he was in the city. He arrived just in time to catch a glimpse of the sorcerer king himself, leading a captive that was bound and gagged, and most likely headed to a dark cell. Then he saw that it was a woman.

Her arms bound behind her back and her feet tied to those same hands, she was being pulled through the air like she was on parade. Her long red hair dragged on the ground and the guards following kept poking her with their sheathed weapons. Sickened at the level of treatment shown to her, Grafton acted without thinking. He crawled out of the alley and stumbled into the rear guard, as if on accident.

"Apologies, my good man," Grafton slurred drunkenly, "I be a wee bit lost at the moment." As he spoke, he slipped the man's keys from his belt, as well as the guard's curved southern-style dagger. Grafton saw their leader stop, confusion showing on his handsome face. The sorcerer king turned slowly as the men pushed Grafton around, attempting to goaded him into something foolish so they could attack him legally. *Legally,* Grafton thought with a chuckle. *Like they even know what that word means.*

"All right men, enough. Let the drunkard be and let's get this traitor to her cell," Ran'cian commanded, turning without waiting to see if they listened to him.

Grafton was about to start killing these ignorant guards when the wind picked up, making him crouch down and huddle in his cloak. How he hated the wind! He saw the sorcerer king walk away with the girl in tow. He felt powerless. It was then that he decided that he wasn't leaving the city until he freed that woman.

Don't even think about it Grafton—he is too powerful for you to go against, the voice in his head echoed.

"Shut up!" Grafton screamed in frustration. He rolled and got out of the wind, hiding behind a pile of boxes and garbage as the guards turned the far corner. *Ugh, how can anyone live in filth like this?* he thought as he disturbed a homeless man from his drunken slumber. He waited there for another few minutes as the wind started to die down, then made his way around to the front of the palace. He wasn't usually the kind of guy to save a maiden in distress, but seeing that girl tied up like that stirred something in him. Not that he wouldn't usually save someone that was in trouble, but if they were that guarded, he usually wouldn't risk it. This was an exception.

He took the next two days and carefully memorized the guard patterns, the timing of their shifts, and the rooms in the palace that he could get to without being noticed. It was easier to get in than he had thought, as he could slip in along with some of the servants. *Then* he was ready.

GREAT LIBRARY, GOLDEN PALACE

Xalrin paced around the library, once more looking for what had eluded him for the last two days. He *knew* that somewhere in here were the books he was looking for, but none of the librarians would help him. In fact, he was already ignoring the stares of the people in the library with practiced ease, as no one was particularly thrilled that the sorcerer king had lifted the ban on his being here. He was sure that they were gossiping away as to why the ban had been revoked, but he didn't care; he had more important things to do. He was researching a very dangerous magic—the summoning of demons—and he couldn't attempt it without the right books.

Demons were tricky and not at all like most stories make them out to be. Most people think demons were horned creatures, with tails and wings and covered in flames. The stories often said they were summoned with magic into chalk outlines that supposedly kept them bound and restrained. If only it were that easy. Demons were beings of immense power that lived in between the worlds and could only reach out to this world through magic rituals that called them either into the world in their own form —which was rumored to be disastrous —or into an item that could contain them. Demons came in varied shapes and sizes and the thing they craved more than freedom was souls. The powerful elven arch-wizards of old had dealt with demons, and it was their notes that Xalrin was searching for.

He stopped in the back of the library and scratched his

head. *Didn't I just walk by here an hour ago?* he thought, looking at a dark hallway that led to another set of bookshelves. He swore that he hadn't been down there yet, but it looked awfully familiar. He took a step and then turned and started walking back to the front of the room. He caught himself after three steps and stopping with a cold realization. *Now why did I do that? I wanted to go down that hallway. Unless...* He now had an idea as to why he hadn't been able to find what he was looking for; it was hidden away by powerful wards.

Xalrin stomped back to the hallway and felt it. It was very subtle, but it was there. It made him feel like he *had* to go somewhere else—and it might've still worked if his mind wasn't just a little bit broken. He called upon his *sight* and looked again at the empty hallway, almost falling backwards at what he saw. Before him was a strand of magic threads, tied together to form a barrier and laced with other magic to keep people away. It was so intricate that he probably could study it for ten years and not know how it was done. Unfortunately, he didn't have the time for that.

He walked up close to the ward, fighting the urge to flee, and studied the webbing. He couldn't break it, not without the knowledge of how it was done, which he lacked. If he tried without knowing how the magic worked, he could get burned... or worse. So, if he couldn't break it, could he force his way in by just bending it a little? Sure, it would set off alarms, but he reasoned the creators were long dead by now.

"Obren ethir, pry yaw dosit ansis'ren!" Xalrin whispered, keeping his voice low while still filling it with power. The command to force his way in was tricky—no one in their right mind would bend a spell instead of just breaking it—but a moment later he saw a very small opening and took it, squeezing through the webbing of magic threads. He felt a physical resistance as he did. He stumbled as he finally passed the barrier, small flames licking his robes and blood trailing down cuts in his arms and legs. He patted out the flames and healed his cuts with ether and looked at the end of the hallway.

No longer was there a bookshelf, but an old door. The door was an iron bound, wooden door with a simple lock and bar. He undid the lock with a quick spell then lifted the heavy bar and opened the door. He walked in and lit a sconce on the wall with another spell, looking around the dusty room with awestruck glee. He had found it! It was a small room, only about thirty feet across, but filled with books on what seemed to be demonic concourse and scribbled notes of past endeavors. The elven archmage who had sealed the room—and it had to be an archmage with that warding spell outside—had left their notes for any to find that could gain passage. He sat down and started to read, ignoring the time and his own hunger. Xalrin had found what he had dreamed of, and there was no going back now.

THE WAY OUT

Cirith lost all track of time in her dank, dark cell. Still gagged— this time with an iron mouthpiece so that her hands could be freed—she had lost access to any magic she could count on. Unlike some bards' tales, magic required the caster to ask, or in her case command, the elements to do things. Waving your hand around didn't accomplish anything short of swatting flies or looking dashing. She rolled over on her damp cot, squirming on the mattress and trying not to cry. She looked around for the hundredth time at her surroundings and wondered how she got to this point in her life; she never thought of things like this, but she had nothing better to do.

Her dismal cell was only a seven by eight room, made of stone with a cot, a pot for her bathroom needs, and very little illumination. Some torch light spilled in through the thick iron bars lending the room a sense of gloom that even a dungeon shouldn't have. It also had a leaky ceiling that dripped on her at night. Cirith had tried moving the cot to the other side of the room, only to find that it leaked there as well. Tears welling up in her green eyes, she turned over and stared at the stone wall instead, if only to hide her tears from any who would come calling. No one had of course.

She expected Ran'cian to come most days and brag or ridicule her, but she had been left alone for so long that she couldn't even tell how many days she had been here. She tried to count the meals, but they were so irregular that she gave up. Why did Declan go to Xalrin for help? He should've known better than that, even if he *was* desperate to help her. If she knew anything about the sorcerer king, her love was probably dead now, and her life was all but over. *If there was only some way to get back in Ran'cian's good graces,* she thought, her desperation forcing her to think of what she could do to stay alive. That was when she heard the first noises from down the long dark hallway.

LOWER DUNGEON, GOLDEN PALACE

Grafton spun, placing his knives deep into the neck of the guard that had seen him. The knives sliced his vocal chords so that he couldn't cry out and splashed the walls with thin trails of blood. Couldn't be helped. He would've had a clean run too, if this lout hadn't changed his mind and turned around, bumping right into the damn near invisible thief. Then another guard rounded the corner and saw Grafton. *Damn,* he thought, throwing one of his knives with pinpoint accuracy and hitting the man square in the throat as well. Unfortunately, the guard didn't go right down.

Grafton was on him in seconds, slicing with his other knife as the man fought to fend him off with his sword while holding his throat. The close stairwell they were in prohibited the man from a wide swing, so the favor was in Grafton's court with the small, light weapon. Dispatching the guard, he ran down the stairs to the dungeon and *almost* barreled into another guard. He hid along the dark wall, breathing calmly and trying to regroup.

The incarnation of shadows had made it into the building easily, making his way around the maze of hallways that made up the Golden Palace. He had taken his time mapping his route in the last two days, and it had proved invaluable in getting this far. Dumb luck had struck though, so now the plan was sliding away from him faster than a fat merchant down a hill of ice. In another few minutes the bodies would be found and he would have more guards than he could count down in these hallways.

It's not too late to cut your losses and get out of here, the deep voice boomed in Grafton's head. *It's probably a trap.*

"I'm not leaving that girl to rot in this place," Grafton whispered, refusing to think his words to this being in his head. He rounded another corner and saw the last doorway down to the dungeons. He ran on the balls of his feet—knives out and ready —and slammed into a mousey looking man in a black cloak coming the other way. The two tumbled down another set of stairs, Grafton trying to knife him quickly before he could speak any magic. When they finally stopped rolling down the stairs, Grafton plunged both of his knives into the man's chest and eye, but not before the man screamed. Grafton was good though, hitting the man's lung and almost killing him instantly through his eye, but the damage had been done. "Some days you just can't win, even when you rig the race," he said as he wiped his knives off on the man's cloak and ran on, looking from cell to cell for the woman. He had no idea who she was, but no one should be treated like an animal.

He saw her jump up as he neared her cell, his feet padding

softly on the stone floor. Unable to call out, she banged her metal gag on the bars to get his attention. He came to a stop right in front of her and bowed, flicking his hands out to open the lock with his stolen set of keys. "I am Grafton, the Incarnation of Shadows, here to set you free," he said, feeling a bit heroic for the first time in a long time. He wasn't supposed to reveal what he was, but he felt that if she knew who he really was she would trust that this wasn't some sort of a trap. She looked at him with an incredulous look then shrugged, exiting the cell.

You shouldn't have told her who you were Grafton.

The voice in his head sounded annoyed. He knew that Incarnations were supposed to stay in the proverbial shadows, as it were, and he was technically motivated to do that literally. While the voice never influenced him directly, it tried to give advice when it could. Grafton knew someday his rebellion would get him in serious trouble, but hopefully not this day.

Without a word, they ran down the halls and made their way out of the palace, dodging the guards who were now running everywhere looking for a killer. Grafton dragged the woman along and hid when he could. He didn't want a prolonged fight while trying to protect her, but if it came to that, he was ready. They had almost made it all the way back to the ground floor when he heard the booming voice of the sorcerer king. He crept close to the wall as they neared the voice and all he could think of was the voice in his head telling him, 'I told you so.'

NO GOING BACK

Ran'cian was livid. Someone had infiltrated his palace and killed his guards with such efficiency that they weren't even discovered until the guards changed. You would think someone would've heard or seen something, but no. That meant an assassin or even worse—an elf. *Like my day hasn't been bad enough already,* he thought to himself as he followed his royal guard down to the dungeons. He hadn't gotten far when more guards came running up.

"What now?" Ran'cian asked, projecting his annoyance with a scowl. It was then that he recognized one of the guards as Braslen, a veteran who had earned his respect for being honest and telling things straight. Unfortunately, his partner must've been new.

The younger guard started babbling as they approached. "It wasn't our fault Lord, we couldn't—" The man stopped as Ran'-cian took away his air with magic. The air fled his lungs as he gasped, clawing at his throat for air, and he fell to the ground flailing in panic as no air came. Tears fell as he thrashed on the tile, ripping skin at this level of near death. After agonizing minutes of pain and horror, he died at Ran'cian's feet.

"I don't want to hear why you couldn't," he said to the body of the young guard, "I want answers. Braslen?" Ran'cian asked the rather stalwart guard, ignoring the horrified looks from his royal retinue.

"We searched the lower dungeons, Lord. Cirith is gone, her cell opened, not broken. As if someone had a key." Braslen held his ground and his eyes showed no panic.

"Very well. Lock the palace down; not even the nobles can leave. I'm heading to the front now." Ran'cian turned and was about to head up when he looked back to the trusted guard. "What was his name?"

"Noram, sir."

"See that the next one is trained a bit better, Braslen." Ran'-cian walked away, leaving the guard to let out a breath loud enough for the sorcerer king to hear. He couldn't help but smile at the effect he had on his subjects. He raised his voice to all who could hear him as he walked to the front. "Find this assassin! Now!"

UPPER HALLWAYS, GOLDEN PALACE

Cirith had seen the sorcerer king stop and kill the poor young guard ruthlessly and without compassion. The evil man watched with a small smile on his face as his subject writhed in agony. *It isn't our fight*, she thought as she mentally went over her options. She could stay with this man, who claimed to be an ancient and powerful being—but what would wait for her out there? She would be hunted and eventually brought down anyway. In the end she placed all her bets that if she give Ran'cian a gift, we would give her her freedom. She eased her head back and, as the man who rescued her turned to look at her, Cirith bashed him in the head with her iron gag.

Seeing him go down, but still fighting to stay conscious, Cirith stood and leapt out of the side passage, waving her arms at Ran'cian. The hit had been hard enough to vibrate her whole head and she almost lost consciousness herself with the impact.

Royal guards swarmed over her as her lord came walking over, clearly shocked. With a whispered word of magic, he released her gag along with a cautionary wave of his finger not to try anything.

"Tha...thank you." Her voice sore and ragged from disuse. She cleared it several times before she continued. "This man said he was the Incarnation of Shadows, and I... I believe him." She knelt before Ran'cian, hoping that this gift would be enough to spare her life and hopefully get her back in his good standing.

Ran'cian patted her on the head lightly. "Indeed. You have done well Lady Cirith, all sins are forgiven." He flipped the man's body over and nudged the back of his head with his foot. "Bind his hands and feet, as well as his mouth, and bring him to my conference room." The sorcerer king turned to Cirith, tilting his head as if to say 'after you'.

"Thank, you my lord," Cirith said, getting up and walking after the royal guards. She could feel her lord's presence behind her like a hungry dragon, his voice close to her ear as he spoke to her along the way.

"Relax, Cirith. You get to watch me try and break into his mind. That way he can see who betrayed him right before he loses everything he holds dear in that little head of his."

Cirith didn't acknowledge him, couldn't acknowledge him, as she was far too busy wrestling with her own conscience over what she had done. She went over it time and again on the long walk to the conference room, trying and failing to justify her actions. She had to survive, get out of that cell at any cost... but could she live with what she had done? Cirith Ellwood hung her head and cried silently feeling, for the first time in her life, what others had called remorse. *What can I do though? Rancian is far too powerful,* she thought to herself, drifting to thoughts of Declan. She decided to ignore it for the meantime, enjoying the freedom she had gained at the expense of this man's life.

SECRET ROOM, GREAT LIBRARY

Xalrin arranged the candles in a small circle around the blade on the table. He was still in the secret room and had found everything that the ritual called for in the various niches and chests scattered around the cluttered chamber. It was like this place was designed specifically for this task. Before starting, he had packed up everything that was relevant in a small chest and laid it by the door just in case everything went to the deep Hells and he had to flee. It shouldn't come to that though; he had pored over everything that was here and knew just what to do.

The hard part was figuring out which demon he wanted to contact.

There were only a couple of them named in these writings, ones that the elven archmage had researched specifically. He had found one named Yngilithol, a harsh demon that took the form of a great horned beast bent on destroying all life as we know it. Another named Faerlythiv, a demon whose form was long tendrils of black smoke or darkness that fed on the souls of magic creatures. Lastly, and the best candidate on this short list, was Xilquiliv. This demon looked like a huge black mass with tentacles that enjoyed sifting through the memories of its victims and breaking them down slowly through fear and self loathing.

The ritual was intended to either call them into existence physically—a horrible idea, as stated before—or bind them into an object so that they could be used to achieve goals similar to their own. The elven archmage was researching a way to bind one of these demons into a quiver of arrows so that every arrow would allow the demon access to a new target, turning a host of mindless souls on their own forces. *And people say I'm twisted,* Xalrin thought as he closed his eyes and started to recite the litany.

He'd chosen a knife as his primary object, but had gone one step further. You see, once the demon is in the object, any contact to skin would grant the entity within access—the worse the wound the quicker it would happen. So he had encased the knife in stone, kind of like a sheath, keeping the demon bound with its weakness. Like Incarnations, every demon also had a weakness, usually connected to the elements they detested. Xilquiliv's was stone or rock, while others were wood, water, and even sunlight in some cases. As he pored over the words, flowing from his lips with practiced ease, he felt the power enter this world only briefly.

The room shook and after only a brief couple of seconds it was done, the knife vibrating only barely as the demon tested its boundaries. "I'll find out how to duplicate you later, first let's test you out," he said to the empty room as he gathered his chest and the candles, leaving quietly back to his rooms in haste.

SACRIFICES MADE

Ran'cian paced back and forth in his conference room. The man had healed up nicely in the eight hours he was left under guard and now he could begin to try and infiltrate the man's mind. *What secrets might an immortal being like an Incarnation have?* he pondered, as he flexed his arms. Stretching wasn't necessary, but it made him feel better. He saw the man struggle once more and smiled, relishing in the fact that he was going to do something that no one had done before: break an Incarnation. He wasn't sure if Cirith was boasting about who the man was or not, but seeing the man's wound heal like that convinced him.

Ran'cian had read about these legendary beings years ago, in the libraries' deepest vaults on history that were normally off limits to the normal folk of G'harr. Being from a noble house did have its benefits, as did his tremendous power in sorcery. "Bring her in," he said flatly, focusing on the man before him. He had the man tied down in wet, elven leather. No one could snap that, no matter how strong they were. It was meant to flex with you and then constrict once more.

Cirith was led in, her manner hesitant. When she looked at the man, their eyes met and his narrowed as he figured out just who had betrayed him. She mouthed the words 'I'm sorry' before turning to Ran'cian. "My Lord," she said, bowing her head.

"So, you weren't really being held against your will—it was all a plan to capture me?" Grafton said to Cirith as he tested his bonds once more. He stopped and looked straight up at the ceiling. "Shut up."

"So," Ran'cian started, unsure of what exactly was going on. The man seemed to be having two conversations at once, yet he heard nothing. Was the man crazy or was he actually talking over great distances to someone else? His god maybe? "What is your name? Or do I just call you the Incarnation of Shadows?"

"My name is Grafton, and if I get out of these restraints, I am going to do my best to kill you. And I promise that my best is beyond anything you've seen yet," he said, anger clearly present in every syllable.

Ran'cian laid his hand on the man's arm. "It wasn't a trap. She really *was* going to be executed. She just did what any loyal G'harran would've done in her place. She saw an opportunity for saving herself and took it. Isn't that right my dear?"

Ran'cian walked around so that the man couldn't turn his head to see him and chanted under his breath. He commanded the ether to slowly seep into the man's mind, forcing its way in quietly so he didn't break the man right off. *Let's see what we can get for free first. Then we break him,* Ran'cian thought as he held that spell and commanded the ether to also seep into the man's memories. Two attacks at once would melt anyone else's resolve, but he was still getting resistance. Most sorcerers couldn't maintain two spells at once, but Ran'cian wasn't most; he was one of the best.

GRAFTON'S MIND, THE GOLDEN PALACE

Grafton felt the tendrils probing his mind and closed his eyes, trying to block him somehow. If he could only get free, this would be over quicker than his time at being a hero. They had taken all of his knives, but he could take anything small and use it as a weapon.

I'm doing my best at keeping him out, Grafton. But like I said before, the man is good. I may be a god, but if I use that much power, I would just melt your brain altogether. Only my brother could do that and not kill you, the voice said, sounding saddened by the situation.

Grafton heard the king casting yet a third spell, and the sorcerer's magic finally began to break through. He could actually feel him snapping pieces and healing them before they could heal themselves. He could see wooden doors being forced open and a dark figure rifling through books looking for something. He knew the man was taking memories... taking who he was.

"Ah that's it. Just hold still and this will be over shortly," Ran'cian said, his voice calm and relaxed yet seeming very far away.

The man felt pain and started screaming, calling out for someone to help him, someone whose name he *used* to know, but couldn't remember. Hells he couldn't even remember his *own* name right now. He knew that he was dangerous though and that he would kill whoever was hurting him. *Why isn't that voice talking to me anymore? Wasn't there a voice in my head before?* Then the man hurting him snapped his head up as something came flying at him, end over end. A dagger!

The lady—Cirith, that was her name—moved quickly, throwing another dagger that thudded into the chair near the man's head. She had given him a weapon; he knew that much. She followed that up with words—*a spell, maybe?* —that seemed directed at him and in that moment the leather binding his arms dried up, becoming brittle within seconds.

The man hurting him had his hands up and ready, the torture he was doing forgotten. "Bad shot my dear. You nobles should practice your aim more often," he said as he snarled a command at the air to strangle her.

"She wasn't aiming for you," the man said, snapping the now dry leather restraints and grabbing the knife in one fluid motion. He turned, twisting his back at an impossible angle and slicing the blade across the torturer's throat. The man pulled back at the last minute, but he had cut enough to stop him from talking that gibberish anymore. "Run!" he called out to the girl that he had tried to save. *What was her name again?* She had helped him, but if he had tried to save her, why was she free and he was in straps? His mind was a garbled mess, yet he knew some things—like he had to go, now!

He kicked his feet out and snapped the foot restraints as well, rolling up and grabbing another knife, killing the two guards as the woman whose name he had forgotten ran for the hallway. He saw the man that was hurting him stagger backwards and go through another door, holding his throat.

"Teach your grandmother to eat dirt," the man called as he followed the girl into the hallway. He turned and grabbed her hand knowing exactly where he was and where the exit was; how, he couldn't say, he just did.

UPPER HALLWAY, THE GOLDEN PALACE

Cirith ran, disbelief flooding her that they had actually made it out. She couldn't explain why she had helped this man, other than to make up for Declan's death. As they turned a corner, she saw the man responsible for it all in front of them: Xalrin.

Cirith let go of her savior's hand as they ran and saw him keep going. She called upon the heat around the other sorcerer, trying to ignite his robes so that he had to focus on putting it out, rather than attacking her, but he was quicker and countered with a shield of cold around his body. She was going to cast again when she noticed the blade he was holding and froze.

The black blade was sheathed in stone and as he held it the

stone cracked and fell off. She could *feel* the evil pulse out and thirst for her, almost calling to her very soul. That thing was wholly evil and it was quivering in the sorcerer's hand as if it would fly to her on its own volition. She came out of her shock and heard him cast; she tried to counter, but she was a second too late. Half stunned, she could barely move as he came at her. "What... have you... done?" she asked brokenly, as she fought the ether that had paralyzed her.

"I was on my way to Ran'cian's conference chamber to show him my new toy when I saw you turn the corner. I *knew* that you would try and kill me—hells below I would've tried to kill me too—so instead, I decided to show you first," he said as he sauntered over to her, the blade almost bouncing in his hand. He lashed out with the blade, cutting her on the arm, deep.

Cirith felt the presence invade her and screamed inwardly, knowing that her very soul was being consumed and quickly. "Run... Graf..." but that was all she could get out before she was completely frozen. She could still see, however, and watched her savior look back and shake his head. Grafton turned and ran, disappearing altogether in a blink of an eye. Then her soul was being torn apart and she was gone.

EPILOGUE: WHAT COMES TO PASS

Ran'cian stumbled into his room and gasped for air through his wound. He couldn't believe he'd underestimated that bitch. Calming down and closing his eyes, he croaked out a quick command to the ether to heal his wounds. Once his neck healed, he took a minute to breathe normally before he called his royal guard. The Incarnation was, no doubt, long gone, and tracing the being with magic would probably be impossible; so instead he chose Cirith.

Locking on to her, he honed in with his *sight* and froze as an inhuman presence stared back at him. "No!" He quickly broke the link before whatever that was followed it back to him. He took off at a run in the general location of where he had *seen* her, panic over what could be in the palace driving him faster. *What in the deep Hells was that?* he thought to himself as he went through the halls, trying not to lose the iron control that he was famous for. He found her surrounded by guards and noticed with his *sight* that her very essence was drained: her soul, so to speak, was gone.

Well, that problem is solved. But who did it and how? he asked himself so as to not show his subjects that he was just as clueless as they were. It would be days before he realized that Xalrin was also gone, mysteriously and without a trace, even through magic. The twenty-year-old sorcerer king went on with his rule, trying not to think of what enemies he had made, or what had been unleashed into the world because of his tampering.

NORTHERN BORDER OF LYTHINALL

Xalrin kicked the horse faster as he crossed the border into Lythinall. He had fled once he realized what would happen to him when Ran'cian heard that he had slain a noble. He wasn't thinking when he did it; he was too excited to see his new toy in action. Worse though was *how* he had done it. *At least she was older than my other victims,* he thought as he looked for a place to rest for the night. He looked down at the blade at his side, once again encased in stone. The demon had been drawn back into the weapon after it had fed and he had hastily encased it for safe keeping.

After a couple hours he came upon a ruined outpost that had fallen to nature and the ravages of time. Perfect. He set up shop and rested for the night, getting ready to conduct more experiments on his blade and to make more if possible. Oh, the fun he would have...

ANOTHER FIGURE CROSSED the border into Lythinall just a day ahead of Xalrin. The man knew only that his name must be Graf, for that was what the girl had called him before she had died, and that the wind physically hurt him if he stayed in it too long. He slept in caves when he could find them—or back alleys in towns—curling up in the piles of refuse and garbage to avoid the dangerous gusts. It also kept him hidden and he found that people generally looked away when he walked by.

Graf made his way across Lythinall, avoiding the capitol and heading east. Though his mind was a mess and he couldn't remember much about his past, he remembered *certain* things, like geography and names of places. He knew that he was special, but the why or how eluded his unstable mind. He knew that he used to hear a voice in his head, but now it was silent and never answered him except for the odd whisper in his dreams or when he was resting. He eventually found a dry river bed and followed it to a hidden cavern. It led into a city called River Vale and he easily lost himself among the frontier people of the growing city for many years. It would be a long time before Graf would be found and remember who or what he was... but that is a story for another time.

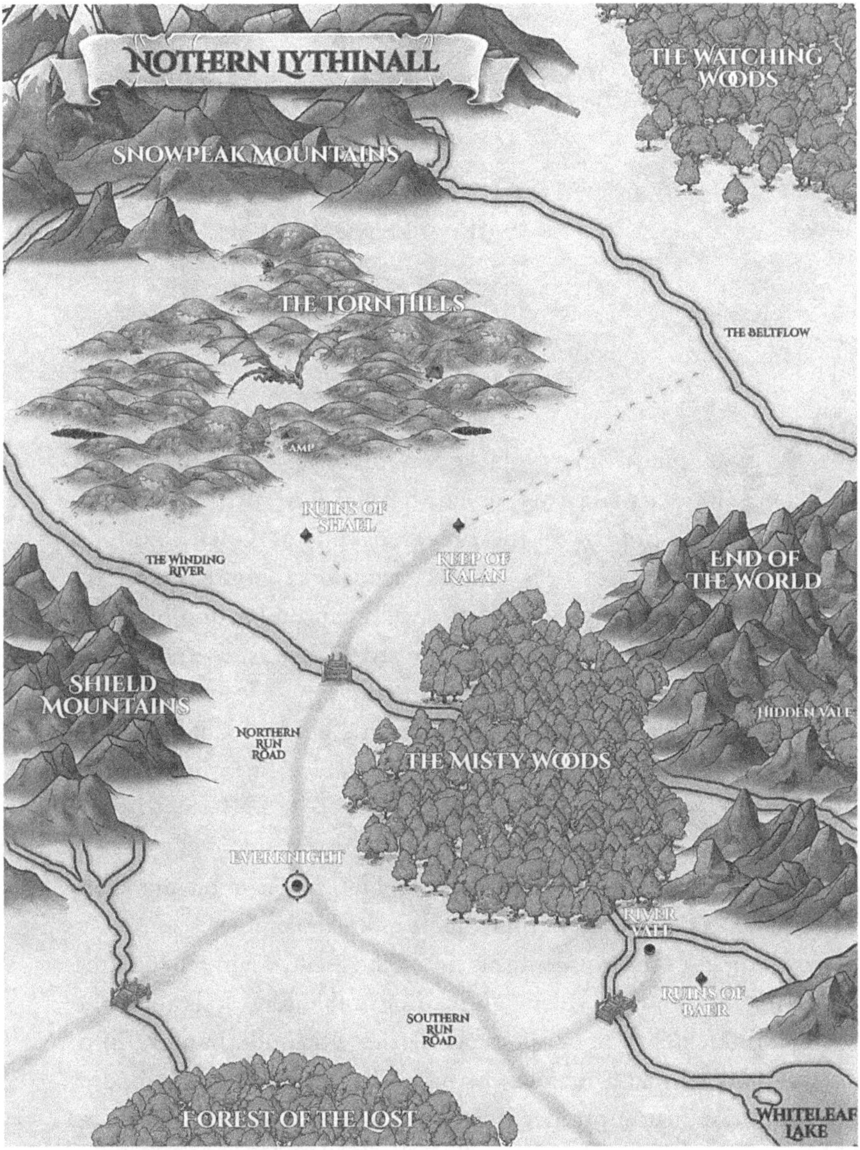

NOTHERN LYTHINALL
THE WATCHING WOODS
SNOWPEAK MOUNTAINS
THE TORN HILLS
THE BELTFLOW
AMP
RUINS OF SHAEL
THE WINDING RIVER
KEEP OF KALAN
END OF THE WORLD
SHIELD MOUNTAINS
HIDDEN VALE
NORTHERN RUN ROAD
THE MISTY WOODS
EVERKNIGHT
RIVER VALE
RUINS OF BAER
SOUTHERN RUN ROAD
FOREST OF THE LOST
WHITELEAF LAKE

MORLAN'S TALE
THE SWORD OF LEGEND

His black boots clacked across the gold tiled floor louder than usual as he stormed into his throne room. Ran'cian Ashren was the sorcerer king of G'harr and—as powerful as he was—those accursed Companions of Everknight had saved the day once again by besting him. He spun in a fury, knocking his steward Jalren aside and sitting upon his throne before the court could bow. He wasn't in the mood. He glanced up to see the petrified looks of his court and smiled. *All right, that made my day a little brighter,* he thought as they all frantically tried to bow and get to their places.

Straightening his white silk doublet, he scanned the room just to make everyone that much more uncomfortable. "Now, what does everyone want this time?" he asked, trying to hide the irritability from his voice—and failing at that too. Gods above, he couldn't catch a break if someone threw it underhand to him. He noticed that a member of his court, a very tall man, hadn't cringed in fear but rather stood straight and confident. Before he could ask, his trusty steward stepped up and announced the newcomer.

"May I present the Lord Yalinar, from Miran," Jalren said, raising his voice and bowing low as he finished.

"May it please the court," Yalinar said, bowing himself.

"You *must* be new here if you think this is my 'pleased' face," Ran'cian countered as he studied the Miranite.

Miran was a nation to the south east, on the other side of Lythinall, and they were strongly opposed to magic. Actually, 'strongly opposed' was an understatement. They feared it with such passion that there were rumors that they had burned down an entire town solely because there was an elf sighting... and no one thought the rumor unbelievable. The newcomer himself was almost seven feet tall, and whip lean. His long black hair was bound in a braid behind his back, and his white robes were adorned with a bright yellow sash. "What might G'harr do for you this day?" Ran'cian asked after a long pause.

"I come to let you know that we have signed a new truce with your neighbor, Lythinall. We hope to secure our treaty with your nation as well."

"With your hatred of magic, it surprises me that you would treat with them. They have an accord with the elves still, do they not?" Ran'cian asked rhetorically, knowing exactly what answer he would get. It was rumor only that Lythinall still treated with elves, but he had his sources. Besides, he took pleasure in pushing people's buttons.

"It *would* bother us, were elves still around, but we know they left a long time ago," Yalinar said, distaste clear upon his face. He was so ruffled that he started to wring his hands openly, like he was cleaning them.

"Yes, well, thank the gods above they're gone," Ran'cian said, winking openly at his steward. "But I digress. Was there something different in mind for this treaty or just a friendly renewal of the old?" Ran'cian knew there was *something* Miran wanted, or they would've sent a courier, and an expendable one at that.

"Well, now that you mention it... there is a certain enchanted sword my lord would like you to retrieve for us."

"A sword you say? What sword is this?" Ran'cian was intrigued; for a society that loathed magic, knowledge of a magic sword seemed beyond them. *And why have me get it?*

"It is the Ninetieth Sword of legend and its existence offends our lord Lorenal. It must be destroyed at all costs," The ambassador said, making the sign of Davalar as he said this.

Ran'cian whistled silently at the name. He knew of the Ninetieth Sword and its twin blade—any sorcerer worth his tomes knew *that* story, but to actually know *where* one was? "And you know this sword has been found... how?" he asked dubiously, silently wondering why the sword would perturb the ruler of Miran. The man was an expert swordsman, rumored to be trained by the best of the best.

Yalinar cleared his throat and relaxed a bit. "A travelling bard came through, working some magic. We, of course, tortured him for the information of why he was in Miran, but we got nothing," he said, turning and pacing before the throne. "Yet, before he died, he told us of the Ninetieth Sword in the hands of a great beast named Garentifranor, somewhere in northern Lythinall. Perhaps he wanted to use it as leverage; it availed him not."

Now Ran'cian understood. "Ah, and you can't send anyone because of the treaty you signed."

"Sadly, yes. We had already signed it when we received the information. We asked the king about it and he just quoted the treaty back to us."

"Let me guess. You knew I wouldn't have any problems sending people in after it?"

"Precisely." Yalinar seemed pleased, his face brighter now and he stopped pacing.

"I'll do you one better. I'll sign Miran's treaty *next* month when they send someone else and get the sword myself in the meantime," he said, standing slowly and stretching his arms behind his back. The rest of the court took a collective step back, knowing that he was capable of anything. "That would be one hell of a bargaining chip when I declare war on Lythinall and ask for your lord's forces to back me, wouldn't you say?"

"Well! I can tell you that Miran won't be sending anyone in another month. What shall I tell my lord was the answer *today* then?"

"Obren fra, bin dosit kithin," Ran'cian whispered as he stepped down and walked towards the man, asking the air to bind him tight and lifting him up high. He smiled as the ambassador struggled. "They will have to send another delegate. You see, brigands killed you before you arrived," Ran'cian said, with a mock air of sadness, "but don't worry, I will send someone to let your lord know and send my assurances that you will be avenged." He turned back and the court jumped by the audible snap the man's neck made, then they jumped again at the wet thump of the body hitting the floor. "Now, someone tell the researchers to find this Garentifranor."

GOLDEN PALACE LIBRARY, G'HARR

Braslen Erel strode down the hall, intent on his orders. He was an older man, forty-three this month and trying to perform his newly appointed duties as Commander of the guard. His short black hair was combed neatly to one side, and his blue eyes had worry lines that never seemed to go away. He passed a pair of guards that snapped to attention as he passed, saluting by holding their fist to their opposite shoulder. "At ease, men," Braslen said as he strode right passed them. All the rank and file had been much easier when he was just a guard. *Can't go back now*, he thought. *Once you impress the sorcerer king there is no saying no.* He had always been known to tell it how it was and with honesty... and look where it got him.

Braslen turned the corner and slammed the doors open to the library, and received a stern look from the older caretaker. He ignored the man and walked to the back, headed right for a table in the corner. "Mil, the sorcerer king needs your help."

Milaren Grells looked up, her deep brown eyes fluttering behind her thick glasses. Her hair was a mess and her shirt was unevenly buttoned. She frowned and took a breath to retort, but never got the chance.

"No, I don't want to hear it. You know as well as I do that you're going to do it, so spare the grumbling and just go see him," Braslen said as he turned around, but only took one step before she surprised him.

"Happy birthday, Braslen," she said, putting her book aside. She stood and smiled, adjusting her glasses and walked around the table.

"We can't do this here Mil," he started to say, but she walked right up to him and kissed him. Not just the peck on the cheek kiss, but the 'I need a cold shower' kiss. Murmurs went through the library like flames in dry grass and soon even the caretaker was talking.

She pulled back after twenty long seconds and held him at arm's length. "What? I can't kiss my husband?"

"You know we're separated."

"No—*you* wanted that. I never agreed."

"Look, with my new position it's dangerous for you to be married to me. If someone wants to get to me, they will hurt you." He closed his eyes, praying that something like that never happened, but he couldn't get the image of his predecessor's family out of his mind.

"He was dirty, Braslen, and you're not."

"Still. I don't want you to be put in that position," the

captain of the guard said with an air of finality. He knew things about Milaren that he wasn't about to bring up, but someday they would have to talk. "Now, go see Ran'cian and please just do as he asks this time."

Milaren harrumphed as he walked away. "Hey it was one time... and it was my book!" she called out uselessly.

Braslen closed his eyes as he walked back to the barracks. This day wasn't going to go well, he could just feel it. Hells, tomorrow didn't look too good either.

TO THE RESCUE

The horse's hooves thundered down the Southern Run road, the dust from long days of no rain leaving a cloud behind the five riders. The summer sun beat down on them without caring how important their mission was, and the wind didn't seem to even try and visit them. The man at the head of the group seemed to not be bothered by any of this, and in fact wasn't even thinking about the loss of comfort. He was tall, well over six and-a-half feet tall, and was all muscle. He had golden locks and intense, blue eyes that seemed intent on his destination. Arian Everknight was the prince of Lythinall and the leader of the Companions of Everknight, though you would never know that if you heard them squabble amongst themselves.

"Are we there yet?" the young man coming alongside of him asked in a mischievous tone over the sound of the horses. Tanan Norhil was dressed in a black tunic with black breeches, sporting a long dark blue cloak. He was the one they called on to get into places that required a bit more discretion.

"Tanan, why do you do that? You know he hates that." The man that came up on the other side of the prince was also over six feet tall and his corded muscle stood out prominently through his woolen shirt. He had shoulder length brown hair that looked like it could use a combing, but not one of them dared to get close enough to try it. Gareth Whiteheart was what some called a sword for hire, and a damned good one at that.

"Someone has to keep Mr. Prince Charming on his toes," Tanan said, pulling the reins and dropping back as Arian turned towards him.

"Listen," Arian called to everyone as they slowed down, pulling their horses off to the side of the earthen packed road. "It's not like we have a map to where this thing is. All I know is that it took that girl and we have to help." He sat in his saddle, the weight of the world on his broad shoulders.

"It's all right, love," a woman's voice said, coming over and placing her hand on his armored shoulder, the warm metal heated by the unforgiving sun making her flinch. "We'll find her, don't worry." The woman had shoulder length, curly brown hair, and piercing blue eyes that could read your every move—sometimes before you made one. She was lithe, but her stare could turn aside a dragon. Maressa Tolimar was hopelessly in love with the charming prince, and some said their love was the stuff of stories. She was a bard and had a way with stories that would leave you speechless.

"I know. It still pulls me though. The way that thug talked so callously about selling her to that... *thing* makes me sick." Arian sat straighter, trying to compose himself and looked at the young healer of their little group. "Wesan, tell me that you can fix her if that thing bites her?"

The little man tried to rein his horse over and failed miserably. He was a small man, almost five feet tall, dressed in dirt brown colored robes and a rope belt. A golden sash, draped over his shoulders, marked him as a healer of Davalar. He frowned at the question, however, and lowered his head. "No, Arian. If the wolf bites her, I cannot help. I can heal her minor wounds, like I've done for you all, but I can't cure that. I'm no priest."

"It might not even be a lycanthrope," Gareth interjected, trying to sound hopeful. "Maybe they got the description wrong?"

"Well, let's just hope the others got what we need and meet us there quickly," Arian said as he turned his horse to the road once more. It was hard to talk while riding, but they couldn't stop like this much more if they hoped to save the girl in time.

"Karsis will be there," Maressa said, "if only to tell you he was right."

"Ha! She's not wrong my Prince," Tanan said laughing at the face the man made at being called that yet again.

Arian sighed and rode on. *Father never said leading would be so taxing on one's temper*, he thought to himself as they rode on. *Then again, he probably had better companions.*

&

"HERE THEY COME," Karsis said as he spied the distant cloud of dust. He lowered his hand from his eyes and smiled at his two companions.

"How can you be so sure?" The dark-skinned archer said next to him. Storn Keragan was dressed in a simple dark green cloak over a white shirt and woolen breeches, which made for a stark contrast to his very dark skin. His black hair matched his deep brown, keen eyes. Compared to Arian and Gareth he wasn't a big man, but he stood over five feet and was well muscled.

"Because he's Karsis the Bard, Storn," a small woman replied, wrapping her arm around the man called Karsis and smiling up at him. Tierra Silverleaf had a slim build and long flowing platinum blond hair bound up in twin braids fell straight down her back, each set with two-inch steel balls that would click and clack whenever she walked.

"Oh yes, I forgot. *The legend,*" Storn said with a yawn, mocking the bard.

Karsis the Bard: legendary rogue, warrior, and general hero of the downtrodden. His name had spanned centuries, his deeds the stuff of history. His auburn curls were as recognizable as his one-of-a-kind burgundy long coat. He had played for kings, slain tyrants, even won the heart of an ancient dragon. That's what most of the songs said. And he should know—he wrote some of them. People had given up trying to figure out his past, since he never seemed to age or even look like he was slowing down in the slightest. So, they made up their theories and invented stories. Rumor had it that the title of "Karsis" was passed down to his heir once the child became of age; others hinted at a pact with demons from the hells.

Karsis stood a hair above five feet with long auburn curls draped over his slender shoulders and his clothes were finely made. He had a ruffled shirt with tiny pockets, and his black pants fell down to his black polished high boots, decorated with tiny charms. But it was his mannerisms that most people found disturbing. That look that said he had seen everything... and still wasn't impressed. It helped that he wasn't bluffing. "It's easy, Storn. No one else would be riding that hard in this heat except for our beloved prince trying desperately to save an innocent girl."

"But you already saved me," the girl said, standing behind them all. Her name was Caerlyn and she was about twelve years old and scared to death. She had long blond hair that was braided down her back and deep emerald eyes that could blink away your doubt. She was dressed simply, in a long white dress adorned only with a rope belt, and her delicate feet stuck out of her sandals.

"Yes, little one, but they don't know that yet," Karsis said, patting her on the head like a pet. Kids weren't his thing, yet there was something about this one...

"I can't wait to see his face when he finds out it wasn't a lycanthrope," Tierra said, twirling her fingers in Karsis's hair. He smiled at her and kissed her then, to the open disgust of Storn.

"Well, I for one can't wait to get back to the city. It's too dry out here for anyone to be running around," Storn said.

"You just want to get back to Kiera," Tierra teased, then ducked as the dark man kicked at her shins. They chased each other in circles around the bard as the others pulled up, shock written on their road weary faces.

"About time you got here. We had to have all the fun," Karsis said, watching the prince cover his forehead with his hand in frustration.

GOLDEN PALACE LIBRARY, G'HARR

Milaren approached the door and scrutinized it closely. The door was an iron bound, wooden door, shut with a simple bar. It used to be locked and barred, but ever since it had been rediscovered, it had been left open.

Years earlier a rogue sorcerer had uncovered the hidden room in the great library and took some of the most important works, then fled the city. Milaren walked in and lit a sconce on the wall, looking around the dusty room with apprehension. It was a small room with books on demonic discourse and scribbled notes from past endeavors strewn about willy-nilly. The sorcerer king had been through this room with a fine-toothed sword and had declared it free of important writings, though she still thought there might be something about that name and sword down here.

Milaren was about to sit down and read when she tripped,

slamming her knee down into the floor with a hollow thud. *Hollow?* she thought, as she rubbed her sore leg. pulled up a floorboard and saw that, beneath it, was indeed a hollow recess. In the space beneath the floor lay a dust covered book. She took it out and sat, opened the book, and began to read. Suddenly she understood why someone would hide this book in a secret compartment. She stared in horror at what was on the pages before her.

Milaren had found the name that the sorcerer king had wanted, but never dreamed what her search would uncover: the name was of a great dragon, recorded by the elves at the time of the truce over six hundred years before.

Garentifranor was said to have been cursed by an adventurer and the sword thrust into his back, forever embedded until it was removed by a worthy hero. Yet that wasn't what had evoked her terror. It was the supposed power of the sword was what had frightened her.

The blade, called the Ninetieth Sword, supposedly bestowed an aura of luck around the wielder, an aura so extreme that the bearer of the weapon almost couldn't lose in battle, to anyone. With a blade like that—and his formidable magic—the sorcerer king would be unstoppable. There were also lists of other hidden books and where to find them, books with even worse secrets hidden away within their pages.

These elves of old really knew how to hide things didn't they, she thought as she closed the ancient book and looked around, suddenly feeling very vulnerable; luck like that would be coveted by any who heard of this tale. *So how did he miss this book when he went through the room?* Trying not to think about that she closed the book and rushed to her rooms to hide it away, desperately thinking of how she could contact the only people strong enough to stop her liege: Karsis the Bard and the Companions of Everknight.

HOME AT LAST

Three days later the Companions, reunited and riding together, came through the east gate into Everknight. They rode through the streets and smiled at the people who waved and greeted them. The Companions were heroes once more.

Arian pulled his horse into the stables and shook the dirt from his armor. They had taken their time and delivered the young girl they saved back to her parents unscathed. The poor thing was wide eyed at the heroes and swore someday to join them, which only made Tanan laugh. They were all filthy from the dust and grime of the journey. Everyone but Karsis; that man never looked dirty a day in his life.

"I need a good bath and an ale," Gareth said as he handed the stable boy a gold coin. The wide-eyed boy rushed to take care of all of the horses, tripping over his own feet.

"You could *always* use those Gareth," Storn said, flinging a pebble into his mess of hair.

Gareth spun and looked for who threw it. Everyone pointed to someone else, then started laughing. "Very funny," Gareth growled. "It so happens that I *enjoy* both of those things."

"Don't we all," Maressa said, walking towards the winding path up to the castle. "Arian, I'll go first so your father doesn't know you're here yet. I'll tell him you're a day behind me so you can hang out with the boys." She winked at him and sped off.

"You're too kind, love," the prince said, watching her walk away with a very un-princely stare.

"Snap out of it, lover boy," Tanan said. "Let's get going and hit the tavern before someone notices you."

"No one will notice him covered in that much dust," Tierra said, giving a mock bow to Arian. "But they will already be gossiping as they saw us riding in."

The prince laughed, then stopped as he realized Karsis

wasn't joining in. He turned and saw the bard talking to a courier and his heart sank. *Oh, come on, we just got back,* he thought, knowing that they would more than likely be leaving again within the hour. Such was their curse: the Companions were known throughout the land and if there was trouble, they would be there. "Well, Karsis? Where are we going this time?"

Karsis paid the courier and turned towards his companions. His usual smile was gone as he folded the parchment and placed it into his pocket. "Nowhere right now, but very, very soon if we want to stop something terrible from happening," he said, whispering to the air to lightly clean his horse's mane and coat. The astounded stable boy whistled to himself and nodded his thanks.

"Well, thank the gods you decided to not be cryptic today," Tierra said, whipping her hair around towards him and hitting his shoulder. The steel balls clacked into the bard and he spun, finally smiling and becoming playful as if a switch had been thrown inside him.

"I'll fill you all in at the tavern. Wesan, why don't you go tell old Ralavin that there wasn't a lycanthrope after all," he chided, seeing Arian's face.

"Sounds good. Oh, and stay out of trouble until I get back," Wesan said, chasing after Maressa.

"Never letting that one go, are you?" Arian asked rhetorically.

"Not any year soon my Prince," Karsis said bowing, then took off after Tierra, playfully chasing her among the people walking in the streets. Tanan and Gareth bounded after them and soon they were all crowded into the Laughing Sprite, at their customary table in the corner of the large common room.

Arian sighed and followed, knowing that this was going to be one of those tendays that he regretted being a prince.

THE LAUGHING SPRITE, EVERKNIGHT

Karsis sat back and sipped his customary wine, wondering if this fame they had was worth it after all. They were well known all across the continent now, from Sirr to Miran, and everyone with a problem tried to contact them.

"All right, Karsis. What is so damned important that it stopped you from making fun of me?" Gareth asked.

Karsis leaned forward and crossed his arms. "If you must know, the letter was from a researcher in G'harr who has stumbled upon a very powerful sword here in Lythinall. The sorcerer king was going to try and get it but she got word to us first."

"Let me guess—you're not going to tell us what it is or what it could do?" Arian said, fingering his enchanted blade. "Sounds like when you told us about Chalice."

Karsis laughed at that memory. The prince's sword, Chalice, had been found on a similar quest that had led to the formation of the group in the first place. "I will tell you what I can actually-ly," the bard said, sipping his wine. "It is one of two swords in a set, made when the world was young—"

"Oh, gods above! Here he goes again," Storn said, rolling his eyes.

Karsis went on, ignoring him with practiced ease. "—and the priests needed weapons to fight the creatures in the dark. They forged two swords at the hour of Ollian's faith, and imbued them with beneficial powers. It is said that whoever holds either of these blades would be able to cheat death itself."

"So, the sword isn't cursed?" Tanan asked, eyes sparkling at the prospect of treasure, yet wary of the possibility of mortal danger.

"It is said that they are the bane of the skilled... so no, not cursed per se," the bard said, draping his arm around Tierra as he drank from his other hand. "Though powerful items like these bring their own problems."

"So why aren't we leaving?" Arian asked.

"Because we have a head start. The sword lies in the Torn Hills and we're days ahead of anyone the sorcerer king could send," Karsis said, waving to the serving maid for another round. Gareth had already drained two mugs and was looking for a third.

"Fine. We leave at dawn," the prince said, an air of responsibility giving his voice gravity.

"I'll go tell Maressa," Tierra said, kissing Karsis on the cheek and dancing through the crowd.

Karsis watched her go, noticing as always that Gareth watched her as well. He knew that look, and felt bad for the big warrior. "A toast then. To the Companions on the road again!"

CASTLE HALLS, EVERKNIGHT

Maressa walked the halls of the castle and reflected on her past. It was just a few years back that she had happened upon a lonely prince and turned his life upside down. She started skipping, thinking back to all the secret messages they used to send each other back when the king and queen didn't approve of their relationship. *Well, I changed their minds real quick now, didn't I?* she thought, as she passed the stairs down to the east wing. She stopped and stared as a young woman walked up towards her. She did a double take; the woman looked just like Cara, Arian's trainer who had retired and moved away to Sirr.

"Cara?" she asked, looking the woman up and down. She was easily six feet tall with short, dirty blond hair, deep brown eyes, and sun-darkened skin. The woman was built slender, but had packed every ounce of that slender frame with muscle.

"No. My name is Carana. I'm Cara's daughter," the woman

said, stopping and holding out her hand. "I'm replacing my mother as trainer to the royal family."

Maressa shook her hand and tried not to make a face as the woman squeezed a bit too hard for her liking. *Going to have Gareth shake hands with her to get even,* she thought as she rubbed her hand to get the feeling back in it. "Nice to meet you Carana. Need help finding your way around?"

"No, I think I can find my way. I was here when I was little and not much has changed," Carana said, as she nodded and made her way down the hall.

Maressa watched her go. Something tugged in the back of her head, but before she could finish the thought, Wesan came up and slapped her on the shoulder.

"Hey, want to go see the old priest with me?" he asked

"Sure, I'll go see the king after that. Besides, I'm sure we are going to have a little time to relax this time anyway." She turned at the sound of running feet and saw Tierra. *Then again,* she thought...

CHANGE OF PLANS

Ran'cian called to the air to bring him his goblet; the fine elven wine inside barely sloshed as it glided across the room to his waiting hand. He took a sip and swished it around in his mouth to savor the taste before he set the goblet down. "Bring her in," he said to the waiting guards. The throne room was empty at this hour, though no doubt those noble sycophants would've loved to see this. Two guards came back in with a struggling girl between them.

"Unhand me this minute!" Milaren screamed, then stopped as she noticed the sorcerer king. Her face went white.

"I see you realize that you're in quite a bit of trouble," Ran'cian said, fingering the rim of his glass. "We found the note you sent. I admit that that was daring, to say the least. Sending it to the Companions of Everknight... you really must be tired of this life my dear."

"I—"

"Save it. There is only one thing that could possibly alleviate your suffering this day, milady," Ran'cian said, turning around and motioning to the rear curtain in the corner.

The heavy red cloth moved and Braslen stepped out, his tear-stained cheeks a stark contrast to his hard eyes and his arms, which he held rigidly behind his back. "Why, Milaren? How could you throw your life away like this?" he asked, his voice barely constrained.

"Braslen, that sword is too powerful..." Milaren started, but her words fell away at his look. "I'm sorry, my love," she said simply.

"Is it more important than us?" Braslen asked, his voice breaking now as the grief started to overwhelm him.

"Braslen... I—"

"Never mind. It's not up to you anymore," Braslen said, his back straightening. He took a book from behind his back and handed it to Ran'cian. "Here you go, my King. The book for her life."

"Ah, that's a good man. You know Braslen, I always thought you were loyal. That's why I keep promoting you." Ran'cian turned to Milaren and gestured to the guards. "Bring her to the border of G'harr in the north and set her free into the mountains," he commanded as she stared in horror.

"You... you're letting me go?"

"I told Braslen that if he could bring me the book you had found, I would save your life. However, you may never return to G'harr," he said as the guards led her away.

"Wait... Braslen! I didn't get to say goodbye," she called as they dragged her from the room, her tears falling unabashedly.

"Than... thank you, sire," Braslen said as he turned and walked for the door, trying to keep his sorrow a secret and failing horribly.

Ran'cian could see the heartbreak on the man's face. He had heard the rumors of their separation and knew exactly why the commander had done it. "Don't thank me, Braslen. The mountains may well kill her yet. But she is at least alive to try and survive. I am truly sorry for your loss though."

"She was dead to me when she betrayed G'harr, my King." With that final statement Braslen left the throne room.

I know better than to compete with those Companions when they have a head start, but hopefully there is more in this book that can help me than they are unaware of, Ran'cian thought as the commander left the room. *And I may have to promote that man to General soon.*

NORTHERN LYTHINALL

Karsis looked at the distant horizon as he rode with his friends. The Companions of Everknight travelled up the Northern Run road, and were making excellent time. For once, the brigands and monsters seemed to be hiding and nothing stopped them as they headed towards the Torn Hills. They took the path to the ruins of Shael—where they had found Chalice two years ago—then continued north. Tanan was on point, with Storn taking up the rear with his bow. This was Koben territory and they knew the dangers of getting outnumbered by those little cretins.

Koben were short, cave dwelling creatures that bred quickly and often. They were dark-green with rough skin covered in dirt and had ears pointing out to either side. They only grew to about three feet tall and lived in the hills and mountains far from society. They often sought to trap any other beings they could, yet ran from shows of brute strength unless they had the numbers. Koben might have been frightening *en masse* if they weren't so horrible at following any direction whatsoever. The few times a warlord or powerful creature tried to unite them into a menacing force, the Koben only made it five miles before they devolved into bickering and fighting amongst themselves, mainly because they forgot why they were all hanging out.

"Now remember friends, this dragon is going to be much older than the ones we faced two years ago," Karsis said as they rode.

"Maybe we can try and talk to this one, Karsis?" Arian asked, fingering his sword in anticipation. "It almost worked with that dragon's mother before."

Karsis winked at the prince. "It *did* work; she agreed to take me flying, didn't she?"

"Do we *have* to hear this story again?" Storn asked, laughing at the faces of his companions.

"All joking aside, that *is* the plan, my Prince," Karsis said, seeing the look Tierra was giving him. "Don't worry—I promise that I won't try and seduce this one."

"Hey, maybe I can get the sword without it even knowing," Tanan said, pulling his horse back to the rest of the company.

"Keep dreaming, Tanan," Maressa said, laughing at his hurt look.

"We will set up camp up ahead and then Arian, Tanan, and I will go see if we can even find this dragon," Karsis replied, liking their chances. "You show up to a dragon with eight people and it just makes them uncomfortable; uncomfortable and hungry. Hells below, you show up at all and they get all indignant sometimes."

❦

A few hours later, the three men were riding slowly towards the deep recess in the side of a low hill. They could see the bulk of the dragon in the distance and Karsis signaled to Tanan to take the high ridge.

"Just distract it and I'll get the sword," Tanan said as he padded off out of sight.

"Yeah. You're good at talking to dragons, Karsis. You distract it and I'll follow your lead," Arian said, laughing at the face Karsis made.

Karsis continued on with Arian and soon they stood before the great beast. To their shock, the dragon wasn't keeping the sword as treasure… it was lodged in its back! *Well, this complicates things just a bit,* he thought as they neared the dragon.

Karsis saw Tanan and winced inwardly, seeing that the rogue had noticed the sword as well. The dragon stirred and spread its great wings out as it stretched its neck. The scales of its massive form were a deep brown and getting darker here and there, slowly turning a deep russet. Dragon's scales changed color with age, and this dragon was indeed old. Another hundred or so years and the scales would darken to red, but even now it was a beast to be feared, to say the least.

Karsis looked at the dragon as Tanan snuck around behind it. *Distract it they said. It will be easy they said,* he thought as he smiled at the dragon, stepping up closer. The impossible task was daunting, yet he *was* the legend here so… He shrugged and kicked the dragon in the shins. "I say there—are you awake?" It worked all too well.

The great beast moved with an alacrity that defied its size, its head whipping around as it lunged to bite the bard, but Arian stepped in with Chalice. With the flat of the blade he struck the dragon's mouth and shouted in his kingly voice. "Stand down and just listen! We mean no harm." Arian then turned to Karsis, "*That's* your plan?"

"It's distracted isn't it?"

HIGH LEDGE, TORN HILLS

Tanan circled the high ledge behind the dragon as Karsis and Arian distracted the huge beast, knowing that if he was caught they would be erecting a headstone for him soon enough. He could see his goal—a sword stuck in the dragon's back up to the hilt. It was almost his. *Odd, ever since I heard of this blade, it's like I have to have it,* he thought as he crouched down, sizing up his target.

Tanan gauged the distance and leapt upon the dragon's back, grabbing the hilt of the sword as the dragon roared. The dragon twisted and writhed as he held on for dear life, until finally he found his feet and stood. Tanan pulled and fell backwards as the blade came free in a flash. He rolled and slid down the deep, brown scales towards the ground with an agility born of long practice. The sword hummed in appreciation and almost seemed alive in his grasp. Now he just had to live to wield it.

The dragon twisted his neck around to bite him, but Karsis whispered and flames gathered around his outstretched hand. The dragon stopped upon hearing the elven words and cocked his head at the bard.

Karsis stepped forward and spread his hands out wide. "Now that the hard part is over, can we talk quietly? Or does my friend here have to start hitting you with the *sharp* end of his sword?" the bard asked, standing the way he always did: like he owned the place.

Tanan gripped the sword and rolled to his feet. He was lucky he wasn't dead: miracle number one. The sword throbbed in his hand and he saw a name on the side of the blade —

Morlan. Somehow, he *knew* it was meant to be his. He turned his gaze to the standoff and walked in front of the dragon.

"Feel better without *this* in your back?" Tanan asked with an air of accomplishment. He couldn't believe he was doing this, but when the dark one rides...

The dragon's eyes went wide at the sight of the sword. "That sword has been in my back for over a century. Usually, you humans are obsequious in my presence, but you fools don't seem to care," the dragon said, clearly feeling better. He stretched his wings like he was working out a cramp and straightened to his full height. "I have been guarding that sword for a *very* long time. Now I will take my leave, humans; go in peace." He beat his wings once, twice, then lifted up into the sky and flew off south towards the Shield Mountains.

As Tanan watched the dragon fly away he laughed, all the tension melting away. "Well, that could've gone horribly wrong," he said, sheathing the weapon in his old sheath and sitting on a rock. His old sword would make a good mantlepiece in the Laughing Sprite.

Arian scowled at the rogue. "Wrong? The dragon could've swallowed us right down his throat if he wanted. I hope that sword was worth it," he said, looking around for his horse.

"Oh, it *is* worth it Arian," Karsis smiled, brushing off his long coat for no reason.

COMING TOGETHER

Karsis and his companions walked back to their camp, victory still fresh in their minds, and saw that the girls were waiting for them. Yet something was wrong. The two women seemed complacent and lost, and neither Storn, Wesan, nor Gareth were anywhere to be seen. Karsis swore softly and scanned the scrawny trees, while Tanan circled in the darkness. Something bad was here.

Arian pulled Chalice as he walked towards the fire, determined to save his love, yet stopped when Karsis held up his hand.

Karsis scanned the trees as something leapt out of the shadows with a yelp. Tanan had flushed it out with the point of his shiny new blade. It was a deceitful little Koben. "Well at least it wasn't a gnome," Karsis said distastefully.

"Oh, great masters! I was just sitting in the dark, wondering to myself why the stars were so small when this one stabbed me." The koben smiled up at the Companions as he babbled on about his innocence. It was comical, since he was only as tall as an elven amphora.

Karsis pointed to the creature with an exaggerated pose, "Release them and we may let you live," he said, drawing his sword with a flourish—mainly for show, but also to be ready, as Koben rarely travelled alone.

The little creature sighed and gathered up his tiny pouch. He pulled a root out carefully, watching the swords trained on him and shivered as if a mistral-wind had blown; he wasn't cold, he was scared. "Have them chew this root and they will come around," he said, sitting down after Karsis took the root.

Karsis put the root in Tierra's mouth and made her chew it. She came out of her daze in a rush and when she saw his face she blushed. "Saved me again, love?" she asked.

"Of course, dear. And I always will," he replied charmingly. He went about giving the root to Maressa, while Tanan and Arian watched their guest.

Maressa came around and saw the koben smiling at her. She drew her sword and lunged, barely missing the creature as Tanan pulled him back out of the way. The thing hit the ground and let out a belch as he landed.

"Wait Maressa! We're not done questioning him yet," Tanan said, pulling the creature to its feet by the ears. He turned the creature around and stared at him intensely. "Now where are the rest of our friends?"

"There are two down there, under my tree, but the last one is around the back because he doesn't fit. You can have him too, if you want." The koben said, as if he were talking about the weather.

"Must be Gareth!" Karsis said, laughing.

Tanan watched them pull the others from the koben's hiding spots and stole a glance at Maressa. He tried not to stare, but she was beautiful. Beautiful and *taken*. Arian was smitten with her and she, him; yet Tanan would always remember that he met her first... and loved her first.

"So why did you waylay our companions, foul creature?" Arian asked, stepping up like a fired up noble. "Did you plan to take their souls?"

"Don't mind our friend. Arian needs more fiber in his diet, so he tends to get all worked up," Karsis said, laying his hand on the knights' shoulder.

Tanan walked over, shaking his head. "Seriously, why attack an armed party? It's not like your kind at all, unless you have the numbers..." *Crap, I missed it,* he thought as he spun quickly to go back to back with Arian, pulling Morlan.

The koben streamed out of the woods as if that was the signal and came at them relentlessly. The companions formed up and tried to work together, but even though they had been together for over two years, they still weren't used to fighting as a team yet. Tierra kicked and caught Storn's leg by accident when he stepped in front of her, then Arian stepped out too far and got separated in the throng of little bodies. All the while Karsis sang and danced with his slim sword, killing all who came against him.

Tanan knew what they needed to do, though he also knew most of them weren't fond of the idea. They needed someone to take charge. "Karsis, take lead!"

"Maressa, Tierra, go get the prince! Tanan, Gareth, to my side," the bard said, ending his singing.

"Okay, Karsis." Maressa said, grabbing Tierra's arm and slamming into the koben in front of the prince.

"What do you have in mind, Karsis?" Gareth asked, swinging his axe with devastating accuracy. The man was a powerhouse with that weapon.

"Spearhead," the bard said with a knowing smile.

Tanan leapt up next to him without question, still staring at Maressa, as Gareth's eyes lit up with understanding and laughed. They were usually reluctant to listen to Karsis when Arian was here, and that usually led to them having problems like this.

"All right, now—let's give the girls some back up," Karsis said, moving forward with the other two fighters as one. They piled behind the women and forced the koben off of their flank, giving the girls a free shot at the ones keeping Arian busy. Once they had all gathered together, they drove the creatures into flight, and soon were left alone; besides the moans of the dying, all that could be heard was the sound of the wind through the.

"My love! You're all right," Maressa said, wrapping her arms around Arian as he tried to sheath his sword.

Tanan looked around and saw the piles of dead around him. He had always been good with a short blade, but this time he was almost as good as Karsis. He thought of the fight and replayed some of it back, realizing that they tripped more often than not when they came at him, and always left an opening.

Koben weren't competent fighters, yet something seemed off. He remembered what Karsis had said about the sword allowing whoever wielded it to cheat death. He walked over and caught the bard alone for the moment. "Karsis, I'm worried."

Karsis flashed him a charming smile. "About how women find me more attractive? Or about how everyone wants to listen to Arian in a fight?"

"No—I'm more attractive and someday we'll learn to trust you completely. I'm worried that this sword is going to make me rely on it more than I want to," Tanan said, keeping his voice down for fear of embarrassment.

"Oh dear! Good looks *and* brains," Karsis said, clapping him on the shoulder and walking with him. "We'll just have to train without it so that you become just as good on your own; then it won't matter."

"Won't it be... mad if I did that?"

"Tanan, it's a *sword*. It might be magical, and very powerful, but it is not sentient," Karsis explained, rolling his eyes. "Just don't drop it, it hates that."

"It does?"

"No, Tanan! I'm messing with you."

"Well stop it. I've had a stressful day." Tanan smiled and sheathed the sword, feeling pretty good about the days to come.

EPILOGUE: KING TAKES SHIELD

Karsis pulled into Everknight on his horse and watched the others dismount and joke with one another. They had found the sword and didn't even encounter any resistance from G'harr. He looked to the southwest and frowned, wondering what Ran'cian had been thinking. Did the sorcerer king know that he couldn't have reached the sword first, and if so, why had he given up trying to recover it? Or was the letter a plant to keep them distracted from something else? The bard sighed and let it go. There wasn't anything to do now—they would just have to wait and see what came of it.

"Hey, come on Karsis. We're going for drinks, then up to the castle," Tierra said, sliding behind him and wrapping her arms around his waist.

"That sounds great, but I may have to leave before that. Let's start with drinks then see," he said, kissing her hands. He couldn't shake the feeling that that something was wrong. *I'll just have a couple of rounds, then head to Alrin and see what I can find out,* he thought as he followed the companions through the streets to the Laughing Sprite. He envied the other's ignorance of the larger picture sometimes, yet he couldn't tell them the things he knew; it would ruin their fun. And besides, if he told them all he knew about what was coming, it would spoil most of his plans...

GOLDEN PALACE, G'HARR

His black boots clacked on the stone floor, the sound echoing in the tunnel as the sorcerer king made his way down to the dungeons. He walked by the cells, their occupants moaning in various states of despair and injury, and ignored them with practiced ease. The book he had liberated from that traitorous researcher had told him of even more books hidden around the palace. It irritated him that they were hidden from detection by magic, which was why he missed this one in the first place.

He was down here looking for another such hiding place, though he had been down to the dungeons countless times before and never noticed anything. *Damned archmages and their paranoia,* he said to himself as he neared the dead end at the back of the long row of cells. He cocked his head to one side and whispered a command to the ether to show him the lines of magic and was surprised to see a great web of threads protecting a door. Once he knew right where to look, it was easy to spot. Ran'cian chuckled to himself and broke the threads, then unlocked the door with another spell. Stepping into the room he was staggered by the sheer size of it.

He turned around in amazement. The room was at least forty feet in diameter and lined with bookshelves. A small table sat in the center of the room. Seated at it was a skeleton in a high backed chair. The clothes had rotted away from the skeleton's frame, yet the quill in its bony grasp remained. Ran'cian walked around and peered over the shoulder of the body to see what the corpse had been looking at. Closed and covered in dust was a book titled 'Dost Frein en Krist.'

"The Fall of Evil," Ran'cian said quietly. He asked the air to blow the dust away and lifted the book away from the skeletal hand reaching for it. He flipping through the ancient pages delicately. It seemed to be a book of prophecy, and a copy of an older text at that. He could tell mainly from the handwriting throughout the tome; different styles and hands had copied these words down. He stopped at one passage and smiled, knowing that he had stumbled upon something very significant.

The beast long locked away shall be freed with malice and hate, but can only be stopped by what it despises. No one, be he man, elf, or incarnation, may fight him and live, unless they are touched by the one who is none of these, yet all of them.

THE BOOK WENT on with other cryptic phrases which he ignored, knowing that to delve too deeply into prophecy could drive one mad. The words were always frustratingly vague and tended to lead you away from their true meaning... unless you were the one that had the visions.

Ran'cian closed the book and glanced around at the other

books on the shelves. Nothing else really stood out as important, yet he would send his trusted researchers down here, the ones that were left that is. *On second thought, I think I will keep this place to myself. Fool me once and all that,* he thought as he locked the door behind him and asked the ether to shield the door once more, weaving his own threads into a careful net that would fry anyone attempting to dispel it. There were still two more hidden rooms to find this morning and he still wanted to sit down with this book and see what he could make of some of it.

Ran'cian smiled as he walked past the moaning bodies lying in their cells once more, noting that one had died since he had been in the hidden room. He made a mental note to have the guards clear the body out and went up into the palace once more, a slight bounce to his step. He may have lost the sword but he had gained something else.

"Sir." A guard came to attention as he came running up. The young man looked scared to death. Given Ran'cian had dealt with bad news in the past, it was hard to blame him.

"What is it now?" Ran'cian asked, clearly perturbed.

"There is another delegate from Miran in the antechamber awaiting you," the young guard said a bit breathlessly.

"Ah, a little early but that's fine." Ran'cian straightened his back and clapped the eager guard on the shoulder, almost making the man whimper. It still amused him that everyone thought he was going to kill them. "Alright, lead the way and let's go see if we can get anything out of *this* one, shall we?"

THE BORDER ROAD, LYTHINALL

Karsis rode in silence, trying to clear his head of the song that was stuck in there. He was still mostly drunk, yet he had to head south to figure out the sorcerer king's next move. He tried to think of what the man could've wanted by *not* sending someone after the powerful sword—after all it was ridiculous to not even try—and had a revelation.

It's like elven khoss, Karsis thought, remembering the elven game of strategy. *You move your shield to get in range of their king and when they move it safely out of range, you take it with your sword instead.* Yet that made him think of the counter to that move as well. Baiting the shield so as to surprise it with the king in attack mode. Was that what the man was doing?

The bard shook his head and laughed, surprising his horse at the sudden outburst. It didn't matter; there were moves for that as well. *Besides, I still have to figure out what the 'leaves of silver bearing elven fruit to battle the darkness' means,* he contemplated as he patted his pocket. His favorite book, 'Dost Frein en Krist', was getting good, but, as with all prophecies, it was a bit hard to decipher.

Karsis the Bard kicked his horse into a canter over the bridge and on to Alrin and whispered to the ether to change his appearance. If he was going into G'harr he couldn't be recognized, or he would be in serious trouble. His hair changed to blond and his curls fell away, becoming straight. His face darkened a bit to that of a hard southerner, and his eyes were now deep green. His clothes were turning burnt gold, and his coat was fading to white. Once that was done, he tied the magic to his soul and rode on, singing that ridiculous song that was stuck in his head as the sun set behind him.

THE HIDDEN VALE
THE COUNCIL OF
TREES

❦   *6*   ❦

CHASING THE DARKNESS
THE STORY OF KARSIS & THE FAERIES

He was almost there. The wardens were right behind him, but if he made it to the woods of S'ren-Sellare, he knew he could lose them. Not for the last time, he cursed his misfortune of choosing the high king's daughter as his latest target. *How was I supposed to know who she was, all dressed up in that dark cloak?* Jalafryn Silverleaf smiled at the thought, exasperating as it was. The girl had lived a long time and it filled his ears with pleasure to prolong her agony like that. In the end, her last breath was bliss to him.

Jalafryn dashed across the field of high grass toward the forest, and his elven ears picked up the sound of shouting. They could *see* him! The wardens were all wizards of Tir-Lanan, the elven homeland, and they were good at using their *sight*: magically sending their vision out across great distances. He had shields up, but they still pierced right through to find him. *Well, when the dark one drives...* he thought, and spun to face the group in the distance. He called upon the elements around him and felt the darkness pulse around his heart, like a comforting embrace. "Ash'anti fra hadar lae kith!" He spoke the elven words to hold them with the air, yelling it so that the wind knew

158

he was truly in need. Elements were choosy; you really needed to let them know just how badly they had to work.

The distant screams indicated that his spell took hold, but they were wizards too, so it wouldn't be long until they countered their way out of it. Jalafryn turned and sprinted for the trees, calling to the air once more to speed him along. He hadn't used magic until now because he was trying to stay out of their tracking spells, but now they knew he was here, so it was time to pull out all the stops. He was almost at the tree line when he heard a 'pop' of misplaced air. A tunnel opened in front of him and a female tumbled out. She exited, still moving as fast as when she had entered, and she used the momentum to roll and come up with her enspelled blade at the ready. She was lithe and dressed in wizard leathers, holding her slim sword in unshaking hands.

She must've called upon the ether to bring her here... that takes specialized training. I'm impressed. He stowed his thoughts away and threw his hands out, pointing at her and calling to the grass around them. "Ash'anti gres, sistren dosit shiran." He hadn't done this in a long time, using the very grass as a weapon, but he had no choice; she looked competent with that blade, far more than he was.

The female warden looked at him and her brow furrowed. "You're not worried? How powerful can you be, that you do not fear the wardens?" she asked. She quickly tried to counter his spell, but the grass at his feet straightened and pointed toward her, leaping out of the soil like daggers. They burrowed into her, in at least seven places, and she screamed in shock as much as pain. She looked down at the three long blades of grass buried directly in her heart. She looked up but her eyes were already vacant.

Jalafryn ran past her, scooping up her sword and plunging into the forest. The trees of S'ren-Sellare swallowed him up as he left the wardens behind. He found what he was looking for soon enough—a faded old mushroom ring that would lead him into the heart of Lythinall. It's too bad that the faeries left all those centuries ago; he had always wanted to meet one. Now all they had were the stories and songs that the faerie folk had left behind. It just wasn't the same. However, he had done some digging and had found that they didn't all flee to another dimension, as first thought; they had hidden themselves away.

Jalafryn shrugged and stepped in the ring, vanishing as the despairing cry of the wardens signaled that they found the girl's body. He smiled as he transported to another place, and out of their grasp.

WHAT ONE FINDS

It was a cool autumn day and the road to Havenar was finally finished. He hated walking new paths before the king's men had finished flattening them; the ruts did terrible things to his shiny boots. The wind was coming off of the Snow Peak Mountains, bringing with it dark omens of a frigid winter—not that he hadn't seen those before.

The man stood a hair above five feet, with long auburn curls draped over his slender shoulders and the clothes he wore were very finely made. Especially his coat—he was very fond of the coat. He had a ruffled shirt with tiny pockets and the legs of his black pants fell down to his black polished high boots, which were decorated with tiny charms. Yet his mannerisms were what most people found disturbing. That look that said he had seen everything and still wasn't impressed. It helped that he wasn't bluffing.

The man's name was Karsis the bard: legendary rogue, warrior, and general hero of the downtrodden. His name had spanned centuries, his deeds the stuff of legend. His auburn curls were as recognizable as his one-of-a-kind burgundy long coat. He had played for kings, slain tyrants, even won the heart of an ancient dragon. That's what all the songs had said. And he should know—he wrote most of them. People had been trying to figure out his legacy for years, since he never seemed to age or even look like he was slowing down in the slightest. So, they made up their theories and invented stories. Rumor had it that the title of Karsis was passed down to his heir once the child became of age. That one always made him laugh.

The town of Havenar was relatively new, being one of the many frontier towns that had sprung up once he and his fellow Companions of Everknight had all but tamed the northern lands. For over eight years they had ridden together and righted wrongs. They had been a force for good and righteous might, and woe to the monster that reared its ugly head when they were around. The Companions of Everknight had freed slaves, defeated vampires, and even dealt with their share of dragons.

Karsis sighed and kicked a pebble out of his path as he strode down the packed earthen road. Now the Companions were retired, with their leader becoming King of Lythinall and the others settling down as lords of the three outposts. Even Gareth and Tierra—who were due to give birth any day—had moved to the northern town of Daelyn to start a quiet life together. Not that he was jealous; he had moved on from her and was happy for Gareth. He knew they loved each other, and he had never really felt *that* for her. What *was* killing him was that everyone had something to do except him.

The legendary bard lifted his head and noticed a column of smoke rising from where Havenar should be and instinct kicked in. He whispered to the air to speed his steps and ran full out. Thanks to the training he received at the hands of the elves he had almost near-perfect control over magic, and it had saved not only his life, but his companion's lives more times than they could count. His jacket billowing out behind him, he arrived at the gates of the town in the time it would take a horse to travel the same distance. He could see that the tavern was awash in flames.

"Help! I can't find Tomas!"

Glancing toward the cry, he saw a woman running in a panic and raced to meet her. "Calm down a touch and tell me what is going on. Is Tomas in there?" He pointed to the engulfed building, praying that he was wrong. He wasn't.

"Yes! I had him in my arms and then he was gone!" She was wailing uncontrollably and could hardly catch her breath.

"Well, lucky for you that I'm here," Karsis said, brushing by her and heading for the front door of the tavern. It looked like the town guard, and possibly the mayor, were trying to put out the flames with water buckets. The only reason he guessed it had to be the mayor was because the man looked like he had been sitting behind a desk for the last ten years.

The mayor tried to step in the way as Karsis came up, and almost tripped doing that. "Hold it there, mister. You can't just walk in *there*. Are you daft?" He was pudgy and out of breath just from helping direct the men around him. Gavin Holsted was the Mayor of Havenar and he did not seem to be having a good day.

"Well, that's where you are wrong and it probably won't be the last time that happens today," Karsis said as he spun around the pudgy man and grabbed a bucket from a shocked guard's hand. "Ash'anti wan sran ea jren dosit fir!" he yelled at the elements to shield him from the fire as he strode into the flames, never flinching. He had to hurry; this spell wouldn't last long.

"Now, if I were Tomas, where would I be?" Karsis asked himself as he dodged a falling beam and danced to the stairs amid the blackened tables and chairs. This building would go before his protection did, at this rate. "Tomas! Oh, Tommy boy!"

he called out, ducking into what he could only assume was one of the larger guest rooms; the large flaming bed was the only hint he had to work with. He listened for the telltale cry of someone being young and frightened to death, and was mildly surprised at what he heard. The only thing making noise—other than the fire—was a mewling under the bed.

"You have *got* to be kidding me..." Karsis slid down to his knees and looked under the flaming bed. There, crying its throat horse, was a cat. "Tomas, I presume?" he asked as he laughed and reached for the cat, whispering quietly to calm the tiny beast down. "Now for the fun part. Getting us both out of here," he quipped to the cat as the roof started to buckle above him.

REMAINS OF THE BLACK STALLION, HAVENAR

The Mayor looked on as the roof fell in, piece by piece, sending flames shooting up into the sky along with more smoke. They had tried to quell the fire to no avail and now the men all stood there watching with bated breath to see if the man would survive. The stranger hadn't come out yet and probably wouldn't at this point. Why the man went in after old Grace's cat, he would never know. "Well, let's pull back men, this thing is done..." Gavin never finished that sentence.

The side of the building cracked loudly above the sound of the roaring flames and crumbled away as an outline became visible. There, standing in a doorway-sized hole in the side of the tavern, was the man, holding a smoking bundle. He leapt up into the air and floated down silently as the building wailed its last cries behind him. The man landed with a soft thump and handed the bundle to the woman who had come running to him. "I believe this is yours, madam. Careful, it's a bit warm." The cat was struggling to get out of the blanket and as she landed kisses upon the feline, the man walked away.

"Hey, mister!" one of the guards called out after him. "Aren't you Karsis the bard?"

Gavin's mouth dropped and hit the packed earthen street. Karsis the Bard! Of course, it would have to be; he knew he had seen that coat somewhere before.

"Well, you will have to stay with us, great bard. It's an honor to have one of the Companions of Everknight on hand to save the day." Gavin walked quickly to the man's side and elbowed him in the arm. "Are you here chasing the guy that did this?

"Sorry. I only... what now?" Karsis spun on the mayor with a speed that shocked the pudgy man and gazed at him with those eyes, the ones that had seen everything. "Did you just say that a man did this? What did he look like?"

Gavin sputtered under that stare. "Well... he had long white hair and... was dressed in traveling leathers like we've never seen before." He grew more confident as he realized that the bard wasn't going to kill him. "He got upset with the accommodations and the next thing we knew he was walking out of the burning tavern saying we deserved it."

Karsis stood staring at the mayor for what seemed like years. "Sorry, I haven't seen an elf in decades so it was a shock to hear one described." He patted the mayor on the shoulder like a parent reassuring a child and turned away. "Don't worry, I'll track him down." Karsis started walking, leaving them to call out after him. He ignored them, more interested in the rogue wizard as he walked into the setting sun.

O'ER HILL AND DALE

Jalafryn had been traveling for days and that man was *still* on his trail. He wasn't even trying to be inconspicuous—the guy was just walking along, playing that damned harp. Jalafryn had even thrown a couple of spells back that should've taken care of him, but they were countered before they even got there. He had used his *sight* to glance back at his opponent—what else could he call him at this juncture — but it wasn't an elf... it looked like a *bard*.

Jalafryn walked a little faster, not wanting to flee yet. He was more curious than worried, but he needed to get to the Misty Woods before night fell. He pulled his cloak a little tighter and thought of what else could be done. *Well, I've tried air, but he countered it. Then I tried using the heat around him to burn him, and he countered that... How about earth?* The dark hearted wizard turned and used his *sight* once more to get a good look at the ground around the man. The man came into focus, his small image growing larger as his *sight* got closer. "Ash'anti dir heath dosit kithin!" he called to the earth, asking it to encase the man. He was hoping to catch him off guard, but he wasn't prepared for the response.

The man following him shot up into the sky like a dragon, just as the earth around his feet rose up and tried to swallow him. He crested his upwards flight and then started to fall back down to earth, chanting loudly to the moisture and the air to combine.

Jalafryn spun and ran, but it was too late. A hailstorm of ice shards came roaring down, pelting and slicing into him as he tried to dodge. Jalafryn limped on as the man floated and touched gently down in a walk. To add insult to injury, the man put away his harp and took out a lute and began playing it as he followed. Jalafryn closed his eyes and chanted to the ether to heal his superficial wounds. The cuts and scrapes closed up and only the icicle sticking out of his hand was left. Curse that man! How was it that he had such control over the elements?

Jalafryn had trained for decades under the arch wizards in

Tir-Lanan, and even some of *them* would be hard-pressed to call down such ruin, never mind while free falling! *It's at least ten miles to the woods*, he thought as he turned and ran on, calling on the wind to speed him along once more. He couldn't keep this up for long, it still strained the body, but he could make it to the edge of the woods at least. He just hoped that the man couldn't go for long either.

Sprinting onward, Jalafryn risked a look back and saw the man actually gaining on him. *What manner of creature inhabits this being?* he thought as he sped over the high grass toward the woods. He put his head down and called upon hidden reserves, pushing on and trying to gain some ground. He needed to get into that forest; he was looking for a three-forked tree, and the mushroom ring he needed would be under it. He had researched over half of his life and delved into some very dark books for this moment and he wasn't going to lose the chance now. This ring was supposedly the very ring that the faeries used to leave the world, and once he found them, he would get his revenge on them for hiding away all these decades.

KARSIS WAS HAVING MORE fun than he should be having. He had been following the renegade elven wizard for a couple of days now and he wanted to gauge the dark wizard's ability. So far, he wasn't impressed, not even a little bit. He had countered everything that the elf had thrown at him—and easily at that. So easily that he suspected that the wizard was toying with him. So, he put away his harp and began to play his lute, hoping to infuriate him. When the elf took off at a run that could only be augmented with magic, he stowed the lute and cast his own magic. Karsis moved with haste, having the wind carry him along as well. He was starting to catch up to the wizard, and when he was close enough, he actually laughed aloud at the elf.

"Ho, ho dear elf–a little tired today?" Karsis asked, smirking to himself at the irony; he should be tired as well, but he was hardier than most. After all, he *was* Karsis the Bard.

The elf cursed. "Who is it that wants me so badly then, human?" he asked as he neared the edge of the woods.

"Me? Well, they call me Karsis. Mayhap you have heard of me?" he asked, slowing down as they neared the woods. A couple more minutes and then the dark wizard would've had some cover, not that it would help him. The elf probably thought he would have the advantage in the woods, as his kind could navigate through the trees with a ghost-like ease.

"Can't say that I have." The elf canceled the wind and stumbled to a halt at the first tree, his grace and nimbleness keeping him from hitting it full force. If he tried to run through the trees that fast, he would just be asking for it.

"Really?" Karsis tried not to sound genuinely surprised, but by the gods above, he was. "Well, if you had, you would be both impressed and worried," he bowed with a flourish, bending at the waist and drawing his sword in a blink getting closer to the elf. "Now. I don't know why you burned up that tavern, but if you have started doing things like that... well, then you have already invited the darkness into your heart. That sound about right?" Karsis watched the elf's face go from indignant to incredulous and Karsis had to smile at the effect. "Didn't think I knew about your magic or history? Well, poor elf, I'm full of surprises." As he spoke this last line, he lunged forward, slashing at the elf, just trying to gauge his response.

The elf danced back easily, scowling at the proclamation. He drew his own sword in a flurry of parrys and ripostes, yet didn't seem all too familiar with the thing, as he stumbled with the grip for a second or two. It seemed like he hadn't relied on a weapon in years, having used magic to solve everything.

Karsis swung his own sword with lazy strokes, having fun baiting the elf. Sooner or later, he would have to finish it. The elf upped the game and threw a tree at him using the air and Karsis had to dodge and roll to avoid it. It was on!

Back and forth they stomped and lunged through the woods, their breath coming in ragged, short bursts. Karsis thought he had him now, but the sound of rushing water came to his ears and the elf smiled.

Great, now what? Karsis thought as the elf slowly sheathed his sword and backed away with his hands in the air. "Let me guess. You surrender and now I'm going to have to spare you cause I'm one of the good guys. Am I close?"

The elf frowned. "Actually, I rather did think that. Isn't that something you humans do?"

"One—I'm not just *one of those humans*. And two—I don't." He lunged, plunging his sword into the man's chest and out his back, then spun around while pulling it back out again in a spray of blood, aggravating the wound. The elf gasped and fell back, clutching at the hole in his rib cage, then stumbled on a weird tree and fell into the water. Karsis ran to the edge, but the elf had slipped under. *Well hells! I wanted to make sure he was dead.* He had lost count of the times his foes had left him for dead, only for him to come back and save the day anyway. He hated that he might be doing the same thing.

Karsis looked down and saw a small ring of mushrooms hiding by the weird tree. The tree had three branches shaped like a trident or a fork, and the ring was so small that only his foot could fit in it. *I remember something about these things. They were supposed to transport you somewhere?* he thought, and of course he couldn't resist placing his foot in the ring, just to see. Karsis the Bard suddenly disappeared from the Misty Woods.

HIDDEN WONDERS

The Queen's Glade was beautiful this afternoon, with the rays of sunshine piercing through the canopy of the tall trees and the birds trilling their singsong melodies. Irilyn stretched her wings and yawned, truly enjoying this moment, as she had many such moments when she came here. She had received a special message from a mysterious source telling her to come.

You will meet the one who will bring the faeries together, the message had said, and she didn't recognize the writing. It was scribbled on leaf parchment and had been rolled up in vines. *Very mysterious indeed,* she thought as she strolled around her glade, waving the rolled parchment around like a wand.

Irilyn was the Queen of the Faeries and she looked the part. She was almost five feet tall with glorious gossamer wings and a very thin gown that just grazed the ground. Her feet were bare and her long, flowing golden hair seemed to move on its own as if there was a light wind.

"Ah I see you got mah note there, pretty lady." The voice was odd and had a tinge of a strange accent that kind of flowed exactly how rocks falling down a hill didn't. Hargon stepped out into the glade with his group of followers and gave a wicked smile.

"Ah, Hargon. I should've recognized that voice." Irilyn turned to face the korred and winced at the sight. The Hidden Vale was home to all creatures fey, but the korreds were the proverbial bottom of the water hole.

They were short, stocky creatures, towering all of three feet in height and their hair was a tangled mess of locks that hung in braided strands down to their feet. Instead of clothes, they wore the leaves they enjoyed hiding in... and that's all they wore.

"So why are you here and what do you mean *your* note?" Irilyn had a bad feeling at seeing others coming out of the forest and surrounding her.

"Well, that was the joke there, mah Queen. The note says that you will meet the one that brings us all together... and that would be me." He received a round of hoots and hollers from the other korred around the glade and mocked the queen by bowing to them. "You see, when you're dead, then I can proclaim myself king and unite us all under my auspesh... auspecias..."

KARSIS HAD APPEARED JUST OUTSIDE of the grove and had witnessed the exchange, barely believing his eyes. Faeries! He hadn't thought they were any still around. Now, however, he was irritated that these little beasts wanted to kill such a beautiful creature, and most people didn't survive irritating him.

"The phrase you're looking for is 'Auspicious rule.' And that won't work, you ragged little man." Karsis strode out into the glade with his usual flair, bowing slightly to the faerie Queen and drawing his sword in a blink as he spun in a circle to flourish his longcoat. "Now, who wants to be the first one to die horribly?" he asked those surrounding them.

Hargon shook with barely contained rage. He stomped right over to Karsis, waving his finger impertinently and motioning for all the others to join him. "Oh, I will try my hand mistah, and boy will you—"

Karsis whispered to the vines hanging from the trees all over the glade and gave them quiet direction as the korred came at him.

The thing's throat was gripped by fast-moving vines and squeezed until his eyes rolled into the back of his head. As that happened, Karsis spun, slashing one, then another advancing korred, scattering them to the forest as quickly as they had appeared.

"Well," he said, a little smirk on his face. "That wasn't as interesting as I had hoped." He saw that the queen was kneeling next to the dead thing on the ground, whispering something of her own, then holding an empty vial to the sky. When she was done, a fine mist rose from the ground and wound its way into the bottle, bringing with it sparkling motes of light. These motes danced around the bottle as the mist settled into a deep red liquid.

Irilyn smiled at him, then looked to the trees. "Go with peace, Hargon, and know that you will save someone someday, like you wanted to save all of our people, no matter how wrong you were." She got up slowly, her brow furrowed in thought. "Have you come to unite our people?

"I do not think so," Karsis started slowly, "but you never know what I can accomplish before supper," he said as he walked toward her, not wanting to spook her now that there was no immediate danger. "I am called Karsis the Bard, and I have absolutely no idea where I am at the moment." He smiled warmly and noticed that she was staring at him with an intense look in her eyes.

"Well. You are in the Hidden Vale, just east of the Misty Woods, once called the Mist'rien by the elves of old." Irilyn boldly skittered forward and grabbed his hand. "My name is Irilyn, Queen of the Faeries. Come with me to the Council of Trees and you will be named and welcomed, Karsis," she said, smiling and tugging gently, guiding him.

They ran among the forest, laughing and skipping and soon they arrived at the Council of Trees. How long it took them Karsis couldn't say, as the thick canopy occluded the sun at times and made the gauging of the hours impossible.

They entered a massive clearing filled with all manner of sylvan creatures. Faeries, pixies, sylphs, and dryads flanked the clearing, and in the center stood a massive tree. Its canopy covered the entire clearing, and the sun peeked through here and there in bright beams of light. Buzzing faeries of all shapes and sizes flittered above their heads, and a beautiful throne of gleaming wood sat at the base of the tree.

Karsis was in awe at the wonder before him. He had only heard stories of the faeries and was astounded that they still existed, and this close at that! They had left the world, some thought to go sideways to the moon. Others supposed that they went backwards into time, but on some level Karsis always thought that they just had hidden themselves away. *Gods above, I love it when I'm right,* he thought as they neared the throne.

Irilyn let go of his hand and ascended the throne, slipping on a crown of leaves. "Friends of the Trees, this man has saved your beloved queen and for that he is given the title of Defender of the Trees." She stopped, as the cheering outburst was almost deafening.

Once it calmed down a bit, Irilyn cleared her throat to silence the remaining faeries. "Now then, we will have a Revel in his honor and may we all remember that though leaves may fall, the roots keep us standing."

"The roots keep us standing." The crowd repeated back, as if in awe.

Irilyn turned to Karsis and handed him the vial that she had filled in the Queen's Glade. "Take this, wandering hero. For with it you may yet save a soul who was otherwise lost. It has the power to banish all ailments and restore any wound." She took off the crown and stepped down, unfolding her wings and smiling. "Tis going to be a merry Revel, come partake in our dancing and song, fair traveler."

Karsis laughed merrily, spinning and letting his longcoat fan out behind him for show. He was going to have fun here; he could just tell. Karsis pulled out his harp from the inside pocket of his coat and the faeries gasped in awe. The pocket was bigger on the inside and could store things without seeming to. And he had all manner of things in there.

While he was thinking about it, he placed the vial of... of... *What am I going to call this special vial anyway? I know, 'The Vial of Eternity.' Has a nice ring to it.* Playing a merry tune, he danced away after the queen and joined the rest of the faeries at the Revel.

SOMEWHERE IN THE MISTY WOODS

Jalafryn started losing consciousness. He fought to stay afloat, but he could feel his arms going numb already. He called, in broken sentences, for the water to keep him up, then concentrated on healing his wounds. It took him a long time of drifting with the steady current, but he did it. He finally pulled himself to the far bank and crawled up into the dirt. Then he was out.

When he awoke, it was pitch black and the forest noises were close. He still couldn't believe that the man stabbed him after he had surrendered — he was sure that humans fell for stuff like that. Jalafryn got up and started walking. He would go all the way back and look for that tree and find the mushroom ring. The man was gone for now and with him out of the way, he could get back to his sweet revenge. Once he found the faeries, they would pay for thinking that they could just hide away from the elves like that. It took him awhile, but he found the mushroom ring and with a tentative step, he too disappeared.

TO FINISH WHAT YOU STARTED

Karsis came out of a hole in a tree with a fuzzy mind and blurry eyes. He hadn't slept, but gods above knew what he *had* done last night. He had tried to stay away from the drink—he liked to be clear headed in strange places—but he was unaware that the food was just as intoxicating. Once he started to feel the effects he gave up and drank anyway. He looked back into the tree and saw Irilyn lying there with her wings tucked in.

I shouldn't have... but she was just too pretty to turn down, he thought as he reached up to feel what was on his head— something was itching and sticking him in the forehead—and found a thorny wreath set upon his brow. *Oh, that can't be good. I don't remember this at all.* He turned to see at least five faeries coming toward him carrying baskets filled with what seemed like fruits, breads, and strange mushrooms.

"Oh, you're awake! Did you rest well, my King?" The satyr carrying a basket of bread set it down to embrace him. "My name is Panilis and I have to say, I've never embraced a human before," he said, letting go and staring down at his hooves in embarrassment.

"Yes, I am. Yes, I did, and... wait, what did you call me?" Karsis distinctly heard 'king,' but he swore that Irilyn was a *girl* faerie. She had all the right parts; he knew she did, he'd checked. Twice. They couldn't be talking to *him*.

Panilis smiled and winked at him. "I said 'King'. You are, after the proclamation at last evening's revel, The King of the Faeries now."

Karsis turned on his heel and went right back into the tree. "Irilyn, I think something happened last night that I don't fully remember." He shook her gently and she came awake with a broad smile on her face. That was one of those smiles that said she knew exactly what had happened. Right then, he had missed something, he just knew it.

Karsis looked into her eyes and smiled. No, this wasn't all bad. He would stay for a while, then see what his duties were and find a way to adventure once more. It was what he did; just ask Tierra. The talented warrior of the Companions had fallen for him, but in the end he simply wasn't the settling-down type, and he had hurt her... used her even.

"Oh Karsis. Last night you married me and announced your love to the Trees themselves. You were given the Seal of the Trees as proof and agreed to stay here for a year and nine days." Irilyn got up slowly and put her arms around him. She seemed so at peace, yet she barely knew him. Then her face fell and she turned away.

Karsis saw her expression turn from bliss to worry in the space of a heartbeat. "What is it Irilyn? What are you thinking about that weighs so heavily on your mind?" he asked, genuinely concerned.

"I recently told my daughter that she would soon be queen and had to prepare for the time when I left this world." The queen took a deep breath and continued. "Nine moons ago, I received a dream vision that I would sacrifice myself for the faerie realm and my daughter would have to take over as queen. I fully expected it to be at the Queen's Glade, but you saved me from that."

"So, she took it badly?"

"Of course, she did! She always goes to cool off and returns shortly thereafter. I expected her to be here this morning, but something is wrong this time." Irilyn started crying as she moved past him. She stopped outside of the tree and bowed her head as the group of faeries moved aside and made way for their queen. "Karsis, my daughter hasn't been here in two days."

She walked away before he could interject and summoned

the faeries to her. She called for them to search, and asked for one in particular named Avaryn. But no one had seen him.

Karsis walked to the edge of the clearing, not wanting to intrude, and sent his *sight* up and out over the canopy. He was trying to sense a presence out in the forest, alone and scared. He didn't know what this faerie looked like, but he figured he would give it a shot. He *was* that good after all. Karsis sent his *sight* back toward the Queen's Glade and *sensed* someone... but it was no faerie. His eyes went wide at the realization of who he was looking at and he ran through the crowd of faeries, shouting for Irilyn.

"Irilyn! There is a dark wizard here! I have to go, though I will be back. You have my love!" Karsis rushed out of the throng of faeries and back the way they had come. He had an excellent memory when he needed it and he ran through the trees with an alacrity that would astound the fey folk.

QUEEN'S GLADE, HIDDEN VALE

Jalafryn stepped into the Hidden Vale with an astounded look upon his face. This was it; he was certain. Then he spotted a group of nymphs flee into a tree and he knew all his research had paid off. He closed his eyes and started chanting—trying not to cry as his emotions soared inside of him—and laid out the objects he kept in his neck pouch. Thank the gods above that it was enspelled to stay dry.

He placed the objects in a circle and sprinkled them with the powder made from the blood of a virgin elf—thank you, high king's daughter!—and chanted the forbidden ritual. *It* came just as he had read, with the ground shaking violently as its herald. The ancient books he had studied had said that the ether contained fragments of doorways into the in-between, where demons lived. There were two ways to summon them. One way was to bind them into an object, while the other was to just unleash them into this world, manifesting in their chosen forms. This second way was only hinted at and had never been tried, on the grounds that it was an extremely bad idea. But he had waited over one hundred years to try it. There was no turning back now. It was suicide to stop the ritual once it had begun, yet for his revenge, nothing else would do.

The being called Faerlythiv came into this world: long tendrils of black smoke snaked through the trees, winding around and around like it was trying to get a scent. It stopped and shot off like the wind. Jalafryn smiled and thought about the faeries being consumed by the demon and how it was fitting for their betrayal; they never should've abandoned the elves... or him. He came out of his reverie and turned when he heard footsteps coming through the trees.

There was the man who had run him through, already drawing his sword and lifting off of the ground and floating. "You're too late, bard—I've already released their doom." Then he had to dodge as the bard called to the branches to strike him.

"What have you done? They vanished long before you were even born, how could you hate them so?" The bard asked as he called to the air around him.

"I've had a hole in my soul ever since I learned about them... they should've been here for me, for all elven kind to laugh and play with." Jalafryn explained as they danced through the branches casting spell after spell at each other.

"You had a bad childhood so you're condemning them to death? Enough talk—your long life ends now!" The man shot a dead tree straight at Jalafryn and the dark wizard barely dodged in time.

This bard wasn't listening to him at all. *Maybe he didn't care that the faeries left us all behind, but I will never forgive them.* Jalafryn called to the ground below to rise up under the bard and knock him off balance, but the man just floated higher once more. Jalafryn knew he had to try something stronger. He soared up through the trees, climbing steadily. He would take this to the treetops and see how this human fared against the full power of the storms.

❧

KARSIS WASN'T sure what the dark wizard had unleashed, but he had to trust the faeries to hold it off until he could dispatch this insane elf. Who knew what else he could do? He saw the elf soar up through the treetops and smiled, asking the wind to bear him upwards as well. He knew who would win; after all, he was Karsis the Bard.

Karsis soared after him and grabbed a branch to pull himself out of the way as an electrical discharge blasted by him. It wasn't lightning, but it was the closest thing you could get with static electricity. He grabbed a handful of branches and asked the wind to send them at the elf. They rocketed out of his hand and splintered against the arms of the black-hearted wizard as he tried to protect his face. This elf was slow; Karsis knew how he could win this.

He called to the air high above to start swirling the clouds, then flew closer to the elf. He knew when nothing happened the elf would grow confident and assume the magic had failed; boy, would he be surprised! Another shot of electricity went by and Karsis called to the clouds once more, this time with urgency, and finally started to see some results. The spell he was casting took time but could be devastating. The wind was starting to move him back as he laughed and held up his sword to take the last bolt right on the blade, gritting through the pain. He had him now. "Goodbye, foul wizard," he whispered through clenched teeth.

"Well, well, it looks like your magic has failed you human, and now—" Jalafryn stopped, with a quizzical look on his face. His hair blew around in a twist as the wind dragged him along. He looked up as the wind picked up even more, finally realizing what the bard had done, and saw his doom coming straight down for him. The descending funnel slammed into him, pushing him down with the force of a tornado. Karsis had focused the wind downward instead of along its natural upwards pull, which took considerable skill and command. Jalafryn hit the ground at a speed that would make a dragon cringe and stopped moving altogether, his shattered body lifeless.

Karsis floated down silently as he dismissed the cloud funnel. He saw the wizard's body and asked the earth to swallow him deep. It took a little while for the ground to bring the body deep enough to satisfy the bard, and when it was done the sun was setting fast. Karsis turned and started the long walk back to the Council of Trees. *Well, that's one loose end tied up. Now I just have to stop whatever he unleashed,* he thought as he gathered his strength. That spell had drained him and the jolts of electricity hadn't helped either. He would need another Revel at this point—maybe two.

TO THE RESCUE

Lurien was young for a Faerie, over fifty winters this year, but she knew that this was the year that everyone would be watching her. She was a little over four feet tall with pale skin and bright eyes. Her long blond hair sparkled next to her transparent wings and she always had a bounce to her step. Lurien loved to giggle and flutter through the branches on a warm spring day, but all of that would be gone soon. Her mother, Irilyn, Queen of the Faeries, had told her that she would be leaving for twilight soon. Lurien would have to rule the Council of Trees and be in charge of and protect all of their people.

There were nymphs, sprites, dryads, korreds, satyrs, pixies, brownies, kelpies, nixen, selkies, and sylphs... and there were many different types of each as well. All of the faeries made up the Council of Trees and they would all bow to her.

She sighed and swatted another branch out of her way. She didn't want to be trapped on some dusty throne. Lurien only wanted to flitter and fly around and sing her songs to the birds. The day that her mother told her, she grabbed her slim sword, packed a few tiny wooden figurines, and flew away. She knew that the other fae would be fine. They would call out to the goddess Syll, who would protect them, while she flew away and had fun. *Then why do I feel so lousy?* she thought to herself

It had been two days since she had left and her mood had only gotten worse. Then the sound of crying came on the wisps of the breeze. Flying over a small pond, she followed the sound of weeping to a small bush. Lurien peered inside and saw a tiny sylph caught in some barbed vines. Taking out her sword, she cut the vines and watched the faerie fly away in haste.

"Wait!" Lurien called out, as the sylph hesitated and turned to her, as if waiting for a reason. "Why are you in such a hurry, little one?" Lurien asked as she flew up, sheathing her sword.

"Youhaven'theardyet?" The faerie sputtered so fast that Lurien could barely understand her, "Wemustsavetheprincessshesmissing!" The sylph flew off in a rush and almost ran into at least three more tangles. Lurien never even caught her name. Curious now as to what this little faerie was saying—she only made out a little bit of the words and 'princess' was one of them—she flew back the way the faerie must've come, retracing the trail of broken branches and debris. It took a turn of the sun before she arrived. What she saw took the wind from her wings.

WESTERN REACHES, HIDDEN VALE

Liana, the sylph that had been caught, was a tiny faerie with gossamer wings, curly hair, and a ton of energy. She was flying through the forest after being released from that horrible tangle and was searching for the missing princess. Her queen had told them to go find her, and Liana couldn't go fast enough. She loved quests!

She paused as she heard a strange noise coming from the tree line. Curiosity got the best of her, as it always did, and she flitted over to see what could be making the noise. She peeked out from behind the tree and her little eyes widened. A unicorn! Liana couldn't contain herself—like she ever could.

"Ohmygoddessohmygoddesslookatyou!" She flew out and circled the great creature's head four times before slowing down to really look at him. He was huge, and also stuck in a huge pile of mud...slowly sinking. "Uh oh, how'd you get in there? Oh yeah, you can't talk. That's okay, I'll talk for both of us!" She giggled a bit and landed on his back, petting his mane and humming a tune. *Where is that tune from? I can't remember. Was it...*

Little one, focus please.

Liana jumped up, beating her little wings and looking everywhere at once. She had heard that in her head, and didn't know what it was.

Calm down little one, the voice said once more. *It is I, the unicorn. My name is Avaryn, and I need your help.*

His voice sounded just like she imagined a unicorn would sound like... rainbows and candy. "Hello Avaryn. Hey the queen told us to look for you too!" she said, then frowned. "Wait, what can I do? I'm just a little thing." She circled his head again, landing once more on his back. "Oh, I know, you're stuck! I'll help you get out then we can... then what? Oh well, we'll figure that out later." She flew straight up into the branches and looked around to see what was near them. *Ah-ha! Vines.* She started tugging on the many vines, really wishing she had a slim sword like most other faeries, but she wasn't big enough.

WHAT IS YOUR NAME, *little one? So that I may address you.* Avaryn tested the strength of the quicksand he was sinking in again, just slightly, and it still held him tightly. He didn't like to let others know that unicorns could get trapped so easily, but he could not fail. He looked up to see the little sylph struggling with the vines and shook his head. He hadn't seen those, and now he felt silly.

"My name? Me? Oh, I'm Liana, and... these... are... hard to... move!" With a snap, the vines gave way and coiled around Avaryn's head. "Ha! I did it!" She flew down and started wrapping the end of the vine around the great unicorn's neck. "Now I'll tie it to a tree branch way up there..." She sped off like a shot, and looped the vine over a big branch and zipped back down, stuffing the vine into Avaryn's mouth. "And poof! Just pull!" She zipped around in a circle, proud of herself, and laughed happily, dancing from sunbeam to sunbeam. "Why did you get stuck in that mud anyway?"

Avaryn pulled hard, feeling the vines tighten around his powerful neck. With the vines holding him up, he could pull his legs free, one at a time. *I was searching for the missing princess when I came upon a dark energy. I tried to stop this foul being, but not before the darkness drifted off into the forest.* With two legs out, Avaryn climbed the rest of the way out of the quicksand, and pranced a bit, getting the feeling back into his legs. He neighed loudly, rearing up and stomping most of the mud from his hooves. *Now Liana, bravest of the sylphs, we must ride to save the queen!*

"Me?" Liana's face lit up at being called brave. "I'm going to ride a *unicorn!?*" She yelled, then took a breath. It didn't really help. "I'mcominghurryletsgo!" She flew onto him and kicked her little feet into the side of his neck, doing absolutely nothing except to make Avaryn smile.

Avaryn neighed and took off, galloping in the direction that he saw the ancient darkness drift off into. He had never seen anything so... evil. It was like the very essence of hatred and pain. After galloping for a full turn of the sun, following the trail of cold lifeless faeries discarded on the unforgiving ground, Avaryn could see it. As if it was aware of him the coil of darkness sped up.

Hold on Liana, I'm going to teleport to catch it. He could only do this once every day, and had to wait until now since he used his power already before getting stuck; it couldn't have come back at a better time. He gathered his energy and *poof!* he was ahead of the dark thing. He lowered his horn and pierced the tendrils of darkness, but to no avail. It kept flowing right around him, dragging at his very soul as it did. Avaryn danced away before any true harm could be done, almost hearing something like a whisper, a beckoning evil within the tendrils.

"Avaryn, look at it go right around the trees! Why doesn't it just go through them?" Liana asked. She grabbed a dead branch and snapped it off, flying at the darkness, curiosity written on her tiny face. She stabbed at the flowing tendrils with her improvised sword and it wailed in agony, like some sort of tortured soul. In the blink of an eye, tendrils lashed out and smacked the little faerie, sending her flying head over heels back to Avaryn.

The unicorn caught her in his teeth and flung her behind him. The darkness sped up even faster, shooting away through the forest toward the court. Avaryn could sense that it wanted to consume him, yet it wanted something else first... he felt the touch of dread creep along his spine. The queen! *Liana, grab bark as we pass the trees and wrap my horn with it, we've got to catch it before it reaches the queen!*

She did what he asked, and every time they passed a tree the little faerie reached out and snatched some bark, molding it to the shape of his horn carefully and tying it with scraps of vine. They had been chasing it so long that she lost track of time. Then they heard the collective gasp as the darkness reached the court. Avaryn neighed out a challenge through the forest, a challenge of courage and hope.

COUNCIL OF TREES, HIDDEN VALE

Lurien stared into the clearing of the Council of Trees. There, at the foot of the queen's throne, were hundreds of faeries, all of whom were listening to her every word. The queen was standing, addressing the faeries with a serious look on her face.

"And finally, the fate of Avaryn the unicorn is *still* unknown. He left to find the princess two days ago and has not been back since; I fear him lost." A collective gasp ran through the many faeries. Irilyn raised her hands, calling for quiet once more.

"I have to believe that the dark wizard Karsis looks for is the cause. We must find my daughter and Avaryn." The queen broke then, sobbing quietly while trying to keep her composure, and finally sat down heavily with a wave of her hand to dismiss the faeries.

Lurien was ashamed. She never thought that her mother would miss her that much, nor imagined that all of those faeries would care enough to find her. And Avaryn missing! She couldn't take it. Lurien flew out in a rush and embraced her mother, crying, "I'm so sorry mother, I flew away, I wasn't captured or anything. It's all my fault, I never meant to hurt anyone."

Before anything else could be said, a gasp went through the crowd as a darkness came rushing into the court. A being made of dark tendrils and horror incarnate rose up and flew at the queen with a hunger that all in attendance could *feel* in their bones. Lurien was terrified. As it drew near, the queen spun to shield her daughter, drawing her own sword.

"Face me, darkness unnamed, for thou shall have no power in this glade!" Irilyn shouted above the growing tumult of the panicked faeries. The being rose in eerie quiet, the faeries stunned silent waiting for the dreadful outcome. The queen looked ready to die for her people, and somehow it seemed one of those perfect moments.

Yet, on the wings of hope came a neighing over the leaves, a charge of courage and love. Avaryn crashed into the court as debris flew from his mud-stained coat.

A tiny faerie hung from Avaryn's long mane. "Use wood my Queen! It is harmed by *wood*!" she shouted, her tiny voice echoing above the quiet of the terrified faeries.

Avaryn slammed into the darkness and Lurien saw that his horn had been covered in bark. The thing wailed and writhed, trying to escape the horn, but the unicorn danced after it.

The faerie princess, terror forgotten in the face of courage, spun and grabbed a staff from Panalis, the satyr, and leapt out at the tendrils writhing in front of her mother. Lurien swung the staff down in perfect timing—the unicorn's horn pierced the creature once more, slashing through the darkness and leaving a great wound.

She stood there, gasping, as the darkness wailed, slowly melting into the air. Lurien, with her now blackened staff. Having protected her people, she finally understood that such responsibility was never a burden, but instead a privilege. She smiled at the gathered faeries and watched as they slowly went down to one knee. Her confusion turned to a knowing smile as she felt her mother place the crown of leaves upon her head from behind.

EPILOGUE: AND SO IT ENDS

Karsis walked into the Council of Trees to see Irilyn embracing a smaller faerie that now wore the crown. *That could only be her daughter,* he thought and before he could continue, a presence drew his gaze. There, standing impossibly regally, was something that shouldn't even exist: a unicorn.

"Well, isn't this lovely place just *full* of surprises," Karsis said to no one in particular as he strode over to meet the magnificent beast. Karsis had never seen one in person, and since they had supposedly disappeared centuries ago, it was a miracle that there was one in front of him. He bowed once he got within twenty feet and spread his arms out wide to show that he meant no harm.

I know you mean no harm. My name is Avaryn and I thank you for ridding the forest of that wizard, Avaryn said, bowing his head.

Karsis blinked and tried to keep his face neutral. The voice was in his head, despite his best mental shields. "Anything for the faeries," Karsis said, bowing low himself. "I hope you only speak in my mind, and don't actually venture too far inside?"

No, I don't invade anyone's thoughts. Though I can sense that you aren't exactly human, nor even truly fae...you are an odd being. Yet fear not, your secret is safe with me. I know what you did for this realm and you forever have my gratitude. Avaryn pawed the ground in acceptance and lowered his head to the would-be king of the faeries.

Karsis laughed despite the revelation. He had gained

another ally at least. "Why thank you, Avaryn, and I appreciate your silence. No pun intended." He smirked at the great beast then walked toward Irilyn who was now looking at him with a smile as she hugged her daughter.

"I have returned; the wizard is no more. I also see that you all took care of that awful darkness that he unleashed." Karsis's smile widened as a little faerie came flying out of nowhere to buzz around his head.

"Heywhoareyou?" Liana asked, as she tried to land on his shoulder and failed miserably. This one was a bit too excited for her own good. "I'm Liana and I'm a hero. Are you the newkingofthefaeries?" She had started off nice and slow, but ended in a fever pitch.

"Why yes, Liana, I guess that I am," Karsis said, glancing at Irilyn for her subtle nod of acceptance. He liked this excitable little ball of squeak and as she flew around him, he couldn't help but laugh wholeheartedly. Turning in a quick circle to fan out his long coat, Karsis struck a pose and stared at the queen and her daughter.

"So. This must be your daughter," Karsis surmised, as he came closer, hoping Liana wouldn't accidentally fly into him. He realized that the gathered faeries were all crowding around, trying to get a better view.

Lurien gazed upon him with wonder, almost like she had never beheld one of his kind before. "Yes, and apparently I'm the future queen as well. My name is Lurien and you must be the famous Karsis we just heard about." She smiled and held out her hand playfully.

"Infamous, actually, but yes." Karsis laughed and grabbed her hand, twirling her around in a silent dance. "You gave your mother quite the scare; I assume since you're all smiling together it's all settled?" He cocked his head to one side as he looked at her, trying to put her at ease.

"Yes, I... uh... had a change of heart," she unfurled her wings and beat them slowly, lifting up off of her feet and giggling. "So, I heard that you have the Seal of the Trees *and* you're now king?"

Karsis smiled and pulled the seal out of the inside pocket of his long coat. It was a round wooden disc carved with the symbol of Syll. Ironic, actually, since that was the Goddess of not only the fey, but magic in general.

"You mean this? Yes, though I'm not sure what it means exactly. The seal, not the king part. *That* I know what to do with." He let her go and she twirled up and away, among the canopy of giant tree. Then the bard heard Irilyn coming behind him.

Irilyn gracefully sauntered into his embrace and took over dancing for her daughter. "That is to verify that you were worthy of even having a Revel with the queen herself. Only one is ever given out, and if another Revel is ever had, the queen cannot participate."

The day was ending well. The faeries were saved and Karsis was having the time of his life. He couldn't remember the last time that he didn't care about what was next. *A year and nine days—that will go fast. Then I will be on my way,* he thought as he looked around at his new fey friends. 'King of the Faeries.' It had a nice ring to it. *Thank the gods above that I brought my favorite book; it could be a little slow without saving the land every day.* Karsis reflected on this and chuckled to himself. He was living with the faeries; life would never be slow again. *Might as well be living with a family of purple squirrels,* he thought as he spun and danced. And if he lifted off the ground with the other faeries now and again, having a little magic never hurt.

CITY OF EVERKNIGHT

7

KRISTMAS IN LYTHINALL
THE MAGIC OF THE SEASON

She shuffled through the snowy streets, careful not to slip on the ice. Her delicate hands cradled the bump in front of her, the little one inside almost done growing. Lenna Harn was due to give birth any day now and she still hadn't settled on a name. They were supposed to pick a name that suited both a boy and a girl, just in case, but she just couldn't settle on anything good. She stopped at the main crossways, looked up the hill at the grand castle, and smiled; she loved her city.

She had called Everknight her home now for three years, since moving here from the nation of Miran. She and her husband didn't have a lot of money, but they were doing alright for now.

"Morning, Lenna!" Miss Apperon called out from her doorway. The old woman was sweeping dirt from her store out into the muddy snow without even a coat on.

"Get inside before you freeze to death, Miss Apperon," Lenna chided, waving her finger like an old maid. She laughed at the face the old woman made and shuffled on, hoping to surprise her husband at work. She passed down a side street and marveled at the pretty trees that people were putting up for the holiday. With the deep snows coming, and the chill gripping the north, it was almost time to celebrate Kristmas.

Originally celebrated by the elves of old, Kristmas—which translates roughly as 'death no more'—was a celebration of the natural world surviving until the first snows. The tradition held that the trees freeze to hold off the plague that took their leaves, sleeping until the thaw. The beautiful coniferous trees, however, remained vigilant with their full beauty as a symbol of holding off death. The elves of old celebrated this for centuries, finding a tree in the forest and decorating it with string and colored gifts made by their children so it stood proudly, showing all the other trees that it had survived the grip of death. Now people went out and cut down select trees and put strings of bells, pretty beads, and whatnots around them. They displayed these in their windows or outside, for everyone else to see. It was fun to walk the streets and see how everyone decorated theirs differently. Sadly, there were only so many trees that could be cut down every year, so the king gave out passes in a lottery every autumn.

Next year I hope we win so I can show the baby their first tree, Lenna thought as she rounded the corner to her husband's work.

Pellen Apperon worked for the local cobbler, fitting shoes for the folk of the city and helping with repairs. It wasn't great money, but it was enough to keep a roof over them for now. Lenna saw the lights on in the window and started across the street, just as a wagon came around the corner going far too fast. Lenna looked up with a gasp, but there was no time to move. The driver pulled the reins and the floor brake, but the wagon was turning sideways in the snow and ice. Lenna turned her back to the wagon and tried to leap to the side, her arms wrapped around her stomach in desperation; her baby had to survive! She heard a loud crash and suddenly she was knocked down and covered by something heavy. Lenna screamed, fighting to get free, but stopped when a voice called to her.

"You're all right! Just crawl... Now!" a firm, but strained voice, commanded from above her.

She did just that, crawling through the slush and mud-colored snow—cradling her stomach as if it would burst any minute—while crying for help. Once clear, Lenna turned to look at what had happened and screamed in shock. The wagon had overturned and landed on a massive figure who had shielded her from harm. It was a Knight of Everknight!

The brave knight had covered her, taking the load on his back, and she could see that he wasn't going to be able to break free himself. His arms were braced on the slush and snow and he was shaking... he didn't have long before he was crushed.

"Lenna!" her husband, Pellen, called as he raced across the street. "By the gods, are you all right?"

'Help him... please," Lenna stammered as tears streamed down her face. She pointed to the beleaguered knight with a shaking arm. Other men were coming now too, but the wagon was laden with iron, pressing down upon him. Try as they might, they couldn't budge it enough to get the knight free.

"Get... her free," the knight said, his limbs trembling with effort. "I've done my service." He was so consumed with the effort that he couldn't see that she was safe.

"I thought I taught you better than this, Knight Barris," a new voice said. The woman was built slender, but had packed that slight frame with every possible ounce of muscle. "You're not done until *I* say so."

The woman bent down and grabbed the wagon as the others rushed to help once more. Seemingly without their help, she lifted the wagon on one side and held it there. "Get him free," she said in a calm voice. It didn't even seem like the strain bothered her. Once the men had the knight free, the woman tossed it over, the wheels breaking as it righted itself, sending iron bouncing all over the road.

"High General Carana, forgive me," Knight Barris said, bowing to her despite his pain.

Carana smiled and cuffed him on the back of the head lightly. "It's fine. Just don't go giving up on me again," she turned to Lenna and walked over, her hardened visage softening at the sight of her belly. "Is the little one all right?"

Lenna, tears falling freely, hugged the high general, sobbing into her shoulder. "He saved me... saved my baby."

"Well, I hope so," Carana said voice heavy with sarcasm, "It *is* his job after all."

Pellen walked over and clasped arms with the knight, careful not to hurt the brave man. "Thank you, Knight Barris. I owe you everything."

"Nonsense, but a hearty meal would be fine once I'm better." Barris said, winking at Lenna.

Carana went her own way, calling for clean up on the road from some of the soldiers on duty as Pellen walked with his wife and her savior back to the guard station so the knight could get checked out by the healer on duty.

Lenna shook her head as they went, something just starting to find its way into her mind. "So, Knight Barris, how did you get to me in time? I was alone in the street, I swear," Lenna said as they arrived at their humble home.

"Well, I was riding by when I saw the light on at the Cobblers. My boot has a torn stitch and I thought since I was here..."

Lenna smiled and looked up to the sky, eyes closed and

praying to Davalar, god of protection. *It was a holiday of miracles after all,* she thought as Knight Barris bid them farewell and they started home. *And I now know what I will name the baby,* she thought, looking up at the castle once more. *And I pray that young Barris finds his own path in this great city.*

STREETS OF EVERKNIGHT

8

ALONE IN DARKNESS
THE STORY OF SPROUT

His black boots clacked across the gold tiled floor as he sauntered into his throne room. Ran'cian Ashren was the sorcerer king of G'harr and all that he surveyed was his to play with. He so liked playing with his toys, even when sometimes he broke them. *Especially* then. He spun lazily, letting his golden cape flitter out behind him as he sat down on his throne to the petrified looks of his court. Straightening his white silk doublet, he scanned the room and made everyone instantly uncomfortable. He was late, as usual, but not a soul here would say anything about it.

"How fares the day, good Jalren?" Ran'cian asked, speaking directly to his steward and reveling in the slight jump the man made when he heard the deep voice. Ran'cian brushed his long black hair out of his rugged face and laughed a little at the old man's nervous eyes.

"Everything is running smoothly, your eminence. Not a complaint in the last three days." Jalren bowed as he talked, shying away from the deep, ice blue, eyes of the king. "Is there anything that your eminence would like to go over with the court sire?"

"I assumed that today was the day the Merchants Guild was going to try and get more assurances out of me, but I do not see them in attendance as yet." Ran'cian lounged back and crossed his legs, waving his hand and commanding the wind to bring him his goblet. The golden goblet lifted off of the table next to him and floated slowly into his waiting hand. He sipped the dark, elven wine contained in the goblet—heated to his specifications, as usual—and used his *sight* to look out past the room and across his glorious city.

Most sorcerers couldn't use their magical *sight* through buildings, but he wasn't just any ordinary sorcerer. Ran'cian pushed his *sight* all the way to Merchant's Way and saw the group of guild masters hurrying down the packed street. The king frowned and brought his *sight* back, sitting up straight while sipping his wine.

"Guards, go and meet with the Merchant Guild masters and bring them to my private quarters. They are coming down Merchant's Way and they have made this court wait." No one brought up the fact that Ran'cian had also made the court wait and that was how he liked it. "Take their weapons and detain them until I find the time to deal with them personally."

"It will be done sire," Braslen, the Captain of the guard, said. He was an older man, almost in his sixties, but very loyal. He and his guards hurried out, brandishing their weapons the minute they left the doors.

"Lord Ran'cian, do you think that is wise?" the voice echoed from the back of the court and at the sound of it, the entire room went silent. Manoah Toulon was an old noble and a favorite of the court, and it shocked everyone in attendance that she obviously had lost her survival instincts. She glared at them all in open defiance. She obviously thought herself important and that there would be no retribution from the king.

"My dear, I do, indeed, think this is wise. However, one

cannot say the same thing about your outburst." Ran'cian stood and strode out onto the floor, his regal bearing in full force. Nobles fell back, scrambling out of the way like panicked mice and soon the only one left was Manoah. At ten paces he commanded the air to his bidding.

"Obren fra, hadar dosit m'ren ubel!" She flew upwards and tried to scream, but it came out a strangled yelp more than anything with the air rushing past her. Ran'cian held her in the grip of his power and smiled. He looked around then, at the horrified faces of his noble subjects. No, they would never feel this bold again. With an audible snap, Manoah's neck was twisted around and he released the air, letting her body hit the ground with a sickening thud. "Send a message to House Toulon. They will want to bury her before she starts to smell." He laughed at his own dark humor, and the court nervously joined him.

MOANING HILLS, NORTHERN G'HARR

Meanwhile, about one hundred miles northeast of the G'harran capitol, two people were making their way through the wilderness. The sun was getting low and they weren't even close to their destination. Belin and her lover Harvon were on the run and if they were caught it would mean certain death.

Belin was short and very beautiful, with shoulder length blond hair and hazel eyes that could sparkle in the rain. She was one of the sorcerer king's concubines and had fallen in love with a serving boy. The two lovers didn't have a lot of time to spend with each other, but Harvon had some training in minor magic —enough to sneak in to see her now and again—and, of course the unthinkable had happened; she had conceived the king's child.

It sat there in her belly, kicking even now, and Belin couldn't help but smile, despite the dire circumstances she found herself. "Hold on little one. Let's get safe first, then we can enjoy the kicking."

"She giving you a stomping there, Belin?" Harvon quipped as they plodded on through the brush of the low hills. They didn't dare risk traveling the road, in case they were finally missed and the guard came after them. Her lover led the horse that she was riding and stepped over another bush with his short legs. He was all of five feet tall and weighed almost ten stones. Harvon had shaggy black hair and blue eyes—and most certainly didn't belong in the outdoors. He had grown up in the castle of the sorcerer king and learned to serve him from very young.

He would've gone on serving him too, if it wasn't for these damned hazel eyes of mine, Belin thought as she smiled, thinking of the day they met. She was about to comment on that very day when a horn sounded behind them in the distance. "Is that...?"

"I don't know, maybe. Just hold on." Harvon awkwardly jumped on the horse behind her and kicked it to make it go faster. The horse sped off, more from boredom than obedience, and soon they were flying over the desolate hilly terrain. They had another fifty or sixty miles before they would hit Everknight, the capitol of Lythinall, and there they could hope-fully blend in and find solace.

HIDDEN AWAY

She crept down the alley in the early morning light and pulled the hood down lower as she neared the street. People were already bustling to and from their humdrum lives, unaware that she was looking at them. Illiyana Ana'ashlyn had watched this very scene for almost fifty years and still these people confused her. The poor, the sick, and the lazy; they all resided in this glorious city together with the rich, the able, and the haughty. Illiyana was one hundred and seventy-two this very morning and she still looked like she did at thirty: just one of the many benefits of being an elf.

She counted to three when someone walked past and then blended seamlessly in behind them, as if she were there the whole time. Weaving in and out of the sparse crowd, she made her way to the alley behind the bakery and then took her hood down. Her white hair fell softly around her pointed ears down to her slim shoulders, and her silver eyes sparkled in the morning sun. She was almost five feet tall and her slight frame was very lean but rugged. If anyone versed in fighting saw the way she stood, they would know she was dangerous, but she was alone. She was always alone. It had been her choice, all those years ago, but it was better than the alternative. Anything was better than the punishment she would've faced for being born without magic.

No one had really seen elves in over two hundred years, not since they had retreated past the Snowpeak Mountains and never returned, locking themselves away in isolation... yet here she was. The problem was that she had to stay hidden, mainly because she had no idea what these humans would do if they saw an elf. She still remembered her homeland and missed the cobbled roads and marble pillars that decorated most of the buildings. Trees growing in the streets, birds singing in low hanging branches... But her lack of magic had taken all that away from her.

Every elf is born with a connection to the elements; magic was in their very blood, yet Illiyana had been born without any thread of it. Ask as she might, the elements ignored her every time. It was unheard of, unspeakable, and marked her as an abomination. So, before her noble house could drag her in front of the city and call for her death, she left in the night and fled. She had found her way to this blossoming city, called Everknight, and had been here ever since.

Now, instead of sylvan glades and birdsong, all she had was filth-covered dirt alleys and drunks asking for coin. Somehow though, it was home. She dug out a half-eaten cake and sat down to eat her breakfast. *Humans...why do they throw away food when their own people starve in the cold?* she thought as she ate the sweet confection. She was lost in her silent contemplation when she heard the commotion; that was when her life changed forever.

GOODWAY ROAD, EVERKNIGHT

Belin and Harvon had made it to the city, but he didn't look so good. Belin smiled at him and kept her worry to herself. He had taken an arrow in his back five miles south of the border; as they crossed into Lythinall, the guards chasing them stopped and turned back, unwilling to cause a dispute without their precious sorcerer king's permission. Unfortunately, the damage had been done.

By the time they reached the city, Harvon was so bad that the healers didn't know what they could do. Of course, they weren't true healers; they were just the herbalists that helped the poor and needy.

"Hold on Harvon, we'll get up to the castle and they will fix you up," Belin said as she nudged the horse down the road, but they didn't get very far.

"Hey there missus. My name is Spook and it looks like you need our help," a man said, smiling with his missing teeth; it made her skin crawl and put her at ease exactly like a drawn sword would. Spook looked her over and then at Harvon, her lover barely staying in the saddle. The creepy man reached for the reins and tried to pat the horse, but it pulled away.

"No thank you," Belin said. "We have business at the castle. Good day to you, kind sir." She tried to be polite, but fear edged her voice. Belin pulled the reins and tried to go around him, but he reached for her as she went by.

"Now see here, Missus. We don't—hey, come back!" Spook pulled her hand, dragging her from the saddle and sending her tumbling down to the road face first. More importantly, she hit stomach first. His eyes went wide with horror at what he had done, backing away as Harvon slipped off the horse and came around screaming for her, his face a mask of pain. His eyes seemed to focus when she screamed and he stumbled to her side.

"The baby!" Harvon cried out as he helped her into an alley away from the traffic of the bustling street. He sat her down so he could look at her.

Belin could still feel it kicking, even after that fall, and there was a puddle underneath her. Then she felt a warmth on her shoulder and thought that something was leaking on her. When she turned, she saw that Spook was standing over her love with a knife, Harvon's blood covering her like a last goodbye.

"*No!*" she cried out, but the man grabbed her lover's coin purse and left her, running into the crowd. She couldn't move out of the alley and she knew that it was time; the baby was coming and there was no one to help her.

ILLIYANA ARRIVED in the alley just as the woman hit the ground. She hadn't noticed the woman was with child and by the time she did move to help, the thief had already slashed the man's throat. She was about to chase the murderer down, until she saw the woman was holding her stomach and looked to be in trouble. She couldn't leave this woman alone.

"Easy now, I'm here to help," Illiyana said, covering up with her hood so no one noticed her lineage. "What's your name?" The woman's face was a mask of stone as she tried to concentrate on one thing at a time; this was a strong girl.

"I'm Belin. Please... can you help me?" the woman pleaded

"I've helped deliver babies before. A long time ago, but I've done it," Illiyana confessed, moving Belin's legs and trying to get her comfortable.

"Thank the Gods above, I... can't..." The poor woman couldn't speak anymore, the pain was too much. Belin's strength seemed to go out of her, but thankfully they were far enough in the alley that most people just ignored them.

"It's alright. Just hold on and try to breathe." Illiyana would've called out for help, but she knew better. In this part of the city people ignored business that wasn't theirs. Besides, no one wanted to walk in on a murder scene, lest they get questioned themselves.

The baby started to move more and more, like it knew it was time, but it wasn't coming. Illiyana tried every trick she knew to turn and help the child down to no avail. *It must be stuck sideways,* Illiyana thought, knowing that sometimes that could happen.

Sobbing with grief and fear, the woman looked up at her and narrowed her eyes in determination. "Cut me open." It wasn't a question, and there was no room for debate.

Illiyana stared at the woman, mouth agape. "I... what?" A part of her knew that it had to be done—the woman wasn't pushing at all anymore, her strength seemed to vanish in the space of a heartbeat. Illiyana nodded and swallowed hard; you didn't live on these streets for as long as she had, without resolve. "All right."

Illiyana pulled out her knife and wiped it clean. *I wish I had magic to heat the blade, but I'm deficient; I can't even help this woman.* Her thoughts were dark this morning and it didn't look like they were going to get any better by tomorrow.

"Promise me you will look after my baby." Belin was getting weaker, her pale visage almost deathly. "I'm bleeding inside, I think... got to hold on a little longer," she mumbled.

"I don't... a baby though?"

"Promise me!" Belin snapped to a state of awareness, her eyes wide, then started to fade once more.

Illiyana sighed and lowered her hood, revealing her heritage to the dying woman. She could see Belin's shock in the woman's face. "On my honor, as an elf of Tir-Lanan, I do swear lady." Illiyana nodded at the grateful smile on Belin's face and closed her own eyes for a moment to gather the strength it would take to do this; she was horrified.

Illiyana took a deep breath and sliced deep across the woman's belly, just higher than the kicking lump. Praying that she didn't cut too deep, Illiyana set about getting the child free of the mother as the life ebbed out of her. Pulling out the baby was a chore and took longer than she wanted, but soon, bloody up to her elbows, she held a crying little girl. Slicing the cord and putting her on her mother was instinct, and miraculously, the woman hadn't passed yet. "It's a girl."

"Lhana... oh my little... an...."

Illiyana shed quiet tears, but knew they had to leave. By now someone would've at least told one of the knights about the murder and they would be here before long. "Come with me Lhana, let's get you warm," Illiyana said through tear-streaked sobs, cradling the baby and wrapping her in her cloak. She disappeared into the city and reflected on her new charge. *What have I gotten myself into?*

THROUGH THE YEARS

For the first few months, Illiyana had her skilled hands full. Not only did she have to scrounge for herself, but now she had a tiny mouth to feed as well. Add in the fact that this tiny little human would make noise at the most inopportune times and it was a wonder that Illiyana ever scavenged *anything* for them.

She had a small hovel set up where two streets dead ended in a dark end of the city, hidden on a second story roof of a potter. She was always warm in the winter months, and the smoke helped hide her hovel from prying eyes on the other rooftops. Her lithe, elven form was extremely agile, so climbing down a rickety ladder with a child was no problem. Stealing with one, however, was a bit of an inconvenience.

The months passed slowly, as her attention was constantly brought back to caring for this little mouth. Illiyana had taken to calling her just that as well, and she started to consume more and more milk as the months ran on. It wasn't until the fourth month that she noticed something was going on in the streets of Everknight. Word was going out that strangers were looking for something and Illiyana was smart enough to know it had to do with Lhana's mother.

One sweltering summer day, after feeding Lhana some mushed rice and milk, she saw what could only be G'harran soldiers walk past her in the street. Illiyana recognized the black, stylized cut of the cloak, and the wicked looking dagger at their side. She pressed on, then double backed and trailed them from afar.

"Now, Mouth—try to be a little quieter, as I really don't want to deal with these two while holding you," Illiyana said softly to the snug bundle in her arms. As usual, the baby didn't respond or acknowledge her in any way. Turning down the main thoroughfare, she spied them at the bakery talking to the proprietor and motioning to their daggers. *Typical southerners. Threaten and bully the weak to get what they want. I should be grateful that they aren't sorcerers,* she thought as she crept behind a stack of barrels across the street. Wizards were one thing, but sorcerers were an abomination to nature.

Elven wizards cast magic by asking nature's elements to help them, or assist them. Human sorcerers didn't want the years of training to be able to do that. Instead, when they were taught magic centuries ago by a traitorous elven archmage, they found that they could force nature to obey them, commanding the very elements and destroying nature around them in the process. Sorcery was learned much quicker as it didn't rely on the elements wanting to help. Illiyana shuddered in spite of herself. Though she didn't have magic, that didn't mean that she didn't respect it. She watched them turn away and the store owner visibly let out a breath of relief. Then it happened; the baby cried out.

TANTRAL ROAD, EVERKNIGHT

The two men followed the woman with a baby through the twisting streets of Everknight. They were here looking for the runaway concubine and the sorcerer king's child, and those two fit the description. Vellis nudged his companion, Cres, and they walked apart, trying to flank her. They were staying back far enough back so as not to spook the woman, yet couldn't gain any ground at all.

The two men were twins, both standing about five feet with dark hair and eyes. Average on all accounts, they were the sorcerer king's favorite trackers, known for their ability to not stand out. They came together and turned into an alley some five blocks later, knowing she turned down here but seeing no sign of the woman. Then they heard a baby cry further down the garbage strewn back street.

"Stay here, Cres, and make sure no one gets out," Vellis told his brother as he crept down the alley, following the sound. He turned a corner and saw the baby laying on a blanket, still wailing.

Foolish girl. Probably got spooked and fled, leaving this little one behind. Poor thing, he thought, approaching the blanket. Sadly, that was the last thought he ever had as the knife slid quietly across his throat deep enough to almost sever his head.

Cres cried out as he felt his brother's death, and rushed down the alley in a blind rage. Pulling out his daggers, he skidded to a stop as the woman turned, holding a pair of knives. One was still dripping blood all over the filthy ground.

"You should've stayed away," she said with a calm inflection to her voice.

"You will pay for that, girl," Cres growled, advancing with cold, methodical steps. He was still in control, despite seeing his brother's killer. He darted in as he got close, trying to take her by surprise, but she spun behind him, slicing his back and arms. The assassin cried out, more from shock than pain, and turned, swinging his blade in a deadly arc. It did no good. The woman parried the attack easily and actually laughed at him. It was then that he saw the white hair peeking out from under her hood and realized what he was facing. *Oh, gods above! She's an elf.*

The woman cut him twice, not deep but just enough to get

him to understand that he was outmatched. She had to be an elven blade master, a warrior trained with her weapons for decades; clearly she knew her daggers as intimately as any lover.

"What are you after?" she asked, spinning around him again, slicing his other arm. She danced back and deftly parried the next two attacks, as she moved in and sliced his chest and cheek.

Cres kept his silence, refusing to talk. He had to concentrate if he were going to escape this alive.

"Fine." She stepped back, feigning defense and when he shifted his stance, she lunged and took him in the throat and heart in two quick thrusts, burying her blades as deep as the hilt. As he lay dying, his blood soaking his ruined shirt, he saw the woman wipe her blades on his brother's cloak, grab the child and walk away. Cres could hear her talking as his vision faded to black

"We must be careful, young one. Next time they may have a sorcerer."

❧

OVER A YEAR WENT by and Illiyana saw no more G'harrans in Everknight. Now that the little one was bigger, she was *really* restricted to her movement around the city. At almost two years old, the girl was already talking, walking, and *hated* to be carried anywhere—pitching a fit that often drew unwanted attention.

The good news was that she could stay by herself for short amounts of time if sufficiently occupied. Wooden dolls, toys, and even insects, would keep Mouth docile for at least an hour, letting Illiyana go and get food for them both. Unfortunately, Illiyana also knew that as the girl grew older, she would be asking questions about why Illiyana looked different. As much as she hated the idea, she might have to leave the girl to her own fate sooner rather than later.

DESPERATE GAMBLE

Ran'cian ignored the table full of conspirators and stared out the window. He had tried to track down his lost child and that hateful wench and so far had come up with nothing. Well, not exactly *nothing*. He had tried using magic to trace them and learned two very important things. One, he knew that Belin was dead. Two, for some reason he couldn't *see* his child with magic, which was troubling.

The sorcerer king had tried sending assassins to track them down and was shocked when he learned they had been killed. Something was using powerful magic against him and he had no idea who—or what—it could be. The hard part was doing this without alerting Lythinall of his presence in their city. G'harr and Lythinall had a tentative truce after years of border skirmishes, and with what he had planned for the future, he wanted to keep this truce while he could.

"Damn politics," Ran'cian said under his breath as he heard the outward sigh from the table behind him. It sounded like the traitor from Lythinall that had joined their cause, so Ran'cian let the insult slip... this time. "Is there a problem?"

"No, not a problem, per se. It's just that I'm an old man and I was wondering if we were *actually* going to go over anything today before I die of old age." Othren Lawkland had come to G'harr from Everknight wanting to become a spy for Ran'cian. In trade, he had only asked to learn magic the way they did. Othren was the seneschal to the King of Everknight and had the position to cause a lot of harm when the time was right. The man was over sixty winters and had deep, knowing eyes; short, close-cropped hair, and a wit that was sharper than most swords.

"You walk a dangerous line, friend... but I do accept that I have become distracted of late." Ran'cian walked to the table and sat, folding his hands and smiling at the others who seemed genuinely shocked at the admission.

Ran'cian had called this meeting to discuss the newest plan: to raise a powerful elven wizard from the dead for their nefarious plot. What he *hadn't* told them was that they were also going to try and free an even more powerful being with her help. Somehow, though, he just couldn't focus.

Ran'cian held up his hand to stall their talk and waved over a guard. "Tell Suris Arn that I'm sending her on a mission and to come see me here." The guard saluted and left with haste. It had been three years since Belin had fled carrying his child and he was done playing around.

Suris was an accomplished sorceress and knew how to keep a low profile. If anyone could get in and out of Lythinall quietly, it was her. *Still, it's a gamble. Especially as we don't know what is keeping them hidden from my magic. But I will find my child,* he thought as he settled down and gave the table his full attention at last.

"I still say we keep going with the Lycanthrope trials," Denem Vas spoke up. He was a small man, with shaggy brown hair and wild, black, eyes. "We would have no need of raising this wizard if we had our own pack of wolvren to command." People around the table muttered about that distastefully.

A wolvren was twice the size of a large wolf, and had the temperament of a one-armed, blind beggar on an empty street. They were mean and cruel, and killed more for sport than food. The idea of changing into one was repulsive to most of the sorcerers seated at the table, but Denem seemed to have no shortage of volunteers.

"No, Denem—your trials are at an end. I don't mind losing sorcerers as much as I mind losing time. Set-backs cost valuable resources in that department." Ran'cian looked to the next man in line and smiled, but was saved from dealing with anyone else as Suris Arn came in the room.

She was only twenty-five winters but had a command of magic that marked her as an up-and-coming sorceress. She walked quietly over to his side, staring at the seneschal from Everknight with her piercing blue eyes. Othren shifted uncomfortably under her demeaning gaze and Ran'cian laughed.

Suris flipped her long black hair to the side and smiled down at her king. "You wanted to see me, my King?" She seemed intrigued as she waited for the details.

"Yes dear, I have a sensitive mission for you." Ran'cian waved to the rest of the table, giving the sign that the meeting was over for now. They grumbled and left, shutting the double doors behind them. "Sit and relax; you'll be traveling for a while without rest." He poured her a glass of wine from his own bottle and laughed as she raised her eyebrows. "What?"

"You never share your wine, ever. How bad is this mission?" she asked as she sat back and sipped at her drink.

Ran'cian poured his own glass and set the goblet down, sitting forward and folding his arms on the massive table. "I need you to get into Everknight and find my missing child. She disappeared three years ago and I can't find her with magic." He laughed as she raised her eyebrows again. "I know, that's the same reaction I had. *Someone* is hiding the child, and I have no idea who would be powerful enough to do that."

"What about Karsis the Bard?" Suris asked hesitantly.

"No. By all accounts he is in the far north at the moment, annoying someone else, thankfully," Ran'cian said with a scowl.

Gods above how he hated that man. He lifted his goblet and drank deeply, watching her mind work behind those calculating eyes. He knew she would rather risk death at his hands than go after Karsis.

"No—whoever it is, I have faith that you can handle them. I need you, because no one can know that you're there." He finished his wine and sat back again.

"Ah, the truce. Got it. I'll get in, find the child, and get back here without anyone there the wiser." She finished her drink as well and stood, bowing to Ran'cian and turning to walk away. She heard him clear his throat and froze. She looked back and smiled politely.

"Just so you know Suris... the child is more important than the truce. If you have to pick one, always pick the child. Understand?" Ran'cian saw her frown and knew that she was hiding her true thoughts. This was different for him, mainly because his long-standing goals were always more important than any life. He couldn't explain why, but this time was different. The sorcerer king watched her nod and hurry out, satisfied that now he would get results.

GROWING PAINS

Another nine months passed with a very wet spring in Everknight. Illiyana began leaving Lhana alone longer and longer—a little bit at a time—just to see how she did. No one had come around asking for the little girl since those two men, but that didn't mean whoever was looking for her had given up. Illiyana knew the stubbornness of the G'harrans from her history lessons.

She crouched above the hovel, watching Lhana playing with her dolls, and smiled. The girl was becoming self reliant; not totally, but better with each passing day. The little one had turned three winters and was talking with sentences, albeit short ones.

She should be getting hungry any minute now, Illiyana thought to herself as she looked over at her first big test for the girl.

It was a simple thing really: Illiyana had placed a garbage bin with food on top of it by the back door of the shop under the hovel. All the little girl had to do was get down the ladder and take the food back up. Illiyana smiled as she saw the girl look around twenty minutes later and start calling for her.

"Iya!" Lhana looked around and squinted at the sunlight coming in the makeshift window. "Iya, where are you?" She got up and went to the door and peaked out, frowning and stomping her foot.

Illiyana smiled at Lhana's attempt to say her name. It came out like "eee-ya," and was the cutest thing she had ever heard. She never corrected her—she liked her new nickname. She saw the little one notice the food down by the street, then she looked at the ladder. This was it.

Lhana toddled out and tried to step off. The sudden loss of balance made her pull back. Then she turned around and crawled onto the ladder, half slipping and holding on for dear life. "Help Iya!"

Illiyana winced and closed her eyes, fighting the urge to go to the girl. The fall didn't concern her, since she had placed a thick straw pile at the bottom of the ladder just in case. It was the desperate need to protect her that pulled at the elf's heart. But the girl needed to learn to fend for herself, and soon. *It hurts though, not going to her,* she thought as the little one got her footing and made it halfway down the ladder.

She wasn't going to pretend that this hadn't been the best three years of her very long life. Illiyana held her breath as Lhana lost her grip and slid down the last few feet, landing on the straw. The little one started crying and Illiyana was worried that the shop keeper would come see what had happened. However, after a couple of seconds with no one giving her attention, Lhana sniffed back her tears and crawled to the garbage bin.

The little one took the food and ate it right there in the alley, then crawled back up the ladder. It had worked—not like Illiyana had planned, but it was good enough.

Three months later, the tests had evolved into Lhana going down the alley, then around the block. Between tests, Illiyana taught her that she had to stay hidden from other people, and that shop keepers shouldn't see her either, lest they get angry. The little girl was very good at being quiet... but not so good at being invisible. Every time Lhana saw someone that had something nice, she would run over and tug at their cloak and tell them how nice it was. Illiyana would just hold her head in her hands.

The two were out on one of those trips right now, over at the flower shop. Illiyana told Lhana to sneak over and get a single rose from the front window. Illiyana watched as the girl scampered across the street, ducking under a carriage and around a noble with a dog without getting distracted. Lhana was doing well, until she found an elderly man with a cane.

ADDIE'S FLOWER SHOP, EVERKNIGHT

Suris Arn was walking down the muddy streets of Everknight, using her trusted eyes to scan each alleyway that she passed. All she knew was that the king's concubine had run to this city three years ago and had died. The likelihood that the child was still alive was marginal, except for the fact that someone was hiding her with powerful magic. That meant she was looking for a three-year-old and possibly a sorcerer with plans to usurp the throne of G'harr. She was just about to head back to her room at the inn when she froze.

There, in the street ahead of her, was a little girl and an older man. The man had an exquisitely threaded cane and was showing the little one the flowers in the window of a flower shop with such adoration that he seemed like a father figure.

Walking over to the side of the road, Suris found an alley and leaned back against the wall. When the man looked away, Suris launched a dagger and commanded the air to speed it to the target.

The man clutched his chest and stumbled back, blood flowing from the horrendous wound. The weapon was buried to the hilt, straight in the man's heart, and Suris smiled at her aim. The little one screamed and fled towards the opposite alley, leaving the man to lie in the road; now the girl's protector was gone.

Suris sauntered up to the old man amid the screaming people and pulled her dagger free with a smile. She cleaned it on the man's cloak and ducked away, her long black hair falling into her face. Suris looked up to the sky as she walked and whispered, commanding the ether to show her the child.

"Obren ethir, reva ea dost ilkith!" She felt the magic start to swirl around her, searching, then just fade away. She had been *sure* that the old man was the source. But clearly she was wrong.

By now chasing the child was foolish—she had a head start. *I'll wait and keep searching the area. She's bound to turn up again soon enough,* she thought as she blended into the growing crowd before the guard showed up. *Besides, I did learn that it is a girl.*

ILLIYANA SAW the woman and her heart sank. Taking the crying little one into her arms, the elf watched the assassin walk away then look up to the sky, mouthing words. She was a sorceress. That changed things. Illayna took Lhana back to their home and thought about what she was going to do next, how she was going to fight someone with magic when she had none herself. Lhana had to be on her own so they didn't draw attention; a lone child would draw less attention. With a deep sadness in her elven heart, Illiyana knew the time had finally come.

GETTING HER LEGS

She was alone again this morning. In fact, she had lost count of the days that she had been alone. She knew that it was hot, and that it was called summer, but that was all she could get out of the people that walked by her—or all that she could understand, that is.

People talked about all kinds of things when they didn't see her, and it was getting easier to not be seen. She still missed Iya though. She had looked everywhere for her those first couple of days, almost getting picked up by a man with metal skin.... *Nite, I think they called him,* she thought as she stretched the sleepies away. She hardly ever cried during the day anymore, mostly saving her tears for night as she was falling asleep. Sometimes she would even dream that Iya was there with her as she slept.

She got dressed and climbed down the ladder, skipping off to another day sneaking around the city. She had no real purpose, other than to learn the different streets and alleys. That, and it was fun to see all the people. She knew that two streets over was the flower shop, then three more to the new bakery. Across the street from that was the blacksmith and four streets over from there was that little place with the dolls in the window.

Her favorite, though, was the flower shop. As the sun went down each day, she would hunt for scraps out back in the garbage and decorate her hiding place with the flowers she would find. Her little room now looked like a flower forest, but they kept dying so she would need to replace them. After two weeks of sneaking fresh blossoms, she was stopped by a woman at the end of the alley. She almost bolted, until the lady held out fresh flowers.

"Wait, little one. My name is Addie," the woman said, holding out the flowers with a smile. "I've seen you here before. Do you want some more flowers?"

"I would love some!"

"What's your name little one?"

"I don't think I have one." Now that she said it, it did seem odd that she couldn't remember what she was called. *Didn't Iya call me something?*

"Well, I will call you Sprout, because of your love for flowers." Addie laughed at the girl's face. "Where are your parents?"

Sprout didn't know what to say to that. Iya was probably her parent, but she didn't know where she was anymore. "My parents were lost in a terrible storm," she lied. Better to keep people thinking that she had her parents taken away from her then to admit that she lost them. She faked tears and ran past the woman, smiling to herself once she was away. She headed out of the alley and into the busy street, but stopped when someone spoke to her. That's when the fighting started.

ADDIE'S FLOWER SHOP, EVERKNIGHT

Suris Arn had been scouring the city for weeks, to no avail. Oh, she caught glimpses of the girl, but she had learned the hidden ways quickly for one so small and could disappear without a trace. So, imagine her surprise when the little one dashed out of an alley right in front of her!

The little one was only three and a half feet tall and weighed about five stones if she was carrying two of them in her arms. The girl's short blond hair was dirty and her skin was a dark tan from being on the street all the time.

"Why hello there, little one," Suris purred, getting ready to command the very air to hold her in place. She never got the chance. Feeling a presence behind her, Suris spun and parried a knife that was coming in fast, then sidestepped another swing that came in almost faster than she could see it. It still drew a cut across her side, but it wasn't fatal.

"You will not have her, *gos,*" her attacker said, calling Suris the elven word for filth. The woman wasn't holding anything back, attacking with a determination scarcely seen in most warriors, the raging emotions clear for all to see as they crossed her face. The woman spun again, slicing three times consecutively—high, low, low—scoring a hit on Suris's arm and thigh. Still nothing fatal.

Suris Arn knew she was in trouble though. She had faced sword masters in the past, but had never been surprised by one. With no time to gain any footing or defense, she actually had to think about flight. *And just when I found the girl too,* she thought. But her frustration was cut short when a guard came and tried to separate them by force of arms.

Suris spun around him, placing him between her and this wild attacker and for the first time she could really look at what she faced. The woman was heavily cloaked and covered, but she had white hair and a very good move set.

"Obren fra, leven la!" Suris yelled, commanding the air to leave both the guard and her attacker. Shock filled her a second time this morning when it floored the guard, but the woman remained untouched! Her surprise was her undoing, as both knives slammed into her chest, then pulled pulled back out in a spray of blood. The next moment she was looking up at the sky, unaware that she had even fallen on her back. She had just enough time to wonder, *When did the sun go down?* Then she thought no more.

❧

ILLIYANA DUCKED into the alley and sprang upwards, catching the roof of the flower shop and pulling herself over the edge. Thankfully both Lhana and the woman that ran the flower shop had fled at the sound of fighting. The elven blade master sat cross-legged on the hot summer roof and cried, letting all her emotion out.

Illiyana had been watching over Lhana all this time, even sitting with her at night and wiping her tears away once she was asleep. She knew she was doing the right thing, but it was *killing* her. Worse, though, was she had seen Lhana's expression when she had saved her. The little one didn't recognize her. The little girl she had raised as her own had raced away in fear, as if she was one of the bad people she had always warned about. It was these times that she hated her heritage more than anything in this cruel world. After a while she went and checked on the girl and saw that she was crying herself to sleep once more, crying out for "Iya."

GOLDEN PALACE, G'HARR

Hundreds of miles to the south west, Ran'cian paced in his throne room. Suris was late with her report and she was never late. He was excited that she had seen the little girl and was still tracking her; he had a daughter!

Then Ran'cian felt it. The pain exploded inside of him, like twin knives stabbing into his chest, and he fell to his knees in shared pain. He had linked himself to Suris when he knew she was close to finding the little one, just in case she chose to betray him, and was unprepared for the shock of her death.

Ran'cian felt the life ebb from his sorcerer assassin as he slowly gained his feet, leaning on his throne for support. *I'll have to go myself at this rate,* he thought as his frustration mounted. No. He couldn't do that—in fact he couldn't even spend any more time on this until he completed his plans to raise that arch mage. Once whoever it was had been brought back from the dead, he would resume the quest for his child. Nothing would stop him then. *I have a daughter,* he thought as he limped out and walked down the hallways.

EPILOGUE: A NEW LIFE

Two years flew by and Sprout became a beloved regular at most of the shops around Everknight. Living on the street and sleeping in her room on the second story roof of a potter, Sprout knew every inch of these alleyways and streets by heart. Even some of the guards knew of her and helped her with food and clothing. Life was good, but lonely.

She still had those waking dreams that Iya sat by her in her sleep, but she didn't cry as much anymore. Sprout accepted that she lost the only mom she would ever have, and that, somehow, she was paying the price for having lost. When anyone asked about her parents, she made up some horrific story, mainly to make people feel bad for her, but also to make herself forget that she was hurting.

Skipping down the alley on her way to see Addie at the flower shop, she caught a whiff of smoke that didn't seem to be from the usual stacks burning this time of day. Sprout turned around to check on her room, and when she saw that it wasn't on fire, she breathed a sigh of relief and ran for the road.

Taking the twists and turns through the streets, she followed the smoke column in the sky and soon found herself in front of the bakery. Thankfully it wasn't her favorite place to get food going up in flames either, but the blacksmith across the street. She had been by that place a couple of times, but nothing there ever piqued her interest. Now, though, she wished she had gone and checked it out, because it looked like it was going away for a long time.

Sprout stayed for the whole thing. She watched people cry at the loss, and even saw the guard take away two bodies from the shop. That's when she saw the boy.

He was big, much taller than her, with sandy brown hair and big arms like some of the bullies she had to deal with. He clutched a hammer in two white knuckled hands and was crying when they brought the bodies out. Sprout inched over and nudged him softly. "Them your parents?" she asked innocently, immediately regretting it. She was bad at saying the right things at the right times.

"Yes..." he said, breaking down. "I have to get away and get home. That can't be them! It just can't." He ran, clutching his hammer as he swerved through the people on the street.

Sprout ran behind him, keeping up with the boy easily, dodging under people's feet. She saw him burst through the door, calling for his mother and father. Sprout eased her way in and saw the boy staring at a note on a weird black wall.

"I was late today. I didn't mean to be late, but I stopped for candy," the boy said, falling to his knees and weeping silently.

"What does the black wall say?" Sprout asked, not sure what the squiggles meant.

"It says my mother was going down to help my father for the day and if I came home, to get down to the shop." He sobbed again for a minute, then continued, turning towards Sprout with tears welling up in his eyes. "It was *my* fault."

Sprout knew that he had to be real sad. She used to cry all the time when she was really sad. "It's all right. You can come stay with me if you like, since you have no parents now."

"They'll take my house anyway," he said. "I know *that* much about money and I have none." Grabbing what he wanted to take with him, he followed her out in shock, not thinking to even ask her name until they were in sight of her home. "What's your name?" he finally asked, his voice small and meek compared to his size.

"My name is Sprout and this is my home. You are welcome to stay, even though, to you, it will probably be small." She kicked a dirty wooden ball into some garbage containers and cheered as they crashed over. "I won!" She turned with a scrunched-up face. "What's your name?"

"I'm Tomas. I don't mind your place being small. I can always find a place around here and try to build my own. It would keep me busy."

"Oh, that sounds like fun! I know where we can get flowers to decorate it!" Sprout ran up and hugged him, grateful that she was no longer alone. She led Tomas up the ladder and into her room and took the next hour to show him everything that she had collected... twice.

CHILDREN'S ALLEY, EVERKNIGHT

Months went by and Sprout grew to like the company of the boy. Tomas made himself another room, one building over, close enough to Sprout's to still whisper to her at night but far enough to be alone when he wanted to cry. She showed him all the good places to eat and how to get clothes without getting caught.

Tomas was amazed that she was so good at surviving on her own and still so young.

It was in the cold of the winter-deep that year that they both heard crying one night. Sprout thought it was Tomas, so climbed out of her room and ran right into him. He was draped with tons of rotting blankets for warmth and looked worried.

"Are you alright?" Tomas asked, yelling over the whipping wind and snow.

"I'm fine, I came to see why *you* were crying," Sprout said, hands on her little hips. "I usually don't check on you when you cry anymore, but it sounded worse than usual."

"I don't cry... much."

Then they both heard it again. Sprout slid down the icy ladder, holding on with her double gloves and mismatched boots, and hit the ground running, Tomas right behind her.

She could barely see through the blowing snow, but followed the sound of crying. Turning the corner at the other alley way she saw a form huddled in the middle of the alley almost covered in snow.

"Hey look, a real snowperson!" Sprout said, kneeling in the snow and brushing off the person's face. "Hey! You ok?" she asked as Tomas took his fur cloak off and wrapped the person in it, helping them up and getting them walking again.

"C—c—come on, let's get you out of this s—snow," Tomas said, already starting to shiver with the cold. The figure nodded dumbly and followed woodenly.

When they were at the ladder, Tomas threw the person over his shoulder and climbed the icy ladder with one hand. Sprout was always surprised at how strong Tomas was; gloves or not, his grip was like iron.

Stumbling into Sprouts room, Tomas unwrapped the cloak and sat back, rubbing his hands together and warming them up.

It was a girl, about nine winters old—a winter ahead of Tomas—and she had long brown hair tied up in twin braids.

"What's your name?" Sprout asked, trying to get her talking.

"K—Kari," the girl said, still shivering, but not as bad as when she was covered in snow. "I've been wandering for hours and had given up completely." The girl started crying again, small sobs as she tried to continue. "My mother left me a note that said she was gone and was never coming back. It said it was because father left last year with that woman from River Vale and she never got over it."

"Oh no, that's so sad." Sprout hugged her and patted her on the head, not really understanding the whole thing. *At least she didn't lose her own mom though,* she thought sadly.

Kari sniffed and wiped ice from her cheek. "Thanks for helping me, but don't you two have to get back to your families?"

Sprout smiled up with her soft eyes, still hugging her. "Silly, we *are* home. This is where we live. All the time." She let go and waved her arms around like she was showing off trophies. "You're welcome to live here with us too. My name is Sprout," she said, bouncing up and down in excitement. "Or you could live over there with Tomas."

Kari smiled through falling tears. "That would be nice." She reached down and hugged Sprout just as hard. "How is it that I was saved by people so young?" Kari asked, looking up at Tomas.

"Beats me," Tomas said, still rubbing his hands together to keep them warm. "Sprout saved me too."

ILLIYANA WATCHED it all from the roof of the taller building she always used to look in on Sprout, or Lhana as she had known her. It would be impossible to watch her sleep now that she had more company, but it would be good for the little one to have others near her own age at least. "Goodbye, my little Lhana..." She ducked her head down against the blowing wind and leapt down across the snowy rooftops. It was time to start over again across town, but she would check in on them from time to time. What else were parents for?

FOREST OF THE LOST
HUNTER'S CAMP
PETER'S HIDING SPOT
RACE ROUTE
ANIMAL VILLAGE
ANIMAL BURROWS
ANIMAL BURROWS
ANIMAL BURROWS
FINISH LINE
START
ANIMAL BURROWS

9

THE LAST RACE OF THE ANIMALS
LISS HEARS A FAIRY TALE

The little girl ran from the practice room down the stone hallways of castle Everknight with a smile on her tired face. Princess Allissana Everknight was ten winters old and it was time for bed. Most children this age would be fighting bedtime, whining about staying up and not being a child, but this was a special night. This night was when her mother would read her a bedtime story. What made this so special to the small princess was that her mother, the queen, was also a bard and a master storyteller. When her mother told a story it pulled you in so that you felt like you were truly there. Princess Allissana loved stories of knights and heroes, and as she turned the corner to her room she giggled and started skipping.

"Excited as usual, I see," her mother said as she came down the opposite hall and saw her daughter. Maressa Everknight smiled warmly as she followed her daughter into the room with a small case and pulled a chair over to the side of the bed.

"Come on, mother! I want to hear what you have for me tonight," Allissana said as she jumped into bed, pulling the covers up. She silently said her prayer to Davalar, God of Protection, and secretly asked for adventure. "I'm ready."

Maressa laughed as she sat down and pulled her lute from its case and tuned it quickly with expert fingers. "Tonight, dear daughter, I will tell you the tale of the strangest race in the history of the faeries."

"Faeries aren't real, mother. Everyone knows that," Allissana said plainly, desiring a story with intrigue and action for once. "I'm ten now! Don't I deserve grown-up stories?" She was older now and wanted the stuff of true heroes.

❦

"OH, YOU WANT A *GROWN-UP* STORY?" Maressa couldn't believe they had a ten-year-old daughter. Ten years; who would've ever thought that they'd have a precious little girl all those years ago. "I assume it has to be one with action and adventure?" The queen laughed as she finished tuning her instrument, knowing exactly what her rambunctious daughter wanted.

Maressa knew that Allissana had been training with the high general for over a year now and had heard of the exciting stories of fighting. The queen thought about the stories she could tell and settled on one that might instill a lesson on the young Princess. "Very well. I will tell you the dark tale of the Forest of the Lost."

"The forest south of us, mother?" the princess asked. "The one no one goes into anymore unless they absolutely need to?" Her eyes were alight with the possibility of danger and daring-do.

Maressa nodded, knowing all to well the stories people told of the forest. It was rumored to be filled with the spirits of angry animals and vengeful souls. "Yes. I will tell you how it got its name all those centuries ago." Maressa started playing and drifted into that place she went when she wanted to bring others into her stories. Bards knew all the old tales and were tasked to preserve them. They were handed down, from bard to bard, and she had learned most of hers from the most famous Bard of them all: Karsis.

"The story begins with a glorious summer day..."

THE CHALLENGE

Centuries ago, all over Lythinall, the faeries used their magic and blessed certain animals with the ability to talk. Unfortunately, when the faeries stepped sideways to the moon and left this world, they left behind their talking friends. The humans that had been warring with the elves didn't know about these animals ability to talk, and so they hunted them for food and clothes just the same as regular animals. In time, the last of the talking animals fled to the southern part of the forest to escape the humans and lived in peace for many years, hiding and foraging quietly. It was at that time that the big argument started.

Two factions arose among the animals: one that wanted to try and follow the faeries to wherever they went, and one that wanted to stay safe in their forest and hide forever.

Gilliam Shelton was a tortoise with a sharp eye and a very thorough mind. He stood for safety and security in the forest and was adamant about keeping a low profile. He had watched the human hunters around the edges of their hidden area of the forest and spied on them more times than anyone knew. Since he was slow and quiet, they never noticed him laying in the bush, and you would be surprised at what one could hear when you think no one is listening.

Peteren Harefoot was a hare, and as such, had not only fast feet, but a quick wit as well. He wanted to strike out and discover a new place, a place that he was sure the faeries that created them had gone. His fur was a very light brown and his dark eyes darted back and forth as he talked. Never one to sit still for very long, he often ran in circles waiting for others to finish their sentences. Every time he saw Gilliam, he ridiculed the tortoise about how slow he was, and how he must think slowly as well. He insulted him over and over, and even some of the other animals started in after a while.

It was during one such a spectacle, early in the fall, that Gilliam had enough of this.

The tortoise turned upon the hare with fire in his tiny eyes. "Let's settle this once and for all, Peteren! I will race you, anywhere and anytime." The gathered animals witnessing this all sucked in a collective gasp. "If *I* win, then we will stay here and you will leave the forest by yourself, banished to wander the lands of the humans. If *you* win, then I will help you plan a route to find the faeries."

Peteren laughed out loud. "A race? Against *you*? Surely, you're kidding, Gilliam. A slow poke like yourself, against a speedster like me?" Peteren was brimming. He had finally pushed the shellback into a corner and now he had his victory in his sights. "Name the time and place, good sir, and I will leave you in my dust."

Gilliam shook his head back and forth, taking quite a while to do this, then looked the hare square in the eyes. "We will race from here, up and across the human lands and back down, starting tomorrow morning at dawn." He saw the watching animals all cheer at the impending spectacle and knew they would all be there when the sun rose.

"I accept, dear Gilliam, though I feel bad that you will be out there still racing while I'm already back here packing for you." Peteren was already thinking of what he would bring and where they could go. He was so confident that he gathered a group to throw a congratulatory party that very night. He drank and ate his fill and staggered around bragging about how he would win the next day.

Gilliam watched them go and sauntered off to his home to sleep. He would be refreshed for the race the next day and he smiled as he drifted off at the prospect of staying in the forest.

THE RACE

The next day, as the sun rose, Peteren came staggering to the starting line as everyone stood waiting. Gilliam was there, a bored expression on his wrinkled face.

"Tell you what, Gilliam—you start and I'll catch up," Peteren said, making everyone gathered around them laugh.

Gilliam ignored the taunt and looked to Osram the owl, nodding. At the sound of the owls call, the tortoise started his trek, slow and steady. He heard Peteren make a few comments about stretching and even taking a nap, but he knew that this would indeed be a race to challenge them both.

After a few moments, Peteren got bored and decided to just humiliate the tortoise. He took off, rounding the trees and boulders of the forest at great speed, leaving Gilliam in his dust. It was still early and he was already tearing through the bushes like there was no tomorrow.

Peteren was about halfway through the course when he felt a sharp pain in his leg that sent him sprawling across the ground and into a tree hard enough to make him dizzy. He was panting and trying not to scream as he looked down and saw an arrow in his leg! The tip went clean through and was barbed so as to tear if it was pulled out. That's when he heard them: hunters.

"Did you see where the little fella went? I know I tagged that little critter," a gruff human voice called out to someone else.

Peteren was terrified. He hadn't realized that it was so far into fall. It was *rabbit* season! The hare hobbled closer to the trunk of the tree and tried to cover up with some dirt and leaves. Peteren was in excruciating pain but he got his labored breathing under control at last and curled up crying quietly. He didn't know how long he lay there, fearing for his own life, but the next thing he heard made his watering eyes go wide indeed.

"Hey look, Hander! A little turtle."

"No Frantz, that's a tortoise. The difference is—"

"Oh, gods above, Hander! I don't care what the differences are, he's cute! Look at him go. You ever seen one move like that?" Frantz said, amazement in his deep voice.

Peteren couldn't believe it. He thought about making a break for it, but his leg was useless. He would never outrun those humans like this; he had to wait until the hunters left.

❦

Hours later, when the forest grew eerily quiet, Peteren made his way along the route and crawled across the finish line, his leg dragging behind him. The other animals were already celebrating and their cheers made him frown. Gilliam had won and, even worse, Osram the owl had looked at his would and determined that he would lose his. Peteren saw Gilliam coming over to where he was sitting with the owl and knew what was coming.

"Well, Peteren, it seems *I* have won. I want you to take a few days and heal up though, before you have to leave." The tortoise smiled smugly and walked away, knowing that he had gotten the best of the troublesome hare. Gilliam had known that the hunters would be tracking rabbits around this time and had heard them earlier this month at their camp to the north; it was why he selected the route he did.

Peteren nodded in defeat. He had been bested by his own

arrogance and, after a few days, he left. He limped away down the trail on a stump of a back leg and a walking stick.

The talking animals would stay in their part of the forest and he would leave to live in the wide world of the humans, disfigured and slow.

It was three days later that Peteren smelled the smoke and looked for higher ground. He crawled up a high hill, looked back, and saw his old home ablaze, fully engulfed in roaring flames.

He would never know that those same hunters left their campfire unattended and that it sent the flames scouring through the dry branches.

Peteren hid in hollows here and there, scrounging for food, and finally made his way back to see the carnage and search for survivors; sadly, everyone was dead. The sad hare left once more, lucky to be alive. Though no one ever heard from Peteren Harefoot ever again, it was well known that he was the luckiest rabbit ever to lose a race.

THE END?

Maressa put down the lute and noticed her daughter's face. The princess was staring at her mother with wide eyes.

"I can still smell the smoke and hear the poor animal crawling his way back to his home, only to find them all dead..." Allissana started in a hollow voice. "What... what is the meaning of *that* story, mother?" The princess sounded truly stunned.

"What do you mean?" Maressa asked innocently. People often asked that question after hearing heard this story. They always had the same reaction: disbelief.

Allissana collected herself and sat up in bed. "Well, the stories that you used to tell me all had some sort of lesson." The princess had that look on her face like she might know, but refused to see it. They all usually did.

"You wanted a grown-up story, didn't you?"

"I... I guess I did."

"Well, there you have it." At the deeper look of confusion on her daughter's face, the queen smiled, then tucked her back into her sheets and kissed her on the forehead. "You see, a grownup has to learn from their own lessons and take what they can without being told sometimes. Did you learn anything from this story?"

"I think I did."

"Then that's all that matters. Good night Allissana."

"Goodnight mother."

Maressa walked away and started to close the door when her daughter spoke once more.

"Mother?"

"Yes dear?"

"Is that why they call rabbits feet lucky?"

"One would think that, yes," was the vague answer Maressa gave her daughter. She took down the torch and closed the door, whistling to herself as she walked down the stone hallway. It was times like this that she truly missed Karsis.

APPENDICES

ON ELVISH

A BRIEF INTRODUCTION TO THE LANGUAGE OF
THE ELVES OF LYTHINALL

The simplicity of elven is that it actually follows a basic syntax of word for word. Very few things change when speaking; the language follows a straightforward approach to its verbal understanding. Rather than having different words for run, ran, or running, the language simply has one word for run and surrounding words provide context to clue the listener as to how it is being used. In the structure of the elven language, adjectives are generally placed before nouns. In some rare cases the adjective can be after, but only in very rare conversations with some ancient elves. Below is a quick guide on how to pronounce some of the words as you read through.

PHONETICS

Ae is pronounced *ay* (hay)
Ah is drawn out long (aaahh)
Ay is pronounced as a soft *a* (air)
C is pronounced as a hard *c* (Car)
C if with *a* or *e* is pronounced soft (ice)

Ch is pronounced with a hard *ch* sound. (church)

Ea is pronounced *eeah* (leah)

En is always pronounced like *n*

Eu is pronounced soft (eew)

Ie is pronounced *i* (eye)

J is pronounced as a hard *j* (jar)

Ly is pronounced *l-eh* (list)

Ov is pronounced *au* (nod)

Oz is pronounced O (doze)

Ri is pronounced *re* (real)

A SELECTED GLOSSARY OF ELVISH WORDS

All-close/near

Alar—away

Ansis'ren—barrier

Amran—mountains

An—and

Ari—song

A'ren—mind

Ayre—blood

Ashanti—pleased

Ash'anti—please

Balen—steady

Balt—belt

Bin—bind/tighten

Blai—sword

Bli—knife

Boun—restraints/manacles

Braken—shatter

Brek—break/free
Car'cen—there
Cas—house
Cav—tunnel
Ce—a
Ceas—stop
Chal—blade
Col—cold
Cra'del—help
Crean—monster/creature
Dal—arm/arms
Dar—hand
Deth—doom
Dir—earth
Dosan—that
Dost—the
Dosit—this
Doz—sleep
Draco—dragon
Dren—end of
Dwoen—down
Ea—me/my
Eae—mine
Elien—fair
Em'ren—women/human
Ethir—ether
En—of
Ent—into
Eu—us
Faer—faeries
Fer—inside

Fin—over/ended

Fir—fire

Fra—wind/air

Frein—fall

Fros—freeze

Gli—fly

Gol—money/trade

Gos—filth/scum

Gra—bring

Gram—demon

Gres—grass

Hadar—hold

Haeth—encase/enfold

Halven—heat/warmth

Hary—hurry/fast

Haryen—faster

Hir—warrior

Icael—snow

Ice—good

Id—soul

Il—light

Ilkith—children

In—I

Ins—we

Ithin—with

Itim—treasure

Jren—from

Jal—king

Jera—evil

Jol—back/return

Ki—him/her

Kin—brother/sister
Kind—kindred
Kith—people/elven
Kithen—person/human
Kithion—half people
Krist—death
La—them
Lae—those
Lai—love
Lea—these
Leven—leave
Lith—risen people/elf
Liv—alive
Lok—control/enslave
Lythin—heaven
Lyst—lost
Ma—yes/agree
Mas—no/no more
Met—hall or chamber
Miran—isolation or alone
Mist—clouded or cloud
Misten—unclouded
Mith—shadow
M'ren-men/human
Nov—hide/hidden
Novran—secrets
N'roth-high
N'rothen—highest
Oa—the
Oren—words
Obren—obey

Ovra—over

Per—feet/foot

Pera—steps

Pire—cursed

Por—portal/door

Pry—force

Ra—was

Ranen—hills

Relin—rain

Rels—release/let go

Rien—forest/wood

Rienon—stick/branch

Reva—show/reveal

Roan—horse

Roun—circle

Rule—power

Sat—staff

Sellare—protected place

Seren—Land/kingdom

Shir—heart

Shiran—life

Sho—shove/push

Shoran—attack/fight

Sirin—watch/look for

Sistren—take

Sonn—stone/rock

Spir—tower/large structure

Sran—shield

S'ren—safe/holy

Ta—to

Tah—calm

Tann—Song
Tar—will/doctrine
Ter'min—kill
Tol—tell/communicate
Tow—at/towards
Tir—city
Travar—travel/walk
Tur—spin
Ubel—up
Unda—under
Urbis—come
Urn—war
Vi/vin—it/it is
Val—ever
Vam—the dead
Van—orb
Var—voice
Vessan—body
Vew—see/look
Wa—your
Wal—wall
Wan—water
Wanel—float/afloat
Worl'—world
Ya—you
Yanel—rise/lift
Yaw—open
Zat—here
Zren—thank/thanks

THE DARKNESS FALLS

A PREVIEW OF BOOK 3 OF THE LYTHINALL SERIES

She stepped out of the magical portal and felt her heels sink into the earth, the cold dirt spilling over the rim of her footwear and onto her pale skin. She was ready for the crisp air this high up, but was unprepared for this little annoyance. Shaking her head in disgust, she whispered to the earth and pulled her foot free as the soft dirt hardened beneath her. The ground solidified before her like a dark carpet and she smiled despite the filth on her foot.

Madam Ill'lyth G'harr straightened her back and walked confidently down this small path, heels now clicking softly on the enspelled ground. She hadn't been in the Shield Mountains for centuries and it still had the same effect on her: it bored her to death. The scenery was all the same, rocks, rocks, dirt... and if you were lucky, some scrub. This high up nothing grew worth a damn and the only thing that liked it up here were the ogrann. But the ogrann were why she was here.

Ill'lyth turned a corner and saw an ogrann guard standing there with his dumb grin and tree trunk of a club resting on his massive shoulder. Ogrann were about eight feet tall and smelled of rotting meat. They were grotesque and ruthless, never mind packed with more muscles than an elephant. The beasts usually roamed the lower hills making sport in hunting the humans in the outlying villages, but lived up high in the mountains. This was the main reason hunting parties never found the ogrann villages. The various knights and soldiers that protected the lower hills would attack the hunting parties, but never found their homes.

The ogrann finally noticed her and smiled, it's cracked teeth showing bits of some sort of meat still stuck in them. "Hey, it's one of the littles. Have you come to get eaten?"

"Certainly not," Ill'lyth said as she pointed and called to the earth. "Ash'anti dir haeth dosit crean." The ancient elven archmage never broke stride, walking past the brute as the very ground beneath its feet rose up and fully encased the creature. She could hear his last muffled cries as the dirt poured into his mouth and covered his head; she couldn't hide her smile.

Another whisper to the air blew the crude wooden gate wide open as she walked on, her confidence an almost palpable thing. Smaller ogrann—probably children—took off and ran for the larger thatched buildings as warriors came rushing to the front to see what was going on.

Ill'lyth continued, on calling to the various elements as they came at her. One warrior went down gasping for air, clutching his large throat and gagging on nothing. Another suffered the same fate as the gate guard, dropping his spear and trying to fight the very dirt that was engulfing him, all while the other ogrann were fleeing to the rear of the village, putting as much distance between them and this horrible threat.

"Stop!" Kragth came around the Speaking Hut and saw the devastation that was being done to his warriors. He feared that the children had been attacked, but it seemed that this little was only defending itself as his warriors attacked. Thankfully, Kragth was a smart ogrann—in that he had the capacity for *some* forethought. The warriors backed away, except for the ones that died within seconds as the little walked by them. The little had long, bone white hair tied up in a bun, held by a wrought-iron pin, and her long black dress looked ripped up the side revealing her delicious legs. "What does this little want here?"

Ill'lyth was having fun until the big one had to go and ruin it. Still, this was what she was trying to accomplish after all. "I'm here to speak with you, actually. I assume you are the leader of this village?" He was a little larger than the others, and had all of six teeth. His mangy hair was caked with mud and she was pretty sure that was a human femur tied to the end his filthy locks. Interesting to say the least.

"Me the leader. Name is Kragth. Who is you, little?" Kragth was a bit confused. He had asked her a question, but then she asked him one... he wasn't sure if he should've answered, or just smashed her. Leading was hard sometimes.

Ill'lyth smiled and took stock of the size of the village. There were about fifty warriors here, not counting the children and females. The females were scarce, as the ogrann only kept them for breeding and cooking; if they couldn't breed, they cooked them. "I am called Ill'lyth, and I'm here to recruit you to my cause." She saw his look of confusion and laughed quietly. If only her own generals were this stupid. "Here, let me help you." She walked forward a bit, so that she was within arm's reach of him, and closed her eyes. "Ash'anti ethir, lok dosit a'ren," she whispered to the ether, taking control of his mind. She chuckled softly at the clouded nod that he gave her; he was hers now. She walked up to him and took his arm in her own, ignoring the filth and slime for a show of superiority to all his followers.

"Now come dear, we have plans to discuss," Ill'lyth said as he followed without complaint and the rest of the village returned to normal. Within an hour, the children had planted a rock garden on the two large earthen mounds that marked where the dead had fallen.

Inside Kragth's hut she gleaned where most of his warriors were at, then had him send runners out to call them all here. Her forces were laying siege to Keragan Hold as she spoke, so she had to move quickly. She gave him the orders she had readied, detailing the plan as simply as she could for his tiny mind. Once he had the numbers she was looking for—roughly one hundred ogrann—he would start a long, forced march upon the city of Everknight. At this elevation it would take a little over a day's march to get there with their long strides, so if they started after the two days it would take to gather the remaining ogrann, they would get there ahead of her main force. More importantly, they would hit the northern gate, where a meager force would be holding it against the attack.

Feeling satisfied that most of the ogrann in the entire Shield Mountains were now doing her bidding, Ill'lyth walked back to where she arrived and closed her eyes, concentrating on her bedroom at the Golden Palace and opened a portal home. She could've left the old one open, but didn't want any surprises going through when she was busy with the ogrann.

She dreamed of a hot bath and maybe some torture before looking for the incarnation of death, and—upon stepping through and seeing her servants expression—knew she needed that bath. They didn't say anything though; they knew that their lives were more important.

"Bath!" Ill'lyth screamed, sending them all scurrying. Sitting down on her bed, she relaxed for the first time in a long time. The servants would take about ten minutes to ready the water, so she could take a good breather and think. Her plans set into motion, she was confident that nothing could stop her now.

To be Continued in The Darkness Falls

Born in the usual way, Michael D. Nadeau found fantasy at the age of 8 with Dungeons and Dragons. He loved being different people and casting magic. By the late 90's, he discovered his love for reading. His favorite teacher gave him her personal books to bring home, and he couldn't get enough. He had even more ways to explore the great worlds out there, and it was harder and harder to come back. When he was much older, and had created and destroyed more worlds than he could count, he decided to delve into the literary realm. He created Lythinall, a place where he could tell epic stories and invite his readers on the journey with his characters. The Darkness Returns is the start of that journey, but certainly not the end. You can learn more about his works at SkullgateMedia.com as well as his personal website, KarisTheBard.Wordpress.com.

 twitter.com/Salen_Valari

 instagram.com/michael_d_nadeau

 amazon.com/Michael-D.-Nadeau

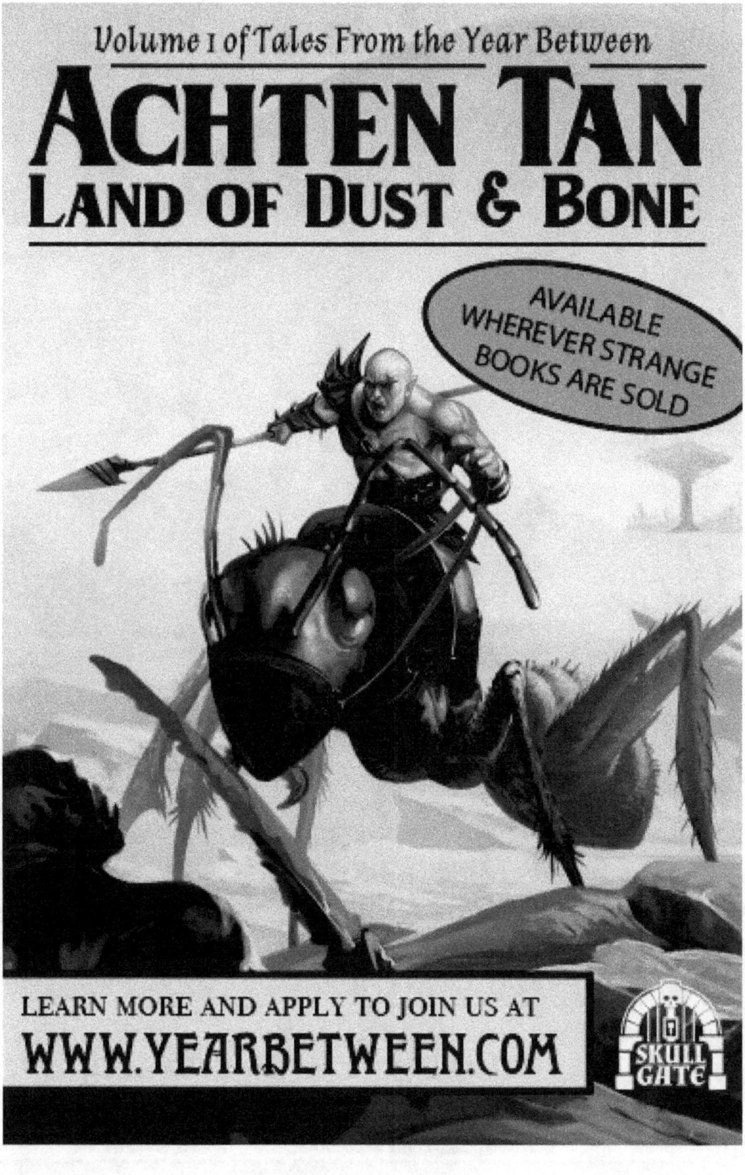
Volume 1 of Tales From the Year Between
ACHTEN TAN
LAND OF DUST & BONE
AVAILABLE WHEREVER STRANGE BOOKS ARE SOLD
LEARN MORE AND APPLY TO JOIN US AT
WWW.YEARBETWEEN.COM
SKULL GATE

Tales From The Year Between, Volume 2
UNDER NEW SUNS
A crew of intrepid space marines...
A pregnant ship trying to get home...
And freaking space sharks.

SKULL GATE

Available now at Amazon,
Skullgatemedia.com and
WHEREVER BOOKS ARE SOLD.
Tales From
The Year Between

9 781956 042993